Readers love
TA MOORE

Prodigal

"I stayed up way too late to finish this book… I can't wait to see who is next on Moore's list to be Lost and Found!"

—Paranormal Romance Guild

"It's not a pretty picture. It's so well written but this book is going to bring out a lot of emotions in people when you read it."

—Love Bytes Reviews

Dead Man Stalking

"The characters are so richly written that it is easy to be seamlessly drawn into the story and to become invested in them."

—Paranormal Romance Guild

"…*Dead Man Stalking* is compelling and absorbing…. This is a world I want to explore more deeply, and in the company of these characters."

—Reading Reality

Take the Edge Off

"Such a great read, one that keeps you entertained the whole way through!"

—Diverse Reader

"TA Moore does a great job combining romance and suspense in this story and I really enjoyed *Take the Edge Off*."

—Joyfully Jay

By TA Moore

Bad, Dad, and Dangerous Anthology
Cash in Hand
Every Other Weekend
Ghostwriter of Christmas Past
Liar, Liar
Take the Edge Off

BLOOD AND BONE
Dead Man Stalking

DIGGING UP BONES
Bone to Pick
Skin and Bone

ISLAND CLASSIFIEDS
Wanted – Bad Boyfriend

LOST AND FOUND
Prodigal

PLENTY, CALIFORNIA
Swipe
Bone to Pick
Skin and Bone

WOLF WINTER
Dog Days
Stone the Crows
Wolf at the Door

Published by DSP Publications
Collared

Published by DREAMSPINNER PRESS
www.dreamspinnerpress.com

Cash in HAND

TA MOORE

Published by

DREAMSPINNER PRESS

5032 Capital Circle SW, Suite 2, PMB# 279, Tallahassee, FL 32305-7886 USA
www.dreamspinnerpress.com

Cash in Hand
© 2020 TA Moore

Cover Art
© 2020 TA Moore
Cover content is for illustrative purposes only and any person depicted on the cover is a model.

Trade Paperback ISBN: 978-1-64405-891-6
Digital ISBN: 978-1-64405-890-9
Library of Congress Control Number: 2020943179
Trade Paperback published December 2020
First Edition
v. 1.0

Printed in the United States of America

To my mum, who always encouraged me to have my head in the clouds. And to the Five, who told me to stop messing around and get my fingers on a keyboard.

Chapter One

BLOOD SWEATED out of the freshly applied magnolia paint in slow resiny drops. It dribbled down the wall in thickening lines and splattered over the polished herringbone-patterned wood flooring.

Mr. Stevens made a choked noise in his throat and covered his mouth with one hand. "It's reclaimed," he said accusingly through his fingers.

Something dipped into the blood and started to smear it in clumsy, rough lines. Cash backed up a few steps and adjusted the angle of the camera to make sure he got Winslow and the wall in the shot. The exorcist was a rail-thin ginger man with dust-bowl bones and a cheap black suit, fresh from a church in Utah. Well, five years down now, but dust behind the ears was his brand.

He was popular in the Midwest. California preferred a more granola approach, bare feet and compromise, while the demographics in the South were split—but you could never go wrong with a snake handler. Catholics, of course, were popular across the board. Priests just gave good exorcism.

CASH PUSHED in close on Winslow's face to capture the way the veins in his temples bulged as he stepped forward. Then he tracked down his arms to show knuckly hands reddened, the skin scalded and cracked, as Winslow thrust the bible toward the wall.

"Begone!" Winslow roared. "In the name of Christ and all the holy angels! I tell you. Begone!"

He slapped the bible against the wall, and Cash pulled back hard to capture the moment—the black book pinned to the wall, framed by the spirit's bluntly unpoetic message.

FUCK YOU.

That was the money shot, which reminded him….

Cash checked his watch and cursed under his breath. It was past 2:00 a.m. already, and despite the number of times he said he'd gotten the kid's stuff sorted out for camp, he hadn't. At all.

He glanced up at the angry rag of a thing that writhed against the wall, squashed out of shape like a bug on a windscreen by the bible. It faltered when he caught its eye—or eye-like thing—and tilted his wrist toward it. He pointedly tapped his finger on the glass face and mouthed, "Camp."

A horrible maw dropped open, misshapen and lined with barbed hook teeth, and a thick, rudely pink tongue flopped out.

"Already?" it said. Well, *said* wasn't exactly right. Spirits didn't have a voice or lungs to fill, but the words dropped into Cash's soul and rattled it with their force. It sounded a bit like someone making fart sounds with a tuba full of loose teeth. And British. "I've been stuck here for months. The two of them are so miserable they didn't even notice for ages. Lost track of time. I'll wrap up."

It winked companionably at Cash and squirmed its way out from under Winslow's bible. Ectoplasmic sweat dripped down its flanks as it reformed itself. Cash swallowed the stingy urge to retch and looked back down into his camera, which placidly recorded the noncreepy side of the world.

Well, less creepy, Cash corrected himself as the blood peeled off the wall and stuck to a sketchy outline of the spirit's horrific shape.

Winslow made the sign of the cross, brandished his bible again, and prayed some more. The spirit thrashed, wailed in a thin drizzle of sound, and put on a quick show of breaking things and pulling hair as Winslow roared scripture. They all had a job to do, after all, and Cash's organizational issues were not its problems. Finally, it exploded in a splatter of blood and wet shreds of something like bloated chicken skin.

Winslow wiped his face on his sleeve and looked around.

"Another evil spirit banished back to hell," he said raggedly. "Good job, everyone. Anyone want Chinese?"

MR. STEVENS wrung Winslow's hand as though he thought he could squeeze the holy out like lotion. Next to him his wife smiled and crossed herself gratefully, probably thinking no one there could see the crispy edges her deal with the infernal had left on her aura. Not the spirit that Winslow had just banished. It had just followed the stench of her soul and gotten stuck like a bug in a spiritual pitcher plant.

No, Mrs. Stevens had traded a pound of her flesh for immediate gratification. Based on how much she seemed to loathe her husband and the fact he hadn't died tragically and weirdly yet, Cash would bet she'd bought stakes in fidelity. Somewhere there was a dirty mistress who was either freshly dead or very confused.

Cash saved their address in his phone. They'd be back before the year was out. Like recognized like, and evil didn't have many friends. The Stevens's would keep having bad spiritual luck until the missus either repented or gave in to the creeping temptation to do more evil. Either way would be good for ratings. Viewers loved a good catch-up show.

He slung his kit into the back of the car—piled on top of Ellie's hockey gear and a pile of discarded sweats and T-shirts that reeked worse than Mrs. Stevens's soul—and slammed the door shut. His phone started to ring as he got into the car.

Ellie.

"I've got everything," Cash lied smoothly as he hunted through the papers discarded on the passenger seat for the equipment list the camp had sent out last month. "I just have to finish up at work and bring it home. Then pack it. It's all under control."

Ellie sighed heavily. "Great," she said. "Dad, c'mon, can't I go to the same camp I did last year? We had horses at Camp Tranquility. There was an Israeli guy who taught us Krav Maga…."

"You might have horses at our camp too," Cash said defensively. "Just… don't get on their backs. Or touch them. They'll want to drown you. It's not personal."

"All my friends are going to Camp Tranquility." The whine intensified.

"Well, they're human," Cash said. He found the warranty for his battery pack, which was useful but not what he was after. "They get to go where they want, and you get to do what you want. As long as the Prodigium doesn't say you can't."

"Urgh."

"You'll make new friends," Cash said. "Horrible ones."

"Not. Appealing."

"Yeah, well." Cash pulled a folded sheet of paper from down the side of the passenger seat and shook it out one-handed. The horned-mountain logo of Medicine Springs Camp was slashed across the top of the page. It was an effort to blend in, but it looked more like somewhere you sent special, murderous delinquents than a normal summer camp. And, well… accurate, but not the look the Prodigium wanted. "Make the most of it. You're going. Just think, your friends will be cleaning up horse crap, and you'll be learning the skills to excel in the corporate world."

"Like what?"

Cash pinned the list to the steering wheel with one hand as he pulled out of the drive. The call blitzed static for a second as it switched to the car's onboard system.

"I don't know," he sighed. "Disposing of bodies. Cut me some slack here, okay? I'm going to grab the… last… things on the list and get home. Now go get some sleep. You're going tomorrow. It's not optional."

Silence dragged out long enough that Cash thought Ellie had hung up. Then she cleared her throat.

"What if I'm not good at being a monster?" she asked in a small voice. "What do they do then?"

Cash hesitated. He knew the answer. It had never helped him much.

"El, you're twelve," he said. "No one expects you to be Grendel's mom right out the gate. Just be yourself, but cooler."

His reward for that was an abrupt disconnection. Cash sighed. As he headed to Home Depot, he tried to convince himself it would be fine. He'd gotten through it, and Ellie was more monster than he was.

That would be enough.

EL HUGGED her backpack to her chest as she got out of the car and watched wide-eyed as sixty kids milled around the two black buses parked outside the school. Some of them knew each other from previous

4

years and clustered together to catch up, as though they wouldn't be on the bus for three hours. Others butted up against each other like adolescent bantams as they jostled to decide who was top dog.

"They just look human," El muttered to Cash as he joined her.

"That's the point," he reminded her. "The humans wiped us all out, remember? The last monster was the Beast of Boston, and they drowned him in salt and sank him in the bay. As far as they're concerned, and we want to keep it that way."

The Prodigium did, anyhow. Cash didn't necessarily disagree— his breed's traditional haunt was bogs and moors, where you got very bad Wi-Fi and no laundry—but it wasn't as if anyone had asked him anyhow.

El rolled her eyes at him. "I know *that*," she snarked. "I listen. Grandma used to tell me about the Beast."

"She probably knew him," Cash said. As he nudged her toward the bus, he added under his breath, "That's probably why he gave himself up to the Church."

"I heard that," El said primly. "Grandma hasn't killed everything she ever loved, Cash."

"The only evidence for that is you," Cash pointed out as he ruffled her hair. "Ready?"

A counselor in a bright yellow sweatshirt smiled at them as they approached, her pen poised over a clipboard. A dozen deaths hung around her shoulders, black rents torn in her aura. They twitched like a fox's tail as El approached her, and her smile was long and sharp.

"Hello. New girl?" she asked.

El nodded and shifted her backpack awkwardly over her shoulder so she could pull the much-folded permission slip out of her pocket. It was initialed, pocketed, and replaced with a yellow strip of paper to glue around her wrist.

"Don't worry," the fox-kin killer reassured El as she put a hand on her shoulder. She winked one bright dark eye. "It'll be great. We're going to have a body farm this year, but keep that under your hat. I'm not supposed to tell yet."

Ellie took a step toward the bus, then turned and tackled Cash. She pressed her face against his chest as she hugged him desperately, her backpack dangling uncomfortably over his arm.

He ignored the *tch* of a passing dowager and hugged Ellie back. She was all bones and smelled of lavender soap, toothpaste, and whatever perfume her human friends had decided was "the best" this month.

For a second he tasted panic in his throat—that he'd gotten it wrong, raised her to *be* human, not just to pass, that maybe he should have left her with her grandmother.

"If I get killed," Ellie muttered against Cash's T-shirt, "just remember I didn't want to go."

She peeled herself off him and stepped back, his T-shirt still pinched in her fingers as if she was going to take him with her. The smile she gave him was halfhearted. Then she looked over his shoulder and brightened up like someone had flipped a switch.

"Uncle Arkady," she crowed with delight as she broke away from Cash. All her fears about camp appeared to be forgotten. The bag dropped to the ground with a thud as she darted away. "I didn't know you were coming!"

Cash turned to watch as El threw herself at her uncle—her tall, well-dressed uncle in front of his very nice Porsche. He waited until Arkady turned back around to pull a face, which he personally thought was admirably restrained. The fox-kin counselor didn't agree; she gave him a look of mingled confusion and disapproval over her clipboard. The Abascals were underworld royalty, one of the few non-Prodigium breeds that could boast no human blood ran in their veins.

At least until some trailer park half-blood by-blow came along and spoiled that for at least one branch of the bloodline.

Cash saw the penny drop in the fox-kin's eyes as she glanced from him to El and then back again. The "really? For *you*?" assessment that he never seemed to come out ahead on.

"What can I say," Cash said dryly as he bent down to grab the backpack and toss it over his shoulder. He grinned at the fox-kin. "I used to be prettier."

6

"You're pretty," the fox-kin blurted out. "Just *weak*."

She immediately went red from her chin to her temples and spluttered a knot of tongue-tied excuses. Cash shrugged it off. She wasn't wrong, not about the weakness, anyhow.

"I guess some people like that. I'll just go toss this in the bus for El, yeah?"

The fox-kin nodded, lips pressed together as if she might blurt out something else rude, and Cash carried the backpack over to shove it in the hold of the bus with the rest. He gave it a kick to make it fit. No one paid him any attention. Even the posturing little bantam monsters craned their necks to see what the celebrity was doing.

"Poor thing," a huldra in Dior, her aura black as tree rot along her spine, said to the redcap next to her—his traditional stocking cap replaced with a Cardinal's ball cap. "I don't know how Donna Abascal can hold her head up. The child might as well be human."

Cash licked the back of his teeth and tasted spite. He wasn't much of a monster. Even if his mom hadn't been a truck-stop waitress with a soft spot for pretty liars, he'd have never made the grade with the monsters-who-lunch crowd. He was a wisp. Even his monstrousness was insubstantial and passing. It was just secrets and a knack for seeing things you weren't meant to.

"At least she's pretty," he said. "Humanity is only skin deep, but ugly's to the bone."

The redcap laughed, a harsh blart of unrepentant mockery, and the huldra went stiff and hard-looking. Like bark. Her humiliation was sour as lemons and fizzed like sorbet as Cash choked it down. He didn't know what it meant—hopefully he hadn't just called a child ugly—he just knew it would hurt.

The huldra grabbed his shoulder and dug her fingers in until his bones creaked.

"Speak to me like that again," she said through thick, cracked lips as she pulled him onto his toes. "I'll take your face and wear it at Halloween."

Cash grinned at her. He didn't have fangs, but he could *feel* them in the words on his tongue.

"I'm sure Belladonna will be glad to know you did what she couldn't," he said. "Probably grateful. Don't you think?"

They both knew the answer was no. Donna would rather her worst enemy—and Cash might not be her favorite person, but there was a long stretch of assholes between him and the person she hated most—walk the earth forever than have some nouveau-evil fey do her a "feyvor." She once described gratitude as "when you have to smile as someone fucks you over."

The redcap, over his fit of the giggles, cleared his throat. "Gret," he said mildly. "Your tail's showing."

The huldra pinked in embarrassment and let Cash go. She brushed her hands together and patted her face to set the humanity back in place. The ghostly flick of her tail under her dress faded away.

"Next time *I* see Belladonna," she sniffed at Cash as she tossed her blond mane of hair, "I'll give her your regards."

She turned and stalked off to push her daughters onto the bus. "Before the good seats are taken," she snapped, her voice thin with distance as she pulled them away from their friends. Cash straightened his T-shirt and snorted.

"Do that," he said dryly. "She'll know you're a fucking liar. I've never even wished that old bat 'many more' on her birthday."

This time the redcap nearly choked as he tried to stop the snort that escaped him. He tugged his cap down farther on his forehead and left quickly.

"Dad," El huffed as she popped out of a clot of suddenly friendly little monsters like a cork out of a bottle. "Were you mean?"

"It's my art," Cash said mildly.

El rolled her eyes at him and then surprised him with another hug. "Uncle Arkady wants to talk to you," she said as she looked up at him. Her eyes were still blue. They'd start to fade now as her monster grew into her. "He said it was important."

Cash kissed her forehead. "But it probably isn't," he said. "So…."

"Pleeeeeeaase?" El begged. "He said you wouldn't listen, but I said you would if I asked."

"Wow," Cash said. "You're not a seer. Not even on the bus yet and you're learning things about yourself."

"Just be nice to him, Dad," El protested. "He's always nice to you. Or he would be if you gave him a chance."

Cash glanced over her head. Arkady was slouched back against the hood of the Porsche, arms crossed and legs stretched out in front of him as he waited. The man was 75 percent leg, and the rest was just shoulders and lean waist.

The last time Cash gave Arkady a chance, it didn't end well. Okay, so it had technically, eventually, ended in El—who was pretty cool. But before that it was mostly screaming, bloodshed, and curses. Cash had enough of that at work.

El pouted at him.

"I'll see what he wants," he said reluctantly. "Only because you asked."

She grinned up at him and bobbed up on her toes to kiss his cheek. "You're awesome."

"How come you never remember that when I'm not doing what you want?"

She shrugged and blinked innocently at him. "It's a mystery."

It was time to go. The proctors came off the bus and checked the kids' wrists as they clambered up the steps. Nobody wanted some kid who thought he was going to fat camp or music camp or whatever getting on the wrong bus.

Not again.

Cash stood with his hands in his back pockets and waited until the bus turned the corner at the end of the street. The other parents chatted to each other, planning murder and mimosas now they didn't have to play human for the kids for two weeks.

He *had* promised.

Cash turned and trudged across the lot to where Arkady waited for him, the dark wings of his aura mantled with smugness. Most people's auras shifted shape with the wind and were mottled, scabbed with bad intentions, or shot through with milky streaks of unexpected kindness. Arkady's aura was purple-black, the color of a fresh bruise, and hung from his shoulders like wings.

"What?" Cash asked as he lifted his hand to shade his eyes against the sun.

Arkady slid his sunglasses down his nose and looked at Cash over the top of them. It was hard not to start in surprise. The last time Cash had looked into—at—Arkady's eyes, they'd been the color of dark honey. Now they were faded down to citrine yellow streaked with pale amber—humanity so thin that, in the right light, you could probably see through it.

"Most people start with 'Good to see you again,'" Arkady noted. "Or 'Thanks for burning one of your last days in the sun to see your niece off,' or even just 'Hello' to kick things off."

Cash tapped his wrist. "I've things to do, money to make, and men to fuck," he said. "So 'what' is all you get. What?"

Arkady pushed his hair back from his face with one hand, fingers buried in the golden-brown waves.

"I need you to do something for me," he said. "For the family. It's important."

"Oh," Cash said. "I see. No."

"What?"

"No," Cash repeated. He knew Arkady didn't hear it often, so he used it in a sentence. "Fuck you, no."

He turned his back on Arkady's expression of offended confusion and headed to his car. Even riding on the cloud of hurt feelings and wafer-thin pride, he was a little surprised he made it. Last time he'd told Arkady no, he'd just been dragged by the collar to the car and shoved headfirst into the back seat.

Maybe they'd both grown up.

Or maybe he'd gotten faster.

Chapter Two

OR ARKADY just drove a faster car.

Cash pulled up outside his house and scowled at the Porsche parked in front of his garage. More people needed to have rejected Arkady in his life. Maybe then he'd be able to deal with it better.

Because you were so good at that, a cynical little voice in Cash's head sneered at him. He sucked in his breath in surprise at how much that stung, like an old scab picked off raw skin. The pain was flat and salty as he swallowed it, like the taste of blood. It sucked that he wasn't immune to his own monster and that it was a dick.

Fine. It wanted to see him reject Arkady? Watch and learn.

The monster pushed against his bones, cold and thin and dubious. They weren't *separate*. It wasn't like the whole "bad wolf and good wolf" parable where human Cash and monster Cash had to fight to see who survived. The monster was more like… an appetite with opinions. It was part of him, but they weren't always in lockstep about what to do.

For example, it didn't think that ignoring Arkady—one of the Abascal—would end well, and Cash was going to do it anyhow.

He got out of the car and pointedly ignored his guest as he stalked toward the house. Before he could get there, the passenger door swung open.

"Get in the car," Arkady said from the shadows inside the cab.

"I already told you," Cash said. He'd stopped, some old hook in his spine unable to resist the habit of doing what Arkady told him, but he refused to look at the car. "No. I don't owe your family anything."

"Casper," Arkady said, voice thick as honey with seduction. The name had been his dad's joke, before he fucked off forever. Casper the Friendly Wisp. Cash had always hated it, and Arkady always made it sound… important. "I need you."

"I don't care," Cash said. "Find someone else to do your scut work."

He bullied his legs forward and ignored the itch of guilt in the back of his skull as he fumbled his key into the lock. The thing was, he did owe the Abascals something. He was the only one who knew that, though, and he had no intention of sharing. It still *picked* at him.

The lock finally gave in and opened. Cash put his hand to the wood, and something hit him from behind and flung him into the house. He staggered forward, tripped over his stack of bags, and pitched face-first toward the floor. Before he could land, Arkady grabbed him by the back of his T-shirt and hauled him up.

Cash dangled there for a second, toes just about on the ground and the seams of the T-shirt digging in under his armpits, and then Arkady let him drop.

"Get the fuck off me," Cash bristled, even though Arkady already had. His monster prickled against his skin, offended at being manhandled in its own lair. Like *prey.* Cash yanked his shirt straight and turned to glare up at Arkady. "What's wrong with you? I told you no. Go bully someone else into doing your bidding. Make a deal. Ask Donna to loan you a minion. Get your *wife* to do it."

That was a mistake. Cash knew that even before the sliver of gold flickered in Arkady's eyes. It burned away a line of honey to leave sulfur, and he grabbed Cash's jaw in one hand.

"Is this why you're being pissy with me?" Arkady asked. He tilted Cash's head back and leaned down to brush his lips over Cash's mouth. It was barely a kiss, but Cash still felt it all the way down to his cock—a hot spill of awareness that prickled his skin and reminded him what it felt like, what *Arkady* felt like. "Because you're jealous?"

"I told you," Cash said. "I don't care."

He was a good liar. When you could see through other people's lies, you picked up what worked and what didn't. He'd always been able to lie to Arkady, even when he hadn't really wanted to. The Abascals had never learned to care about what people really thought or why they lied. Why should they?

Only one problem.

Cash wrapped his hand around the back of Arkady's neck, fingers buried in the short nap of cropped hair, and pulled him down into a real kiss. He chewed Arkady's lips open and chased the salt-and-cinnamon prickle of Abascal magic past his teeth and into his mouth. Tongues tangled, wet and slick, and Cash tightened his fingers around the scruff of Arkady's neck. He could feel the tendons and the long straps of muscle taut under the warm golden skin.

It was rough, impatient, and hungry—all teeth, irritation, and twelve *fucking* years of not doing it. It was exactly the same and completely different. The fine gold stubble that scruffed Arkady's jaw was rough against Cash's mouth, and his shoulders were broader, heavy with lean muscle under his finely tailored suit.

And Cash? How was he different, he wondered distractedly. From the familiar ache in the back of his neck, he knew he wasn't any taller. *Still* familiar, for fuck's sake.

Arkady twisted his fingers in Cash's hair and pulled his head back to bare the tight line of his throat. Cash whined in protest as the kiss was broken, then strangled the sound in frustration. He was always the one who wanted… more.

"I like this," Arkady said mildly as he tightened his grip in dark curls. His knuckles pressed against Cash's skull—not hard enough to hurt, but the thought was there. It made Cash squirm. "You always wore it short before."

"Because assholes pull on it," Cash said tartly.

Arkady chuckled, pulled Cash's head back farther, and kissed his way down until he could nuzzle the thin skin under Cash's jaw. Anxiety peaked in a metallic adrenaline rush as Cash felt sharp teeth pinch his jugular. All it would take would be a little bit of pressure and his throat would be torn out. It made Cash's knees weak, and he swallowed raggedly as the hot flush of hunger washed through him.

The first time they kissed, Cash was sixteen and cocky, sure he was about to wrap the reserved Abascal scion around his finger. It turned out that knowing what he was doing had done him absolutely no good in the long run. Or short run. Arkady had always been a quick learner.

Arkady curled his free hand around Cash's hip and pulled him in closer. His erection nudged against Cash's stomach.

"You're going to do what I tell you," Arkady said roughly.

For a lust-dazed second, Cash almost said yes. He caught the word on the tip of his tongue and tried to squirm away. Arkady let him.

"You're an asshole," Cash said. "I'm not going to get involved in Abascal business again just because you kissed me."

Arkady looked amused as he put his hands in his pockets. "You kissed me," he pointed out. "Casper—"

"Cash."

Arkady rolled his eyes. "If you insist. Cash. You know I still want you now. Are you going to hear me out?"

It was pointless to get annoyed with Arkady for being an Abascal. It wasn't just who he was, it was what he was. The same way that Cash sniffed out secrets to lick at the raw spots, Arkady angled to make deals.

A man had to eat, after all.

Cash still gave Arkady the finger and stalked out of the room. He slammed the kitchen door behind him and slouched back against it to catch a breath that wasn't ripe with Arkady. It didn't work. Cash could smell Arkady on his skin, taste him on his tongue. It was the clean soap and green-tea cologne of humanity, layered over the darker smoke-and-honey-mead smell of his power.

From experience, Cash knew he'd smell the renfaire bonfire on himself long after the green tea had faded.

Worse than that, down in the pit of his bones, where his monster sprawled, he could taste Arkady's *need* like whiskey. Not just the hot cinnamon burn of want, but a dark, smoky thread of genuine concern that plucked at Cash.

"Fuck," he muttered to himself.

"Not until we talk," Arkady said, so close to Cash's ear that he had to be leaning against the other side of the door. "If it helps, this is for El's sake too."

It did.

El was his. It had been made very clear, years ago, that Arkady wasn't. No matter how much he made Cash ache, that wasn't going to change.

"What do you need me to do?" he asked.

"Stop hiding in the kitchen and come out to talk to me," Arkady said. His voice faded as he moved away from the door. "For a start."

Cash pushed himself off the door and padded across the kitchen. He might be going to do what Arkady wanted—he knew full well that "just hear him out" wasn't going to end there, so why pretend—but he didn't have to be prompt about it.

Sure, as long as you don't ask "how high," it means you're your own man and just wanted to jump.

Cash grimaced at how close to the bone *that* cut and how familiar it sounded. At sixteen, he'd definitely believed that. On the other hand, the snide little voice hadn't actually piped up when it could have been helpful—for example, before Cash kissed Arkady. So it could shove it.

He got a beer out of the fridge and pressed the cold glass to the back of his neck. The chill made him flinch, a trickle of condensation icy as it dribbled down his spine. It did absolutely nothing to quench the itch of want that made his skin feel too tight on his wiry frame.

It felt like he hadn't fucked anyone since the last time with Arkady, hadn't felt anything. He had. For a while Cash had even fallen into the old wisp trap of believing that what you ate was what you were. It had felt real, playing human house with Pete and swallowing all that filtered love—right up until Pete started to talk about living together and adopting El.

Maybe Cash didn't hate Donna after all. He popped the cap off the bottle with the edge of the table. If he ever suggested that to her, the old monster would have consumed herself in her fury, like a rat snake eating its own tail.

It had been twelve years, yet Arkady pulled Cash's hair and chewed on his throat and Cash's body apparently decided that this was sex and the rest had just been… filler.

Cash took a swig of beer and headed back into the main room. His own man, that was definitely what he was.

THE HOUSE was clean, but it wasn't particularly tidy. There was a stack of roughly folded laundry on one chair, a plate and an empty glass abandoned on top of El's textbooks for school, and at least three shoes kicked under the table.

Shabby was the word. Cash got paid well enough, but he worked long hours, and sometimes there were long stretches between jobs. There was always something better to do with his money than replace the carpet—a rug covered the burn well enough—or repair the lock on the door.

Somehow Arkady, sprawled bonelessly on the couch with one foot braced on the coffee table, managed to make it look classy. Cash didn't know if it was confidence, power, or really good tailoring, but Arkady made everywhere look like a deliberately staged photoshoot.

In contrast, Cash tended to make everywhere he went look like a recent crime scene. It wasn't fair. That was one good thing about being a monster, though. No one ever told you it would be.

"Okay," Cash said. He pushed Arkady's foot off the coffee table and sat down on it in front of him. "Now what?"

Arkady looked frustrated. "Do I have to kiss you stupid every time I see you to get a civil word out of you?" he asked as he put his foot down on the floor. "Or just every ten minutes?"

Cash smirked despite himself as he took a swig of beer. "I can't promise anything," he said dryly. "But it could work."

He regretted the joke immediately as something dark flickered through Arkady's faded eyes and he reached for him. Cash leaned back quickly until he had half sprawled out over the coffee table, weight braced on one arm.

"How about we just call a truce instead," he said.

Arkady plucked the bottle from his hand and leaned back into the faded red leather of the couch. He licked the rim of the bottle, tongue curved around the glass, and Cash felt the damp kiss of it against his mouth.

"I'm not being a dick," Arkady pointed out. He stopped playing with the bottle and took a drink, his throat pulled tight as he tipped his head back to swallow. When he was done, he set the bottle down and wiped his thumb over his lower lip. "Even though I've as much justification as you, but I'm not here to dig up the past."

Cash looked away. That was a good thing—you could dig up the dead and make them dance, but they were still dead—but part of him didn't want to believe it. He took a breath—the little flicker of magic had thickened the smoke-and-honey smell—and tried to focus. This wasn't how he expected today to go. He should have been on the road to Baton Rouge by now. One of the splatter-rite streamers needed a cameraman for an exorcism on a family out in a nearby town. It wasn't as reliable as the reality-exorcism gig, but it paid better. A week on a Netflix doc in Gramercy, exorcising some cursed workers from the petrochemical plant, would pay for El's camp next year. Although Cash had a feeling he was going to miss out on that.

"You said you needed a favor," Cash said. "What is it?"

Arkady had been the one who wanted to talk. Now he looked cagey as he took another drink of beer.

"Madeline and I divorced," he said. "I assumed you knew."

"Why?"

Arkady gave him a dry look and slowly ran his thumb over the mouth of the bottle in a slow caress. It was fainter this time, the sympathetic connection weakened as the bottle settled into Arkady's possession, but Cash felt the warmth of it. Okay, so they both knew why.

"I don't pick at old scabs," Cash said bluntly. "Unless it's something El told me about after a visit to Donna, I don't know about your life."

Arkady actually had the balls to look annoyed. He washed the bad taste away with a drink of beer and offered it back to Cash. "It turned out we were incompatible, in a lot of ways. A dynastic alliance with no children is… not particularly dynastic."

"Sorry."

17

The corners of Arkady's mouth twisted in a stab at humor. "Why?"

"I never wanted you to be unhappy," Cash said as he took a drink. He couldn't play the same tricks with sympathetic magic, but Arkady still watched his mouth like he could feel it purse against the glass.

"Then why fuck my sister?" Arkady asked, his voice deceptively lazy and definitely venomous.

Cash choked on the beer. By the time he cleared his throat, Arkady had grimaced and dismissed the question with a wave of his hand. Twelve years of practiced responses—everything from the truth to baroque likes—wasted because Cash couldn't get a word out before the moment passed.

"I need a liar I can trust," Arkady said as he leaned back, suddenly the businesslike Abascal son. He crossed his legs, long and lean in gray trousers, and laced his fingers together. "Someone who nobody will think twice about."

It was meant to be cruel, and it worked because it was almost true. A low-key liar who Arkady could trust had been exactly what Donna expected of Cash when she sponsored him. It wasn't as if his mom could afford the fees at Midnight Springs.

Cash had just been too human for it. Not to mention, at sixteen, a horny little bastard.

"Donna has other wisps working for her," Cash said. "One of them—"

"Someone that I can trust," Arkady repeated in a clipped voice. "Everyone currently in Donna's employ is… suspect. They're too close."

"Too close to what?"

"To real monsters."

Cash took a drink. "You're going to need to explain," he said. "The veiled insults aren't really helping me follow."

"I didn't think they were that veiled," Arkady said. His eyes flickered tungsten yellow with irritation, although Cash didn't think it was entirely aimed at him. "Someone is selling information—about us, about our… business—to your colleagues. In particular, business in and around Roanoke. A redcap was nearly caught on camera at a body dump, the Black Witch of Merrimac was doorstepped outside her own house with a list of missing children and a photo of her fifty years ago, and the Worm has lost his seat on the Prodigium after a tip-off led the Jesuits to his latest… interest. He shed his human skin to escape the hunt without exposing us—left the husk for them to fish out of the river—and has to go to ground until he can grow a new one."

There was a pause. When Cash didn't fill it, Arkady grimaced for him.

"Say it," he ordered.

There was A Way to couch accusations among the well-bred and horrifying, a delicate hemming that didn't put any backs up. Cash had been dragged up, though. He knew the rules, but he could get away with pretending he didn't.

"You know Donna did it, right?" he said. The family line had been—for centuries—that Belladonna didn't *want* a seat on the Prodigium, just to live quietly with her children. Everyone knew it was a lie. The head table of the Prodigium had brought their wasted feet down on the matter and blocked her ascension. She *owned* some minor seats outright and was owed by half the rest, but the Prodigium would never let her put her skinny ass directly on a red velvet seat. Not if they could help it, anyhow.

With a local seat suddenly empty, they might not be able to stop her, not without making their objections public rather than just… understood.

Arkady looked away, his profile sharp, the slice of his nose and the set line of his jaw. "She denies it," he said. "To the Left Hand of the Prodigium, to the Black Witch, and to her heir's face."

"And she'd never risk her good name for a lie."

"She wouldn't risk her skin for a lie," Arkady said. He pushed his hair back from his face as he looked at Cash. "My mother is a terror in the night and a curse on the land, but when she came here, she gave the Prodigium flesh and bone, the same as all the other great old monsters of the world. If she breaks one of the Cardinal Laws, *the* Cardinal Law, they'll kill her. And… and besides, how? I can't imagine her sneaking out of the manor to go and meet up with a priest in a bar to trade confidences."

"Most shows have tip lines," Cash said. "People call in sightings. Stuff. All she'd need was a number. Do you really believe she didn't do it?"

Arkady hesitated—just a flicker of guilty *something* in the tilt of his mouth before it was gone—and then nodded.

"I do," he said. "I don't put it past her, and she'll shed no tears for the Worm. But if it was her, she'd have made sure he was dead."

That was true.

Cash chewed the inside of his cheek. Part of him wanted to nope out before he got caught in the politics of it all again, but he was a monster. If someone outed him, then his coworkers would film as Winslow pinned him down and filled his eyes and his mouth with silver and salt. Then they'd come for Ellie. They'd damn her for a monster—even if she wasn't enough of one to fight back yet—and call it a job well done when they tossed her corpse in the sea.

Monsters were selfish things. They could love and be generous, but the thought at the forefront of their mind was usually for themselves. Cash was caught off guard by the sick rush of anger that hit him at the thought of Ellie pinned down by Winslow's bony piety and old bible. He dragged his mind away from the thought of his hands closed around Winslow's flushed throat and scowled at Arkady.

"What do you want me to do, anyhow?" Cash asked. "The sort of people who would know the Worm's comings and goings, his latest conquest? We don't exactly hang out in the same places."

The sort of people tapped to make the Worm's visit to his latest conquest run smoothly didn't send their spawn to camp on a bus. And they had spawn, not children.

Arkady stood up and straightened his jacket with an absentminded tug. "Don't worry about that," he said. "They're all going to be at the estate this weekend for a celebration and to see if Donna is going to join the Prodigium or my father in his grave. All you have to do is see who's lying when they say they think Donna betrayed us all."

"I don't exactly have an invite, so how are you going to explain why I'm there?" Cash asked as he stood up. He didn't like being loomed over. Old resentments left a bad taste on the back of his tongue, and he tried to wash it away with the last of the beer. It didn't work. "Tell them I'm your driver?"

Arkady put his knuckle under Cash's chin and tipped his head back.

"No, you're going to be my date," he said. Cash flinched at the idea. He'd rather be the help than playact that. There was a bleak satisfaction on Arkady's face as he watched Cash's reaction. "To my sister's wedding. Everyone will just assume I want to ruin her day."

Chapter Three

THERE WAS a shop in Savannah that made stationery for monsters. Most of them had email—hell, most of them were on Grindr—but pixels and programs didn't quite have the same... malevolence as vellum and ink, smooth as bloody silk.

It was a family business, the paper shop, although some of the apprentices hadn't wanted to join the family at first.

Arkady had left the invitation propped on the coffee table, against the drained beer bottle. Glossy black ink sketched out the location and date in perfect loops, while the names of Ilyana and her new husband-to-be scored the paper in acid-gold letters. It looked obscenely unfortunate—an omen with an RSVP.

Apparently Jerome would be there, as the groom. No second name. Either Cash was meant to know already, or Donna didn't want anyone to mention it. It was hard to tell without more context.

"Yana," Cash said to the answering machine. "Call me."

He hung up and tightened his grip on the phone in frustration as he fought the urge to throw it into the wall. It wouldn't help. It just felt like it would. Cash scowled, grabbed the bag he'd packed for the Gramercy shoot, and called Tom as he headed down the hall into his bedroom.

"Family emergency," he said as Tom answered. "I can't make it. Get Barrows. Remind him he owes me one."

Cash emptied the bag out on the bed. His jeans, T-shirts, and toiletries were tangled around each other. He liked the old band T-shirts—a very human interest that 90 percent of people didn't want to talk to you about—but inconspicuous at an upper-class monster destination wedding they weren't.

What they were, Cash realized as he dangled a TORN T-shirt from his finger and Tom yelled in his ear, was clean, though not exactly fresh. He'd shoved them in the bag about a week ago so he wouldn't forget them, but they didn't smell like Arkady's skin.

"Dude, Barrows is good, but he flinches," Tom said as he wound down from angry to annoyed. "*You* don't flinch. Remember the *Darling Demon* shoot? She puked bile in the shape of a snake at you, and you didn't even twitch. That's what I need. Fucking steady hand."

"Yeah, well." Cash pulled his T-shirt over his head and tossed it at the hamper in the corner of the room. "Make do with Barrows. I can't come."

"Did you get a better offer?" Tom asked suspiciously. "I've heard rumblings there's some big investigation being shot up in your neck of the woods."

"From who?" Cash asked, phone tucked against his shoulder as he pulled black cotton over his head. He still smelled like Arkady, but at least it was only magic and not skin and sweat.

Tom snorted at him. "Fuck off," he said. "You just dropped me in the shit. Why should I do you any favors?"

"I'd owe you one," Cash said. His voice felt cold on his tongue, damp like mist as he let his power soak into it. Sometimes it worked over the phone, sometimes it didn't. It depended on how susceptible the person on the other end was. "I could put in a good word for you with Winslow. You could follow up on that Utah story with him."

He felt the tug as Tom took the bait, the specter of profitable respectability briefly very real for him. The Utah story, what had come out through official channels, wasn't just sensational, it was tragic… but no one involved would talk about it. Winslow had been there, though, right in the middle of it, with his buttoned-up starched shirt and worn bible. If the good preacher vouched for Tom….

Tom spat the hook right back out. Either the magic had failed or he just didn't know.

"Go fuck yourself, Cash," he said. "I won't forget this, you asshole."

He hung up. Cash sucked the sour reek of spent magic back down and tucked the phone into his back pocket. His bones ached with the first dull twinge of hunger as the monster grumbled with the wasted effort. Cash grimaced. He was out of shape. It was just easier to eat at work—demons always prepared more misery than they could eat—than find the time to make someone suffer from scratch *and* take El to hockey *and* help her with her homework.

Maybe he needed to make the effort, though. He didn't want El to cut her metaphysical teeth on fast food.

Or, his monster slipped into his brain as Cash opened his wardrobe to grab stuff, *show yourself up in front of Arkady, who spends power like it's pennies down a well.*

Cash licked the taste of smoked honey off his lips and thought about the faded glitter of Arkady's eyes. It was unusual for anyone under a century to have worn their skin down that much. Most monsters born under the Prodigium's rule since they decided to let humanity believe they were more or less extinct could still be outside at noon without issue. For Arkady to have shed so much that he burned it off in the morning sun….

That wasn't his business. He pushed jackets and T-shirts aside to grab some of his dressier clothes from the back of the rail. They weren't exactly monster fashion—which favored velvet, brocade, and frills—but they'd do well enough.

He rolled them up, stuffed them into his bag, and pinned them down with his elbow while he dragged the zip over. The invite said the ceremony started on Friday, midnight, which gave him two days to get there. There was no reason he couldn't sniff around a bit first. If he could solve Arkady's problem without having to play boyfriend in front of the monster aristocracy—an idea that made him feel like his chest was being crushed—he'd take it.

Your own man.

Cash had a feeling that mocking echo was his own, nothing to do with the hungry thing in his marrow. He ignored it as he slung the bag over his shoulder and headed out, grabbing the invite on the way through the living room. The paper was thin, smooth, and just a bit too warm as he tucked it inside his jacket.

If his human contacts didn't know who was buying secrets, maybe the monsters would be more help. The Black Witch and the Worm probably weren't going to take his calls, but he knew where at least *one* redcap was this afternoon.

Where else would an upwardly mobile monster enjoy murder and mimosas but at the country club?

THE BOOK and Candle Country Club perched on the shore a few miles outside of Roanoke city limits. If you looked it up on Google, it claimed to be a golf club, but the landscape around it was all bare rock and scrubby, salt-stunted trees instead of smooth and manicured. The members liked to play different games, and no one ever got out of the rough.

The guard at the gate leaned down to peer through the open window at Cash. His eyes flickered over Cash and then around the interior of the car.

"This is a members-only club, sir," the man said. His breath smelled like a meatball sub, and he wanted, so badly, an excuse to punch someone. Cash didn't even have to try to pick that up. The tag on his shirt said West, and he spun his finger in the air as he directed Cash, "You'll have to turn around."

Cash hung one hand over the steering wheel.

"I'm a guest," he said.

West pushed himself off the car. "I'll check the list." He stepped back toward the hut and grabbed a clipboard. "What's your name, sir?"

"I'm not on the list," Cash said. He let West's expression curdle into satisfaction before he pricked the smug bubble. "I'm with the Abascals."

West was human—for now, someone had their hooks in him for him to be trusted here—but he knew the name. He scowled, his disappointment thin and tea-bitter when Cash inhaled it. He clutched his list with both hands.

"Anyone could say that," he said.

"But they'd only do it the once," Cash pointed out. He pulled the invite out of his jacket and held it up. In the sunlight the gold letters trembled as if only surface tension kept them from sliding off the page. The edges blistered—tiny white bubbles of water—and curled. "I have a wedding invite to deliver."

"Who to?"

"Some lucky monster who probably doesn't want to stand Donna Abascal up." Cash tucked the invite away, out of the sun, and grinned at West. The low-grade anxiety that oozed out of the guard wasn't much of a meal, but it took the edge off Cash's hunger. "You have no idea how much she hates when people don't RSVP. She'll bite your head off for it."

They both knew he meant it literally. That part was actually true. Donna didn't value manners particularly—she'd clean her nails with someone's bones at the dinner table—but disrespect she didn't tolerate.

Cash could testify to that.

After a moment of indecision, West swallowed hard and leaned back into the hut to open the gates.

"I'll let management know you're coming," he said.

Cash drove through the tall gates and down the narrow, winding road toward the clubhouse. Halfway down there was a dark, splattered stain on the road where something had died. It might have passed for an animal, but whoever it was had left a handprint smeared across the concrete.

Careless. That was the sort of thing that ended up on Google Earth.

A tall, painfully thin woman waited for Cash outside the club as he pulled into the white-marble horseshoe-curved drive. Her hair was so shiny it looked wet, and when she smiled, she had braces on her uneven teeth. Ena Caldwell. Her mother, Keiko, owned the country club, but she'd worn out her humanity before she even moved to the US. Cash had never met them, but people talked.

26

"I think that's far enough," Ena said as Cash got out of the car. "If the Abascals have business in the Book and Candle, they send Shanko, not some… pretty little gift basket."

"Well, it's his day off," Cash said. "I'm looking for a huldra, Gret, and her redcap friend."

Ena pulled an annoyed face and *scuttled* forward, black "legs" extended from her milk-pale sac of an aura, to grab Cash's shoulder. Her fingers dug down toward bone as she squeezed.

"I don't need wisp trash at my club, fucking my guests," she hissed as she leaned down toward him. "Or picking out their secrets like whelks from the shell. Bad for business. Now I told you—"

She stopped midthreat and snapped her mouth shut. The click of her teeth was audible, and her nose twitched as she sniffed the stink of Abascal power that still clung to Cash's skin and breath.

Cash peeled her hand off his shoulder. "The huldra?" he said. "And I'll tell Shanko you missed him today. He's always got an eye out for a new lady friend."

Ena made a sour face and pulled her hand out of Cash's grip as she backed away.

"I meant no disrespect," she said stiffly. "The Abascals don't usually have truck with your kind."

Strangely enough, that still sounded like disrespect. Cash's monster drummed at his ribs in response to the insult, but he let it pass. Ena could wrap him up in a bow and liquify him over days if she wanted, and Cash wasn't interested in the time it would take to return the favor… although it would be easy.

He could *feel* the water nearby. It wasn't the still, drowning pools wisps favored, but it still cozened at him. Time and cold patience would be all it would take. The water would back him up….

Ena hissed at him, a flash of something black and hairy behind her human teeth. "I'll rip your tongue out of your head, wisp," she warned. "The Abascals have no use for *that*."

"You'd be surprised," Cash said dryly.

It took a second and then Ena caught up. She put her nose in the air and waved her hand brusquely at his car.

"Park *that* in back where no one can see it," she said. "And don't linger. Servants get to obey orders, not enjoy the amenities. Gert and her friend are at the bar."

She stalked off. Cash moved the car. No need to be a dick about it.

CASH HAD just seen half the monsters in the bar at the camp drop-off. A few of them raised a hand to wave him over to their tables, invitations that caught Cash by surprise. He guessed that not socializing with his own kind was on him, not them. That or they'd seen him talking to Arkady. He preferred that explanation.

Uncomfortable, Cash dodged the overtures and pushed his way through the crowd.

A werewolf, Gucci shirt split at the seams over heavy muscles, chewed on a bloody bone like a rib at a party and sipped nightshade with a fancy umbrella in it. He was deep in conversation with a naked hairy woman who dripped a steady stream of water into a puddle around her Louboutins.

Most monsters didn't bother with real human lives unless they had kids—when you had to get human food for them and send them to human schools and teach them to use computers—but they all still had to *pass* day-to-day. That was the Prodigium's rule if you wanted to live in a city where the prey was fat and the Wi-Fi accessible, instead of being banished to a damp cave in the woods.

There were maybe a handful of places in Roanoke where monsters could socialize without masks. Most of them were pretty low-key—a bar that kept a back door open after hours or an empty warehouse with blacked-out windows where the cops didn't bother to answer noise complaints anymore.

The Book and Candle was for monsters who still wanted people to know they were doing very well in the human world.

As the owner gestured grandly, Cash ducked under a segmented arm and found himself at the barstool next to Gert. She flinched when she recognized him and nearly choked on a cherry in her drink.

"Look, I didn't know you were the girl's father," she said quickly, as she dabbed at the front of her dress with a napkin. "But I didn't say anything that other people aren't saying where you can't hear them. No one understands why Donna didn't… act before anyone got attached to the girl. Not like she's never eaten a baby before."

One of her cluster of wannabe socialites giggled through green teeth as she leaned between them to grab a handful of nuts. "Man, who amongst us *hasn't* eaten a baby? *Right*?"

"You have more human in you than Ellie does," Cash said coldly.

"I'm not an Abascal," Gert said. "It's just… not right. If they can't stay pure, how can the rest of us keep ourselves apart?"

Cash glanced at her extensions and the glittery designer necklace around her hollow neck. "The struggle goes on," he said dryly. Without the lash of his magic behind it for bite, Gert missed the jab and nodded sagely. Cash clamped down on his monster and glanced around the bar. "Actually, I need to talk to your redcap friend?"

"Ohhhh," Gert said, eyes wide. She waggled her finger down the bar, toward the end where the stocky redcap chatted to an even stockier troll. "He's down there, but he doesn't like them… little."

She smiled slyly at him with thick red lips as she reached back to pluck a black earwig from her rotted-out back. It wriggled as she crunched into it.

Cash left her to it.

"I figure once Jon's eighteen, I'll just sign all that over to him." Con the redcap was midflirt as Cash got within earshot. "Maybe head over to Scotland, kill a few farmers, and find a cave. Get back to my roots, you know?"

The troll licked salt out of a shot glass and looked amused but horny. Beads glittered in the tufts on his long ears and the matted tuft on the end of his tail as it lashed when Cash put his hand on Con's shoulder.

"Five minutes," Cash said. The troll scowled at him. "It's an errand, for the Abascals."

The troll looked a mixture of worried and impressed as they quickly backed away from the conversation. Cash had forgotten how *easy* it was to move through society with Abascal patronage as a cudgel. It was a shame he couldn't get used to it. One weekend only.

"What do you want?" Con asked as he pulled his cap down over his eyebrows and smeared fresh blood across his pale skin. It looked like he and Gert had stopped for murder on their way for mimosas. "I didn't say anything about your kid. I'm sure she'll do *fine* at monster camp with all our real, meat-eating monsters."

He snort-laughed at his own joke.

"I went to camp too," Cash said. "Trust me, when all your spoiled brat meat eaters cry themselves to sleep at night? Ellie will eat their souls. Don't worry about my kid. She'll be fine."

From his lips, Cash thought miserably to himself, to the Mother of Monsters' ears. Children didn't get killed at camp anymore, but learning to stick up for yourself was a life skill the camp expected them to pick up on their own.

"What do you want, then?" Con asked. He glanced over his shoulder toward the troll and scowled as he saw a dog-headed man buy a fresh glass of salt. "Come on, man. My wife's going to be here soon, and if she has to pick someone up for us, I'll never hear the end of it."

"It's the first night of camp," Cash said. "You'll find someone. I heard that one of the redcaps got picked up by the cops?"

Con's face sagged, and he glanced around. "Where'd you hear that?"

"Guess."

"Yeah, right, well. It's handled," Con said. "Just like the Prodigium wanted. The guy's going to take the fall as a human, do his time. If they give him the death penalty, it'll be a decade, less with no appeals."

There was nothing supernatural about a redcap kill. It was natural causes, if you considered being stabbed natural causes for a human. All they really wanted was the blood.

"How'd he get caught?"

"I don't know," Con said irritably. "He's my brother, not my friend. What's it to you, anyhow?"

Cash leaned against the bar and gestured for the bartender to refill Con's whiskey. "I work the exorcism circuit, and I've heard…."

He hesitated, and Con finished the sentence for him. "Rumors?"

"Yeah."

Con picked up his drink and gestured for Cash to follow him over to one of the black leather booths. The two goblins already there were roughly evicted so Con could squeeze in. He took his hat off and set it down on the table, where it squished against the stainless steel and left red smears on the metal.

"When my brother started to go on about it, I thought he was nuts, y'know? There was someone following him, this car he saw over and over, people going through his trash. I told him he was imagining it, that if anyone heard him talking like that, he'd end up on the wrong end of the Left Hand of the Prodigium. Some of us get like that, you know, if we stay on the edges. Too close to humans but not part of the world? Paranoid."

"And then he got caught."

Con rubbed a hand over his blood-matted hair and picked at the elflocked knots with blunt fingers.

"Danny's *careful*," he said. "Paranoia makes for a bad brother but a good killer. He didn't make mistakes. Plus, I've heard other stuff. Gert's nanny? She had her recycling gone through. They took away the bloodstained papers. Another guy I know, a púca, got freaked out by a dinner date. He said the guy put holy water in his glass and then tried to get him to get into a car. Sheep biting the dog, or what? I thought the Prodigium might be poking around—I heard the Worm was in town—but they do what they like, and you said the exorcists are sniffing around. Do you think someone fancies himself a… Hunter?"

He dropped his voice as he said that and laughed uncomfortably, because it was a stupid idea. Right? There hadn't been any Hunters since the Butcher. As far as the human world was concerned, there hadn't been any monsters since the Butcher. Not *really*. A few insipid monsters left in Europe, a few inbred clans in the mountains—just enough to keep the world interesting but not enough to worry about.

Bigfoot, of course.

"Nothing like that," Cash said. "The exorcists don't want to play around with bloodbaths and hunts. The whole point is they win every week, except for the occasional two-parter, where they win in week two. The monsters who've had trouble, did they know each other?"

That would have been easy, but Con shook his head. "No. Danny was only passing through, and Gert imported the nanny from Finland. Some relative of hers she's sponsoring. They didn't know anyone."

Not entirely true. There was *one* person they all knew, but… there was no way he knew the Worm or the Black Witch. They were *real* monsters, the only one of their kind that was needed.

"Don't worry about it," Cash said as he stood up. "It's being dealt with."

"By Belladonna?" Con asked.

"Sure," Cash said. "Why not?"

Chapter Four

THE PILLOWS in the Roanoke Last Stop motel smelled like mice and KFC. Cash recoiled from it as he woke up, the back of his throat greasy, as if he'd swallowed the ghost of fried chicken past.

Maybe, he thought sourly as he knuckled the sleep out of his eyes, he should have cashed in his invitation to the estate last night after all. Even if the mattresses were the same ones he'd crashed on a decade ago, he'd bet they were still more comfortable than the fucked-into-exhaustion springs he'd spent the night on.

Cash stretched out the kinks in his back and rolled off the bed. He shed his briefs as he headed into the shower for a quick wash in the peeling avocado-green tub.

He stood naked behind the crime-scene-red shower curtain with his face turned up into the tepid stutter of the water. Without opening his eyes, Cash scrubbed with a handful of watered-down lemon shower gel.

His fingers curled around his cock, slippery with suds, and to his credit, he did *try* to imagine someone else. Con and his thick-skinned, heavy fighter's hands, or nice human Pete and his careful touch. Hell, that guy with the cheekbones from the Hunter historical drama on the CW, set back in the glory years of fucking monsters and then killing them.

He had a whole bank of wank fantasies that weren't going to mean *anything.*

It didn't matter. Cash could taste smoke and honey in the back on his throat… like he'd just been kissed. The memory of elegant, too-warm fingers skimmed roughly along the tender skin of his cock, and sharp teeth scraped over his neck in a tease of a bite until Cash's body was just one long wire strung trembling between two aching points.

Cash could have tried harder to edit in an acceptable fantasy instead, but at that precise moment, he didn't want to. He folded his lower lip between his teeth as he stroked down his cock and tightened his grip at the base. It wasn't quite tight enough to hurt, just enough to make him squirm. Until he *ached.*

The water spluttered a couple of degrees hotter as someone, somewhere in the motel turned the cold water on. Cash tipped his head forward so it stung the nape of his neck and ran down his spine. He could almost feel Arkady's body pressed against his, cock hard and hot in the small of his back and stubble rough on Cash's skin as he worried bruises down his throat and over his shoulders.

Cash chewed harder on his own mouth as he jerked himself off in close-enough mimicry of his memory of Arkady. Was it the first time they'd fucked, he wondered hazily, or the last? He couldn't place it outside of the impatient tug of his *need* right here and now. It felt like honey spiced with whiskey, sticky as it puddled low in his stomach but with a burn to it. Like a bad idea, but he didn't care.

Pleasure built like pressure, and Cash lost the slow, almost cruel pace of Arkady's fingers. His hand jerked along his cock in quick, hurried strokes, and Arkady grumbled in his ear at his impatience.

"I would have got you there," he said as he wrapped his free hand around Cash's throat and squeezed. "Eventually. Once you begged."

The thought of that—that scratchy need in his throat as he finally, always, broke and said what Arkady wanted—pitched Cash over the edge like he'd been shoved out a window. He spilled come between his fingers, stringy and sticky as it mixed with the thin lather of soap, and he felt the ghost of a memory bite an approving kiss against his jaw.

Then the last of the hot water ran out all at once and the shower went from sauna to ice bath. Cash shuddered at the shock against his hot skin, spluttered out a "fuck," and rinsed off as hastily as he could manage with the plastic shower curtain trying to stick to him.

He turned the water off—the pipes behind the wall knocked in noisy protest—and dragged yesterday's jeans on over wet skin. The denim scraped the sensitive skin of his cock and made him shudder with a jolt of pleasure that pulled from his balls to the base of his spine.

"Ten years forgetting him," Cash muttered to himself as he dragged his hand down his face and flicked the still-soapy water off his fingers, "and one kiss has him front and center again?"

Or maybe he hadn't done such a great job of forgetting… anything at all, now he thought about it.

Cash snorted to himself, because that was helpful. He squeezed the water out of his hair and pulled his shirt on. The thin cotton wrinkled and stuck to his damp skin. His phone buzzed on the nightstand, and he lunged for it, a sudden burst of paranoia thick in his throat as he expected the worst.

Instead it was a text from Camp Midnight. The kids weren't allowed phones—and unless coverage had improved up that mountain, it wouldn't do any good if they were—but every day the counselors sent proof of life to parents. Cash had forgotten about that, pushed into line with the other orphans and foundlings for a group snap.

Ellie warranted a picture all on her own. She had a black eye— already—and had a dirt-crusted shovel swung up over her head. It looked like she was having fun. The text said, "A little homesick, but settling in well. Has already made enemies."

"That's my girl," Cash said.

He stared at her face for a second. This was for her, because it didn't matter that she had Cash's name. She was an Abascal, and everyone knew it. Better people fear her for it than make her the scapegoat for her family's sins.

Whatever Cash felt—*used to* feel—for Arkady didn't matter. Not that it ever had to anyone else, but now it was a distraction.

He forwarded the message to Donna. Well, to Shanko, but he'd pass it on. The old monster was nothing if not loyal to her.

Cash had packed up his stuff and sat down to pull his boots on when someone knocked on the door—two sharp knocks, a long pause, three staccato raps, and then silence.

Finally. He'd thought he was going to have to leave a message with reception.

Cash stamped his feet into his boots and left the laces to drag as he answered the door. The woman outside pushed in past him without any invitation.

Anna-Beth Fennway wasn't entirely human, but mostly. She didn't need to be invited inside, she could cross running water, and neither silver, crosses, nor iron made her blister. All she'd gotten from whatever monster had fucked her great-great granny, was that she had a faintly off-putting air about her.

That and an instinct for the unwholesome. She worked as a spotter for most of the local reality-rite shows, with a folder of possessed houses and demonically influenced souls. Nobody liked her, but they were happy to pay her.

It was never enough, and she always had a paranoid suspicion that there was worse in the world that she hadn't found yet.

There was, of course. But just because you were right didn't mean you weren't paranoid.

"Hey," she said as she glanced nervously around the room. Her attention lingered on the TV. "What do you want, Cash? I gave Winslow his pick of couples last week."

He pulled an envelope of cash out of his pocket and handed it to her. She picked the flap up with her thumbnail and flicked through worn-edged notes. Her chapped lips pursed as she whistled soundlessly.

"Okay. What do you want?" she repeated, less impatiently and more suspiciously.

Cash left the door open a crack. "Has anyone paid you to follow someone in particular over the last few months?" he asked. "Go through their trash. See who they associated with. Anything like that?"

Anna-Beth frowned and tucked the envelope of cash into a pocket.

"If they did, would I tell you?" she asked. "That's not how you get work."

"I don't need to know who," Cash said. "Just if anyone has."

Paranoia tasted like tea made with limescale-heavy water. It was almost comforting, but there was a chalky undertone that lingered.

Cash's meal of choice was despair—meaty enough to chew as he supped it—but he could use this.

Anna-Beth zipped her jacket up to her collarbones.

"No," she said. "I heard the rumors too, figured that someone would at least hit me up for a couple of hot zones? Nothing. None of the other stringers in town have had a sniff either. If there's someone shooting in town, they already know what they're looking for."

That was what Cash was afraid of. It wouldn't exactly be good news that the humans had pierced the Prodigium's veil of mundanity on their own, but it wouldn't be *Cash's* problem. If it was just some researcher who was here to look for the monster under the bed, they'd have ended up at Anna-Beth's door. Or her at their door.

Roanoke didn't have the most dense monster demographic in the country—that was New York, despite the rent—but monsters had been here since before the first settlers "disappeared." It had been one of the first places to bend the neck to the Prodigium—two things that weren't unrelated. They were integrated, and there were no unusual clusters of disappearances or spikes of violence for someone to track.

For someone to just turn up in town and hit pay dirt? They had to have insider knowledge, and if it wasn't from a stringer? Then Arkady was right.

"My number's in the envelope," Cash said. "If you hear anything, let me know?"

Anna-Beth patted her breast pocket to make the cash rustle. "Unless they pay me more," she said with a thin smile. It was as good as a promise. She liked Cash; he was one of the few people she didn't make uncomfortable. "I'll have a sniff around, ask the usual suspects if they've heard anything. If I find anything out, are you going to be in town?"

"Close enough," Chase said. "My ex invited me to my other ex's wedding."

Anna-Beth raised her eyebrows at that. She reached up and tapped her finger against her neck. "Which of them gave you those?"

Cash's hand flew up to his neck. The skin felt hot under his fingers, and he stalked over to the mirror to peer into it. Hickeys dappled his throat from under his ear down to his collarbone, red-and-blue blotches stark and soft-edged against his pale skin.

Arkady's teeth on his neck, sharp kisses chewed into his flesh.

"The asshole," Cash said.

IT WAS funny how perspective changed a place. Cash had grown up on the north side of the island in a trailer with one bedroom and a view of the refineries out his window. Even the despair around there was junk food—empty calories with no real bite.

Even though there were no walls and the house was literally on wheels, it had been a prison.

Back then Cash had aspired to be Shanko. Everyone on the island, monster or human, was afraid of the tough old man in the black suit. They paid him their debts, they asked him for favors, and he drove around the island in a black Jeep he had other people clean for him. Cash's ambitions hadn't been able to imagine anything more than that.

Until one day Shanko had driven him up the long drive to the Abascal Hotel and Spa, all crushed-white-shell gravel and spiked slate roofs, and Cash had realized this was it. This was freedom—from the low-grade ache in his bones as his monster chewed on him for food, from the hand-me-downs that never fit in the crotch or the pits, from everything—and all he needed to do was be what they wanted.

Shame he'd fucked that up, really. It would have been an easy life. Half-human had always been too human for Cash's own good, especially where his stupid cock was concerned.

Except his cock *hadn't really been the problem, had it? His* cock *had always been happy with what it got out of the deal.*

For a second Cash held his breath, a trickle of pain tangy as a penny on his mental palate as he waited for the body blow. That was the truth, but only half of it. His head was full of silence. In the end, the truth only hurt once. A lie that mattered could be picked open a hundred times.

When Cash knew that, you'd think he'd acknowledge he was lying to himself. He didn't, though, he never did.

These days the estate looked like a trap. A pretty one, with amazing beds, but still just another cage.

Cash pulled up around the back of the hotel and tucked his battered old Dodge into a space in the staff parking lot, between Shanko's new black Jeep and a shiny blue Porsche with a child's car seat in the back. It would have been satisfying to pull his junker up front and watch a valet's face curdle, but he didn't want to be stuck here. Not any more than he already was.

He grabbed his bag from the back and headed toward the worn concave steps down to the hotel's back door. It opened before he got to it, and Shanko loomed up to block the way in.

Monsters were vain things. Most of them clung to their youth and human beauty for as long as they could—decades, centuries—until they could collapse directly into a grotesque old age. Shanko, for all ten-year-old Cash had thought he was an old man, was solidly middle-aged. His hair was short and dense on top of a heavy, sallow face.

There was always a faint smell of old meat around him, worked into the fibers of his shirts and suits. Not the hot, sweet copper stink of fresh meat, but dried flesh.

Old bones and dusty marrow. No one knew what Shanko was. He was just Donna's grubby left hand, her loyal dog for a few centuries at least. There were more than a few portraits of Donna, powdered and pomaded in lace and bloody velvet, with Shanko in the background hard at work with the bits left over.

"I should have drowned you like a rat when you were still small enough to fit in the bucket," Shanko said with contempt. "Do you really think you can fuck your way back into Arkady's favor?"

Cash was two steps up. The few inches of height put him eye to eye with Shanko, close enough, anyhow.

"What makes you think I haven't already?" he asked.

Shanko spat at his feet. The wad of phlegm was thick as chewed gristle. "Because he doesn't stink of bog water and regret," he said. "And you ain't limping."

Cash snorted out a laugh despite himself. "Still a comedian, old man," he said.

Shanko scowled at him from under thick eyebrows that looked as if he'd carved them straight from a cow's hide.

"I gotta do something to break the tension," he said. "Otherwise people just throw themselves at my fucking feet. The girl at camp?"

Shanko didn't bother to learn names, or at least admit he had, until people turned eighteen and their monsters fit under their skins. Before that, what was the point?

"Yeah, first year," Cash said. "She was worried she wouldn't make any friends—"

"She's an Abascal," Shanko interrupted dismissively. "Friends are for people who can't buy or bully minions. *You* have friends."

"And you have neither," Cash pointed out.

Shanko stiffened slightly as the jab slipped past the usual toothless cruelty and caught him on the raw. He scowled at the sting, a horrible knot of heavy flesh on his face, but accepted it as his due. Sometimes he needed a reminder that Cash wasn't an indentured servant anymore and that the Abascals had handed him Ellie like she was a castoff for the charity box before they realized they could love her.

"I got a picture this morning," Cash said. "She's settling in okay."

He pulled his phone out and showed Shanko the picture. It turned out a smile didn't look any better than a scowl on his broad face.

"Good girl," Shanko said. He stepped back and gestured for Cash to come in. "Arkady said to put you in your old room, in the family's wing."

"I don't suppose you'd care if I asked to be put somewhere else?"

"I'd think you were an ungrateful little bastard," Shanko said as Cash squeezed past him. He closed the door behind him and threw the corridor into pitch blackness. His voice scraped ominously out of the darkness, wet as flesh on the back of Cash's neck. "Just like you always were. It's a better room than mine, bog-haunt. I sleep down here, with Belladonna's hounds."

"You should take that up with Human Resources."

"I'm not human."

Cash shrugged and started forward. The darkness faded around him, watered down by a thin pearl-gray film of light as his eyes kindled. It would be hard to lure someone off the beaten path to drown them in a bog if they lost sight of you in the dark. He'd never seen it himself, but Ellie said he looked like a skull nightlight.

"Call PETA, then," Cash suggested. "What did those dogs do to deserve listening to you fart all night?"

Shanko chuckled, the sound thicker in his throat as it crawled around in the dimness. He gave Cash a casual cuff around the back of the head. The clip of heavy bones and thick knuckles against Cash's skull rattled his brains and made him stagger, but if Shanko had meant it, Cash would have been out for the count.

"Be careful," Shanko said, his voice dropping back to something almost human. "Belladonna knows you're here, and she's said nothing of it—not to her son, not to me, not even to her hounds."

Shit.

Chapter Five

NOTHING HAD changed since Cash left.

It would have been creepy if there had been anything personal there to start with. Cash looked around the room in search of something he'd left or a gap he could fill with a memory. But nope. He'd lived here for five years, and even the pictures on the wall had been chosen by someone else.

Of course—Cash eyed the heavy black wood adjoining door— he hadn't really lived here, had he. It had just been somewhere to put his clothes.

He kicked the bed frame. "Still there?" he asked.

An eye rolled out from under the bed, attached to a long braid of sinew. The pupil was a small, fang-lined mouth that mashed aimlessly at the air.

"Where would I go?" it whined miserably in a voice like a thousand gnats that drilled directly into whatever part of Cash's brain handled self-pity. A sort of sick, confusing misery retched into Cash's throat for a second and made his heart falter before his monster got in the way of it. "I'm *bits*. Not even all of them. A housekeeper vacuumed up a toe."

"You shouldn't litter," Cash said. "And I'm back for a couple of days, so you need to shift. I can't sleep through you crying all night."

A hand, disarticulated and clumsily strung back together in no particular order, crap-crawled from under the bed. It splayed flat on the floor and dragged itself out, lungs splayed like wings as it wheezed and burped.

When parents told children there was no monster under the bed, they were telling the truth. Ghosts, on the other hand, loved it under there.

"I live here," it whinged. "Why should I have to leave?"

"You don't live," Cash said. "You *do* moan all night long."

It had picked up an extra eye from somewhere—not human, maybe one of the guests' pets had died—and it leveled all three on him reproachfully.

"I was *murdered*," it reminded him. "Chopped up for *dogs. Evicted.* You never even sleep in here."

"Times change," Cash said. "And it's only for the weekend."

It groaned, fluttered smoke-stained lungs, and laboriously took flight to wobble drunkenly through the ceiling. Splintered ribs hung under it like a daddy longlegs' pencil-stroke limbs and rattled against each other as it moved.

Spirits—like the one at the Stevens's house—were free agents... usually. The gravitational well of a human's bad deeds could trap them in places or people, but they could usually break free eventually. Ghosts were the wrecked bits of souls not up to the commute to heaven or hell.

Most of them were screaming bags of frustrated rage, driven to avenge the slights that ended their mortal lives, even when they didn't have enough of themselves to know what those slights were. They either succeeded in that or an exorcist moved them on. It was different if they were killed by a monster. Then they got left where they died.

The hotel had maybe a dozen official ghosts, like bag-of-bones there, that had stitched themselves together into something like sentience. Then regretted it. Being a ghost sucked.

Cash dumped his bag onto the now unoccupied bed.

"Are you waiting for me to come to you?" he asked.

A low, whiskey-rough chuckle came from the other room, through the door that led to Arkady's quarters.

"That would be a change, wouldn't it," Arkady drawled.

Cash rolled his eyes. Power—whether it was money or monstrosity—warped people's ideas of how the world worked. Arkady had gotten Cash all the way out to the island, but he was put out that Cash wouldn't go the last five feet.

As if he was the one who did all the running. Ever. In anything. Even when they'd been together.

"Fine."

Cash pulled his camera out of the bag and stalked over to the door. Then he hesitated as he reached for the handle. It would be… *weird*… if it were locked. He didn't know if it would matter or not or what it would mean if it did, but it would definitely be strange.

He grabbed the polished brass as if it were hot, and he twisted it. It wasn't locked. The door swung open over thick deep-pile black carpet and revealed a room that was as soullessly luxurious as Cash's was sparse. There was plenty of personality in the thick oil-painted scenes of the homeland hung on the walls and the heavy cherrywood furniture that tried to make the sprawl of a suite seem small.

It just wasn't Arkady's personality.

Or it hadn't been. He didn't know Arkady anymore, it just felt like he did. He stepped across the threshold.

"Happy?" he asked

Arkady looked up from his laptop. He was slouched in a dark oxblood armchair that was all bronze studs and high, carved back. A glass of deep red wine sat on the table next to him, and he still sat with one leg hooked over the thin armrest of the chair. His feet were bare, and Cash nearly choked on his own lust.

His own monster squirmed in his bones, distracted and aroused by his arousal. It didn't want what he did, not exactly, but it was close enough to be hard to separate.

Arkady studied Cash, pale yellow eyes hard to read. "You're late," he said.

"The wedding doesn't start till tomorrow," Cash pointed out. "Shanko won't even have stocked your mom's larder."

Once it did start, it wouldn't end until Monday evening. Monsters didn't gather often. Most of them weren't social creatures anyhow, and the Prodigium discouraged it. So the few events that did draw them together had to carry a lot of weight. A wedding wasn't just about two people making a dynastic alliance, it was an opportunity to politick, to gather information, reaffirm old alliances, and give new slights.

Oh, and to be conspicuously richer and more terrible than your neighbor. Always that.

"You aren't a guest," Arkady pointed out. He closed the laptop and set it aside so he could stretch out more comfortably. His smile was sharp. "You're family, if you squint."

Cash looked around for a place to sit. There was nowhere but the bed, massive enough for five people and unmade, so he *knew* it would smell of Arkady. It felt like a trap.

"You could have the chair," Arkady offered lazily as he watched Cash. "If that would help."

The thought of Arkady in the rumpled bed, all long lines and boneless elegance on silk sheets as they talked, was vivid enough that Cash's mouth dried. He closed his eyes and slowly let his breath out.

"It really wouldn't," Cash said tightly. He sat down on the edge of the bed—it smelled pretty much how he'd imagined, flesh, musk, and the sweet-bitter tang of magic—and tried to ignore Arkady's smirk. "Yana needs to tell Ellie about this."

Arkady blinked. "About the Worm?"

"About the wedding," Cash said. "She's her mother."

"And you're her father," Arkady said. "I hadn't forgotten the details of how she was born, even if I have forgiven *her* for them."

Cash pinched the bridge of his nose. He ignored the old argument that wanted to puke out of his throat to be rechewed. Arkady had been *married* to someone else, yet Cash was still the one cast as the homewrecker. It wasn't fair, but it wasn't relevant either.

"It's the sort of thing a kid is meant to know *before* it happens," he said. "This man's going to be her stepdad, and she's never even met him. Her mom is getting married and doesn't invite her to the wedding? Her uncle keeps it from her?"

Arkady propped his chin in the palm of his hand, elbow braced on the arm of the chair, and listened patiently. A faint, fond smile curled his mouth. Eventually Cash's irritation with that elbowed the annoyance about the wedding out of the way.

"What?" he asked.

"I forget sometimes how human you used to be," Arkady said. "It's cute."

"Fuck you."

Arkady grinned. "You only have to ask." He ignored Cash's annoyed splutter and pushed himself easily up out of the chair. "If this marriage meant anything, even you would have heard about it. It's a sop to Yana's sentimentality and an excuse to host a gathering, since we haven't had a birth, a death, or any significant event in years. She's marrying a nobody, and this wedding means nothing. It's just an excuse to enjoy my mother's hospitality and plot against her in front of her face. If Ellie is upset, I'll explain that to her."

"Sure," Cash said dryly. "Because the cold politics of romance is what a kid who kisses her picture of Shawn Mendes good night will find comforting."

"One day she'll marry for power," Arkady pointed out. "She needs to get used to the idea."

"No," Cash said flatly. "She won't."

Arkady shrugged. "It's years away," he admitted. "We can discuss the details then."

"No," Cash repeated.

"You've gotten very fond of that word," Arkady said.

"So's Ellie," Cash said. "And she's twelve, so all she needs to know is that she has a new stepdad, not about dynastic marriages or the cost of power-brokering your loved ones."

Arkady picked up his glass and drained it. The liquid looked too thick for wine as he licked it off his lips.

"So, what, does she think that, at some point, Madeline and I actually liked each other?" he asked. "That I gave up on us because I just liked the cut of Madeline's jib?"

Well, that question had gone places Cash didn't think he could deal with right then. He looked away from Arkady's mouth. That had always made thinking easier.

"That's pretty much how it works with humans. Once you take murder off the table, people pick misery over divorce more than you'd think." Cash glanced down at the bag balanced on his thigh and seized on that to change the topic. "Speaking of which, it doesn't make any sense to tell people I'm your boyfriend."

Arkady cocked his head to the side. "Boyfriend?" He poured another glass of thick red liquor from a chilled copper flask. "I thought we'd agreed to take it slow and just date for a while. I'm not comfortable with how fast you're moving."

He smirked at Cash's glare.

"It's your sister's wedding," Cash said. "You only take a date to that if you plan to eat them rather than see them again."

Arkady tilted his glass in acknowledgment of that point. "Your plan?"

It was *not* disappointment that Cash could taste in the back of his throat. He patted his hand against the camera. "This year, in addition to the portraitist, you also have a photographer. It'll give me an excuse to mingle, to talk to people, pick out what they want."

Arkady looked curious. "Can't you just tell?" he asked. "Pick out their crimes from their aura?"

"I can see it," Cash said. "It doesn't mean I always understand it. And that's with humans. Monsters are a whole different kettle of sin."

"And we hired my sister's ex-lover, the half-human who outraged our bloodline with his offspring? Why?"

"To rub in that I'm still just the hired help?"

"You were never *just* that," Arkady said, a flash of anger bright in his pale eyes. "And there's just one problem with that."

"What?"

Arkady walked over to the bed and leaned down to cup the side of Cash's neck in his hand. His skin was dry and warm, and the edge of his nail was sharp as he dragged it down over the trail of raw red bruises that Cash knew still looked livid on his skin. It made a shiver run down his spine, and he bit his lip.

"No one is going to believe I'm not fucking you," Arkady said in a low, rough voice that was so thick with *want* that it made Cash's mouth water. "And this crowd aren't the sort of monsters that talk to the help."

Cash swallowed. "That's two problems."

Arkady smirked at him—a flash of white teeth against the dusty gold of his stubble. "Oh, fucking you isn't a problem," he said. "It'll be my pleasure… and yours."

"Don't be corny," Cash said. "You're Ellie's uncle, not her dad."

He twisted his fist in Arkady's sweater, fine-knit fabric bunched between his fingers, and pulled him into a kiss. Rough stubble scraped over his mouth, and Arkady's laugh tasted like blood and whiskey as it rolled over Cash's tongue.

Goddammit, Cash thought with a flash of scratchy, distracted irritation. He wasn't sixteen anymore; he shouldn't still think with his cock. Or anything else that was dumb and horny enough to get him back here.

"Don't," Arkady said, the words chewed over Cash's mouth.

"What?"

"Think."

Fair enough.

They tumbled back into the bed, silk sheets tangled under them and the two of them tangled around each other. The camera jabbed a corner into Cash's thigh, and he had *just* enough of his wits left to move it onto the bedside table. Cash groaned as Arkady palmed his cock through his jeans, the scrape of denim against tender skin almost unbearable. He slid his hands up under Arkady's sweater, and the cashmere bunched around his wrists as he explored the *almost* familiar planes of muscle and bone underneath.

Thicker muscle layered over his back and shoulders now, tight under the stretch of smooth, tawny skin. The new scar on his back, ragged as a hook, was fresh enough to make Arkady twitch when Cash touched it.

"I'll tell you if you ask," Arkady tempted as he licked the bruise on Cash's throat. "All the details."

Cash snorted and moved his hands away from the scar. He reached down between their bodies and fumbled at Arkady's trousers. It was just a button and zip. He knew how they worked, or he had five minutes ago. Arkady laughed against his neck and shifted his weight up onto his knees so he could reach down and unbutton.

"I don't need to know that badly," Cash said. He pushed Arkady over onto his back—all black and honey sprawled out on the sheets—and crawled on top of him. His cock ached, thick and tender under his jeans, but it deserved it for getting him into this. Cash pinned Arkady by the shoulders and leaned over him until he could feel the tickle of breath against his cheek. "And don't creep into my fantasies again."

Arkady looked amused. He stretched under Cash with a lazy flex of muscle just to make the point that he chose to stay where he was. For now. "You know I couldn't unless you want me to."

Yeah, Cash knew that. It just annoyed him more... because how come he never had before? He just glared at Arkady instead of asking that, and *this time* it was Arkady who kissed him—a quick hard brush of lips and teeth.

Cash shoved him back down, although he knew he couldn't enforce it. He tightened his fingers on Arkady's shoulders.

"This isn't a thing. Once Ellie's back—" Cash stopped himself and edited the statement. It was important to word things carefully in the Abascals' employ. Cash had almost forgotten that. "After the wedding, things go back to normal. I'm not back, I'm not *staff*. Deal?"

That was the magic word. Arkady's monster swam up and peeked through the stained glass of his eyes. Scarlet threads tipped with gold needles bled through the dense black of his aura as it flared out around them.

"Deal," Arkady said, his voice rough as gravel as he caught Cash's hips in his hands and pulled him down. The hard, insistent ridge of his cock pressed against Cash's ass. "After my sister is married, we'll go back to how it used to be."

Cash swallowed hard. He knew there would be a sting in the tail. There was always a sting in the tail. The betrayal might help Cash stick to his word.

"This will end badly," Cash said as he pressed a kiss into the hollow of Arkady's collarbone. His mouth lingered for a second as he scraped his teeth gently along the sharp arch. The temptation to leave his own mark on Arkady, to chew a Cash-shaped bruise onto the tanned skin, itched in the hinges of his jaw. He didn't. He never had. "You know that, right?"

Arkady shrugged under him.

"I know," he said. "But not yet."

Fuck it. Every monster parent knew that when the kid was at camp, it was time to play. Cash got to play with all this.

He reached down and slid his hand into Arkady's trousers and wrapped his fingers around his cock. Arkady arched his hips up into the touch, a low, hungry sound rough and raw in his chest as it clambered up into his throat.

"Casper," he said raggedly. "Hell. You feel good."

His cock was thick and heavy. The satin-fine skin creased under Cash's fingers as he gripped the base and felt the pulse of it. It felt as stupid and inevitable as the first and the last times they'd crawled into bed together. Cash tightened his grip to drag a groan out of Arkady and shifted his weight back.

"I could—"

The bell rang. It had been a decade since Cash had heard it, but he'd spent nearly as long answering to it. He'd been a hungry kid with no other options—the Abascal Hotel didn't have vending machines, and the chef would *actually* eat you if he caught you in his kitchen—and his reaction was still a Pavlovian compulsion to answer the summons.

He scrambled half off the bed before Arkady grabbed his arm and pulled him back down. A heavy, slightly too-hot arm draped over his back and pinned him in place. He sprawled out on top of Arkady with ill grace as his stomach rumbled, reminded that a packet of Funyuns and the dull misery of a cheap motel's day residents weren't much of a meal.

"Like you said," Arkady said against his throat, lips curved in a smirk, "you're not staff now, Casper. You're a guest, and that means you enjoy mother's full hospitality with the rest of us. Jeans and a T-shirt that smells like me aren't going to cut it."

No. Belladonna had never been impressed when Cash turned up anywhere with Arkady's scent on him.

"If you want me to get changed," Cash said, "you better let me up. Your mother does hate to be kept waiting."

This time Arkady let him scramble off the bed.

Chapter Six

CASH SHRUGGED his jacket on and raked his fingers through his hair to pull it back from his face. It was only long enough for a stubby ponytail, but it would have to do. Donna hated long hair on men. Or women. She considered anything more than half an inch a temptation for lice.

The adjoining door opened, and Arkady let himself in. He looked lean and dangerous in black, with a dull-red leather waistcoat that exaggerated his lean waist buttoned over a fine linen shirt. A few subtle bits of gold glittered on the waistcoat and around his wrist— enough to satisfy Donna's idea of what wealth looked like.

He looked Cash up and down and frowned. "You look like a banker," he said. "Change."

Cash scowled at him.

"And you look like a funeral pimp," he said. "It's fine. Donna knows what I am."

Arkady snorted and walked over. He pinched the lapel of the jacket between his thumb and forefinger and looked down at Cash.

"Half of the monsters on the East Coast will be here, the ones that Belladonna cares about, anyhow. If we're going to pass you off as my boyfriend, you need to look the part."

"I never let you dress me when you *were* my boyfriend," Cash said.

"At sixteen you're meant to look human."

Cash looked down at himself. It wasn't a cheap suit. It wasn't expensive either, but it was what he'd bought it to be—sheep's clothing, camouflage. But around here it made him look like prey, soft in a shell of a manmade fabric.

"I didn't bring anything else," he said as he pulled the jacket off. The shirt underneath would do. Plain black silk was a bit aggressive, but he didn't need anyone to like him. Just not eat him. "Donna can just deal with having to look at my wrists."

"Wait."

Cash tossed the jacket onto the bed as Arkady walked past him. "I'm not wearing one of yours," he said. "You're an inch taller than me."

"Two," Arkady corrected. He glanced over his shoulder. "And sure, otherwise it would fit like a glove."

He opened the wardrobe and reached inside. Hangers rattled, and there was the distinct sound that expensive fabrics make when they rustle against each other.

"Here." Arkady pulled out a light gray brocade jacket with blue-green highlights and held it out to Cash. "You might as well get some use out of it."

Apparently nothing really had changed. The jacket had been a birthday present. Cash left it behind when he got out, along with most of his things. He'd been young and hurt. It had felt like he'd made a point.

"I didn't know you kept that," he said slowly as he tried to work out if it was creepy or not.

"I didn't, but I didn't make a point to throw it out either. I don't live here anymore," Arkady told him. He looked exasperated at Cash's surprised look. "Did you really pay no attention to what I did for the last ten years? Did you think Donna and Madeline could share a roof?"

Cash shrugged.

He had in the beginning. When Ellie wouldn't sleep during the night—her innate sense that she was meant to stalk the night at war with the expectations of the only day care he could afford—he'd sat up with her and pored over posts on monster.net. It was impossible, despite what the better-bred monsters thought, to live among humans without picking up their vices. Monsters had their own gossip columnists, although anonymity was important—if they crossed the wrong monster, they wouldn't have to worry about being sued. Or alive.

Every time he picked the scab off, he'd been surprised it was still raw underneath. So he stopped. Maybe it wouldn't have hurt after three years. Or six. Cash had never wanted to risk it. What was he going to do? Fight Madeline for his man? Arkady had married *her*, and she could have killed Cash without chipping her manicure. It was safer not to know what he wanted.

He pretended he didn't care until he believed it. That was the same thing as it being real. Basically.

"I didn't want you to be unhappy," he said as he took the jacket and put it on. "That doesn't mean I wanted to know you *were* happy."

It felt expensive on his back. There was a *weight* to a well-made jacket as it settled over his shoulders and found its own shape around him. Cash had worn flak jackets on shoots, and they felt weirdly similar. The coat just had more style.

Arkady caught him by the arm on his way to the door and pulled him back.

"What now—?" Cash started to ask, irritated. Before he could get the rest of the question out, Arkady buried his fingers in Cash's hair. The hair band snapped off as Cash's curls made the break for freedom.

"Don't tie it back."

"Donna won't like it."

Arkady twisted his hand around the curls, his knuckles hard against Cash's skull, and pulled his head back slightly. Just enough to make the point that he could. Blood left Cash's head and puddled, hot and restless, in his already tender balls.

"But I do," Arkady said. He bent down and kissed Cash's forehead with a chaste, hot scorch of skin on skin. "And Donna isn't going to fuck you later."

Cash's hard-on resigned the field on that one. Just the idea of it was better than a cold shower.

"Why the hell would you even bring that up?" he asked as he made his second attempt at the door.

Arkady grinned and slapped Cash on the ass on the way past. "Those trousers hide nothing."

Cash blushed a hot scald of red as he stepped out into the hall with Arkady behind him. It would give the maid on her way by—her arms full of freshly laundered silk sheets—something to talk about later.

IN THE old days the Abascal Hotel and Spa would have been the creepy, run-down manor where the degenerate local gentry took the good-living youths they stole, tempted, or tricked out of their God-fearing ways. Every few generations, the cowed local priest would die and a firebrand young preacher would rock up to the pulpit. Or a bereaved parent would scrape together enough coin to hire a Hunter—mothers mostly, they had always made better plans.

Next thing you know the house was on fire, the local woodcutter had disemboweled the servants, and the surviving members of the family had legged it to the woods through escape tunnels, their pockets full of cursed gold to start again in another county, or country if they'd been particularly florid.

The Prodigium had put a stop to that. Monsters had to blend in—even the rich and even their houses.

It turned out that if a creepy old house was turned into a brutally exclusive luxury spa, beautiful youths would beat their own paths to the door. Not only that, they'd pay for the privilege of being on the menu.

The modern world had its problems, but it did make life simpler.

Arkady hooked his arm over Cash's shoulders as they walked through the hotel, through the crowd of human guests in leisure wear and glitzy cocktail outfits. He slid his fingers inside Cash's shirt, hot against his skin, and leaned down slightly so their temples touched.

"What do they want?" he asked as they passed a mirrored booth. It was full of beautiful women in toweling robes that looked soft as fur. They were all glossy pink smiles and rattly pink drinks as they giggled and clapped, but their auras drooped with the weight of foul gray infection that scabbed the edges.

"What the one in the middle has." He paused as his eyes fell on the one in the middle. Bride-to-be and her hen party, he'd guess, but instead of being flared in excitement, her aura was pickled in close to her body. Like a rind. His skin itched as his monster reached out to taste her, and the voice he'd need to lure her to her death scratched at his throat. Cash swallowed it, like hooks, and looked away. "And she wants him dead."

Arkady glanced over with interest. "Fiancé?"

"No," Cash said. He wasn't sure how he knew that, but… he did. "Someone else."

"Huh." Arkady made eye contact with the woman and smiled. She stared back at him for a second, a flush pink as it spread up her throat, until one of her friends pushed a drink into her hand. She stumbled through the toast, obviously flustered, and Arkady moved on. "Maybe later."

Under Cash's skin his monster sulked at having its prey stolen. It would get over it. Cash hadn't planned to lurk around dimly lit corridors for a chance to lure her into a bad fall down the metal staircase in the Grand Ballroom anyhow.

Not seriously.

There were other monsters there, scattered among the crowd as they browsed the produce section for something that would hit the spot. Some of them were restrictive feeders, like Cash.

Despair was his meat and potatoes, densely filling and calorific, although he could also take a shot of lust like whiskey. The other emotions he could taste, but they were like cotton candy, gone on his tongue before they could hit his stomach.

Others were just picky, well-fed enough they could afford to play with their food. Like the kelpie at the bar, with dark, stupid-handsome features and all-black eyes as he charmed the middle-aged woman in an expensive gown onto his arm. One day she'd die in a car crash, but not tonight. The betrayal hurt more if the lie ran long.

"He's from New York, near Rockaway," Arkady said quietly. "A guest, but one to watch. I heard he made some incautious decisions, and now he works for the Hand."

"Which one?" Cash asked.

"Always a good question," Arkady said, but he didn't answer it. "Come on. We don't want to hold up dinner."

He unhooked his arm from Cash's neck and headed across the floor with the confidence of someone who knew people would get out of his way. Cash straightened his collar and took another look around the bar as he trailed after Arkady. People *did* get in his way. A few monsters stepped pointedly in front of him, their backs turned, as if they couldn't have known he was there. Humans who'd edged out of Arkady's way drifted back into position in his wake.

Cash didn't mind. It gave him an excuse to slow down and have a good look around as he ducked through bodies.

If someone wanted to expose the survival of monsters to the world, after all, where better to send his patsies than a wedding of the great and grotesque? It was the East Coast capital of the Prodigium, no matter whose ass or ass-adjacent body part held the seat, and this would be the biggest event of the year.

Blood would flow.

A sharp heel came down hard on his foot. The tall woman it belonged to gave him a sidelong smirk from behind a thick mane of silver-streaked black hair, just a hint of fang visible.

"Sorry, darling," she drawled in her thickly accented contralto. "I didn't see you there. I was looking for Madeline."

The accent was fake. The Prodigium hadn't allowed any foreign vampires in for nearly a century now. An ongoing familial dispute. Besides, they'd come to camp together. Natalie had granddaughtered in, so to speak, even though she'd been just a human on a promise then.

"Sorry too, you're not her type," Cash said. "I hear she likes her bedwarmers to be, well, warm. How's your mother? Still in New Jersey?"

Her eyes narrowed. The flecks of gray glittered red for a second, like bits of glass. The man with her gave a nervous laugh in confusion. "Jersey, Natalia?"

She blinked twice, and the fangs were gone as she turned back to her companion. Her hand brushed his face, a thin smear of oil left where her fingers stroked over his cheekbone.

"My parents settled there," she said, her voice thick and throaty as she overwrote his memories. "After they came here from the old country? Remember?"

He didn't, but as Cash walked away, he heard the man slur agreement. Eventually the memory would work its way in.

A server with a plate of canapés in each hand hopped back out of his path with a quick apology. Cash stopped to wave her through and caught a glimpse of motion out of the corner of his eye—a tilted elbow and flexed bicep. He waited until the server had gone by and looked in that direction.

The man was human and almost aggressively unremarkable, handsome enough, with stylish-enough fair hair and a suit that hit the exact spot between shabby and flashy. Even his aura was muted and tucked in tidily around his body.

Only the heavy-framed black glasses he wore made a statement. And probably—the man looked at a redcap with a protesting server on his knee and made the same absent-looking adjustment of one leg—a slight clicking sound.

Winslow's casting scouts had the same model glasses camera so the crew could check for frauds and, worse, the unsympathetic. It wasn't "on brand" for viewers to root for the devil to win some asshole's soul, apparently.

The scout picked out another couple and adjusted his glasses again. Cash left him to it and headed over to rescue the server from her persistent suitor with a reminder that Donna's staff was off-limits. The redcap scowled but finally let the woman bounce up off his knee.

"Thank you," she mouthed at Cash.

Cash nodded and touched her elbow. "See that guy over there, with the glasses?"

"Table seventeen," she said without even a glance that way. "The creeper. He takes pictures with those glasses every time we lean over the table. Like we haven't seen *Cheater* and *Mystery Diners*."

"Get his name," Cash said. "His room number too if you can."

She looked suspicious.

"I'll explain later," Cash told her. "Trust me. I have to go."

He left her to clear the redcap's table—he doubted there would be more trouble with the thought of Donna's wrath sharp in the monster's mind—and stretched his legs to finally catch up with Arkady at the huge ebony door with the Staff Only sign. Arkady raised dark blond eyebrows at him.

"I see you found Natalie," he said coolly. "Did she have something to say?"

Cash shrugged as he leaned back against the door and pushed it open with his shoulder. The wards stung as he stepped through, like thorns caught in the meat of his human side.

"Who can make her out with that accent?" he asked. "You have a spy on site."

Arkady stiffened, and his face darkened as he turned to scan the bar.

"Who?"

Cash grabbed his sleeve and pulled him through the door into the corridor with him. "Leave him," he said. "He's just a scout, here to check how cinematic the weird is. If he disappears suddenly, that just proves there's something here to investigate."

"It's not proof," Arkady said. "Not if they don't find the body."

Cash snorted. "That's a good twenty minutes of footage in the final cut," he said. "If he's still here, I can find who he works for later. He shouldn't get anything he can use, anyhow. As long as they're above ground, everyone should have their best humanity on show."

"Should," Arkady said darkly, but he let the door swing shut with a secure click. He peeled Cash's fingers off his arm and lifted them to his lips. The kiss skimmed over Cash's knuckles and made him swallow hard as he tried to decide if the gesture was hot or ridiculous. "See? I knew you weren't just a pretty face."

"Bite me."

"Later."

Cash snorted. He tried to take his hand back, but Arkady hung on to it and tucked Cash's fingers into the crook of his arm. His forearm was taut with muscle and warm through the starched fabric. It felt like it was being absorbed into Cash's bones as they walked down the hall.

"Really?" he grumbled halfheartedly.

"You're here as my date, you go in to dinner on my arm," Arkady said. "It's what people expect."

Cash rolled his eyes but left his hand where it was. If he *had* to play boyfriend for the weekend, he might as well commit to the part. Some things could be ridiculous *and* hot.

The set of stairs at the end of the hall started as concrete and metal but gave way to roughly carved stone as they spiraled down. The light of hundreds of candles flickered over the high wall and glazed the milky streaks of lime that seeped out of the rock. A single fiddle dragged a slow, sweet tune from its strings and was stripped apart and played by echoes until it was an orchestra.

For all its grandeur, the spires and the flocked Victorian wallpaper, the Abascal Hotel and Spa that most people saw was just a roach motel. The real guests—the ones who paid with more than dollars and Instagram lines—stayed down here, in the atmospheric sprawl of tunnels.

There were suites carved into the stone, with the comforts of modern life and the cave aesthetics of the "good old days," and caverns that filled with water at high tide for things that didn't do well dry. Things that were too old or just too strange to pass as human had permanent residency and a very reduced rate for their stay—just the occasional favor, the odd atrocity to show willingness.

Huge strange mushrooms were grown in frilled tiers on the walls, brittle and flavored with the wine made from pallid underground grapes. Cash had never seen it, but rumor had it there was a larder stocked with the descendants of the missing Roanoke settlers somewhere down deep. For the right guests, drunk on mushrooms and wine, she'd lose them for a baying Wild Hunt under a sky of stalactites instead of stars.

It wasn't the only hotel of its kind, although it was one of the oldest. Down here, monsters could dress up like it was the Middle Ages and pretend that one day they'd defy the Prodigium and throw off their humanity. Yet they could still get a Wi-Fi connection to catch up on the next season of *The Witcher* when it dropped.

The Great Hall was full of long oak-fossil tables striated with streaks of amber and the pressed bones of things even the Prodigium didn't have a name for. Servants in livery moved between the tables and served up carved cuts of fresh meat on beaten brass platters or poured glasses of thin pale wine.

Like the Bell and Book, the monsters who came to enjoy the Abascal's hospitality had shucked their humanity, but they'd left all of it at the door. Instead of human fashion that pinched wattled skin and didn't have room for their wings or tails, they were in finery tailored to their monstrosity. A silk fringe tasseled a goblin king's long, naked rat tail, and a harpy wore matched platinum spinner rings on her taloned hands and the long fingers of her bat wings.

It was gaudy and indulgent, all trailing sleeves of stiff brocade in brilliant colors and great gemmed metallic ruffs that framed the grim maws of folklore. Upstairs Cash had felt awkwardly overdressed in his jacket. Down here he looked monastic.

At the center of it all, even though she was tucked away in a booth near the back, Donna Abascal sipped wine and watched the eddy of politics move from table to table. Most of the guests swung by hers to pay their respects and show metaphorical throat. She'd remember them, although it would gain them no favors. The ones who didn't come by she'd remember too, and take her pinch of flesh in some small, petty way.

Ellie called Donna "Grams" sometimes. If any of the cream of the Prodigium in attendance this weekend heard that, they'd choke on their own foot-long tongues.

"Are they all here for the wedding?" Cash asked as they took the last few steps down onto the uneven floor. Like every other rough touch in the caverns, every pothole and stalagmite stump was for the cave aesthetic.

Arkady dipped his head toward Cash and murmured through a faint smile, "Of course. Not all of them are *invited*, but they're to give everyone else the impression they are."

He unlinked his arm from Cash's and put a hand on the small of his back instead as he guided him through the tables. A few of the diners acknowledged them on the way past—a tip of a heavy, horned head or a glass raised in a slime-sticky hand for a brief toast—but others actively turned away to present a cold shoulder.

That was new.

Before Cash could ask, they reached Donna's table. The wig was one he hadn't seen before, short and a delicate shade of red that curled around her ears, but the woman under it hadn't changed. The dust of her humanity had hardened like papier-mâché, dry and delicate. What looked like incipient wrinkles from a distance—the start of crow's feet at the corners of her eyes and marionette lines around her mouth—were actually folds and cracks in the skin. Something paler lived underneath, and every day her maids papered over it with powder and grafts of thin see-through skin peeled from... someone. Somewhere.

There were always rumors.

"Belladonna," Cash said. He didn't bow. At first he hadn't known he had to, and then... well, being a dick was his art. "Even you can't be done with a bad penny, huh?"

She smiled and held her hand out. "Blood of my blood," she said. The voice that came out of that dainty spider of a woman was a low, rough contralto. It was like rotgut in a crystal tumbler. "Sit. Break bread with me. Tell me how my granddaughter fares at the proving ground."

Cash pulled away. Only the hand between his shoulders stopped it from being a step back.

What the fuck was going on?

Chapter Seven

"Hah, she's a scale off the old beast." Donna chuckled as she looked at Cash's photo of Ellie. Her fingers tapped like sticks against the screen, and she sighed wistfully. "It's true, you know. The enemies you make at the proving camp are enemies you have their whole life."

"They really hate it when you call it proving grounds," Arkady said. "It's Summer Camp now."

She dismissed that with an impatient flick of her hand. "Whatever you call it, you never forget your first enemies. It almost makes me regret killing them all at once."

It was never a good idea to have anything less than all your wits about you, dealing with Donna. Cash still risked a drink of the grave-dirt-grown wine to settle his stomach. It had a thin taste and a kick that made his eyes water.

"I hear they found your brother's leg bone in the Catacombs in Paris," he said as he picked over the sushi on his plate. The "they" were the Papacy. "That's half of him reassembled. In another century you'll be able to take him apart again."

Donna smiled at him and slid the phone back over the table. Her fingers hadn't left smudges on the screen, just a faint white powder like the shed of a moth's wing.

"Almost, dear, almost. You can always find new enemies. Sentiment is a drug that even monsters can grow addicted to." She took a sip of her own wine and arched an eyebrow at him. Her plate was cleared, bones cracked open and marrow licked out. "Although we all crave a little hit of nostalgia now and again, don't we?"

The wine had soured in Cash's stomach. He muttered something agreeable and took a second drink. Maybe it would calm the first down to have a friend. Was he dying? That didn't make sense—why

63

would she care? Was *she* dying and this was some last mind game on her part?

"Speaking of which," Arkady interrupted, "is Yana here yet?"

The question flipped Donna's strange mood like a coin. She frowned and sat back in the booth. Despite her slight frame, it creaked under her weight.

"Not until tomorrow. Tomorrow evening," she said, her mouth tipped down in an unhappy pout. "Why come at all, that's what I want to know. Why marry and miss the party? It's the last good time you'll have until your husband gets you pregnant and you can finally hunt him through the woods for sport. Although, of course, some people like their husbands and don't want to bury them under a cursed oak. More power to them, I say. We all have different needs."

She was back to smiling.

"Maybe Yana is afraid that this fiancé will 'get lost' in the caverns like the last two," Arkady said. "She seems to have a thing for men with a bad sense of direction."

"And what will we tell them when they find their way home?" Donna asked archly. "Constancy in this family will die with me. Until they find your father's body, Arkady, I will consider myself married to him… and a subject of the Prodigium."

One of the discreet servers approached the table with a fresh bottle for the table and a message she whispered into Donna's ear. Whatever she had to say made Donna's smile tighten, but not slip. She sighed, drained her wine, and rested both hands on the table.

"If you'll excuse me," she said. "I have to go and deal with a… guest complaint. Please, finish the wine and order dessert if you want it. My larder is open to you. If I'm not back before you're finished, we can speak tomorrow. I'm so glad you could make it, Casper. It isn't truly a family event without all the family there to bear witness if it goes to tribunal."

She slid out of the booth and swept away through the tables, her skirts caught up in one hand. The server left the bottle on the table, bowed, and discreetly made an exit.

Cash unbuttoned the high collar of his jacket and reached for his wine. "Are you sure she isn't the leak?"

"The Prodigium would not consider that a joke," Arkady said. He moved the glass out of Cash's reach and stole a roll of untouched fish from his plate. It disappeared into his mouth, and he eyed the last piece until Cash pushed it toward him. That had always been the trade-off, Arkady didn't order food to consume like a hungry lion in front of Cash, and he got the pick of leftovers. It was a human qualm maybe, but it was hard to enjoy someone's mouth on your cock when you'd seen them crack a femur open with their eye teeth. "And that performance wasn't for you. My mother just wants to make a point."

"What?"

Arkady fastidiously wiped his hands on a napkin. "That Yana's new beau is a fresh pinnacle of disappointment for her, even when compared to you. No offense."

"None taken," Cash said absently. "Donna and I have always known where we stood with each other."

Beneath her and as far away as possible, respectively.

"How does Yana feel about him? Does he make her happy?" Cash asked.

"Does that matter?" Arkady asked.

Cash hesitated. There was more than one way to take that question, and all of them had barbs.

"Not when it comes to the leak, I guess," Cash said. He paused as a bleak thought occurred to him. "I mean, there's no way that *Yana*—?"

Arkady looked grim as he interrupted Cash. "It's in all our best interests to find another culprit, don't you think?"

The Prodigium only had a few laws—it was the best approach to ruling monsters—but they were enforced with the sort of egalitarianism human society could only aspire to. If Yana had done this, she'd pay the price no matter whose daughter she was.

"You wanted a liar for a reason," Cash said grimly.

He had morals. It would have been easier if he didn't, but his mother had thought she was doing the right thing when she taught him right from wrong. He couldn't hold that against her. But if he had to send someone to the salting racks for a crime they didn't commit, he'd do it rather than let Ellie see her mother strung up for jerky.

"I did, didn't I," Arkady said, a faint edge to his voice.

"Don't."

"Don't what?"

"Your mother bought me to be your friend."

"True. Thanks for the reminder." Arkady picked up his glass and took a drink.

"I seduced you because I was a chaotic little asshole, and you were… beautiful," Cash said. "Nothing has changed. I wanted to kiss you, so I did. Nothing to do with me being a liar, or you pressuring me into coming back here."

Arkady looked annoyed. The flash of pinched temper highlighted the lines of his face that he'd inherited from Donna. It faded quickly into a dry amusement.

"You seduced me?" he said thoughtfully. "Huh. Is that how you remember it?"

"I kissed you first."

Arkady leaned back in the booth and smiled faintly, a sly tuck of humor at the corner of his mouth. "I knew you were going to, though."

"Liar," Cash said. "You hit your head on the wall."

"I knew in general," Arkady said. Old amusement twitched the corners of his mouth, a hint of almost sweetness. "I didn't expect you to just go 'fuck it' and try to climb me."

Cash laughed. He felt guilty about it a second after, a bitter chaser to the humor. Sex was one thing—sticky, memorable, and satisfying to the bones but limited by the simple fact it wasn't compatible with his life—but these unearthed shreds of old affection were dangerous. They made him remember all the things he used to want.

Things.

That was dignifying what a single-minded asshole he'd been back then. He'd wanted *Arkady*. He'd have taken the life that came with, but nice pillows and servants hadn't been what woke him sweaty and so hard he ached from his dreams. Like the Prodigium, Cash hadn't liked to complicate things.

His inner monster didn't even bother to come up with a dig in response to that. It just snorted.

"Simpler times," Cash said. It would have been better to sour the moment, but he couldn't quite stomach that along with the sushi. "Simpler us."

Arkady reached out and tucked a dark curl behind Cash's ear. His hand lingered. "Can't say your moves have evolved."

Cash spluttered out half an objection. "That's not…. You haven't seen my—"

"Sir," the server interrupted Cash's disagreement. He was pale. They were *all* pale. No one who worked in the under-hotel was allowed above again. Most of them were night-struck—obsessed with fucking, being eaten, or all of the above by monsters—and eagerly accepted the limitations. Others were dying, but the payment plan made the drawbacks worth it. Once they had been down here a while, there was a texture to their pallor, a greasy rind that fake tan couldn't hide, but this guy was grayish, and his eyes were wide and anxious. "Milady Abascal said to apologize for interrupting, but you're needed."

Arkady brushed his fingers down Cash's throat with a featherlight caress and then sat back. There was a grim cant to his mouth as he drew reserve around him like a coat. He folded his napkin and leaned over to brush a cool, empty kiss over Cash's cheek.

"It's another leak, another monster exposed," he murmured grimly into Cash's ear. "We need to find who did it."

He drew away from Cash and slid out of the booth, tossing the napkin down on the table. An impatient gesture of his hand directed the server to lead the way, and they left. It was a different direction to the one that Donna had taken, but that meant nothing. The under-hotel was a maze of tunnels and switchbacks, and only the Abascals knew all the shortcuts.

Cash looked away before anyone noticed he wasn't just admiring Arkady's ass. He picked up the wine bottle and stared at the label.

It was an Abascal Grand Cru Blanc, vintage 1820, bottled in heavy green glass.

There wasn't enough left in it to knock Cash out if he finished it off, but maybe if he could convince someone to crack him over the head with it....

He considered it. It might not solve any of a human's problems, but monster lore was full of stories where someone passed out after drinking a bathtub of gin and woke to find their problems had sorted themselves out. Usually it was a hundred years on and they had a whole new crop of problems, but that wasn't the point.

But Cash had Ellie to take care of. In a few years, she should be thinking about going to college, stealing her first hearts—or souls, if that's how the gene pool threw down. She didn't need to be stuck luring travelers to a cave for her comatose father to feed on their despair.

He was saving that for his retirement.

Cash put the bottle down and took a deep breath. He hadn't wanted to come back here—and he'd already managed to prove why it was better he stayed away—but here he was. The only way he could justify it was if it was for Ellie, so maybe he should focus on finding the link. Instead of Arkady's ass.

Why not both?

He ignored that. There were times his monster could be useful, an internal narrator who punctured the lies he tried to tell himself. But not when its stomach was rumbling.

Cash slid out of the booth and followed the flow of the servers toward the kitchen. He took his fancy jacket off as he wove through the tables and fished a stray band out of his pocket to pull his hair back into a ponytail.

"Sir?" one of the servers protested as he ducked through the doors after them. "This is the staff area. The guest exit is—"

"I know," Cash said. "Don't worry about it."

The server looked like he was anyhow, but another man in livery pulled him aside and muttered into his ear. It could be that people around here still remembered Cash, or just the good advice that stopping monsters doing what they wanted was above a server's pay grade.

Cash left them to it as he headed into the tunnels.

Only the Abascals knew *all* the shortcuts, but everyone knew some.

THE WAITRESS, Abigail, flicked the ash off her cigarette into the gravel and gave Cash a sheepish look.

"I know," she said. "It's bad for you. I'm going to stop, it's just…."

She trailed off with a defeated shrug and took another quick drag before she stubbed the butt out. It went into the nearby bucket, and she pulled a minibottle of perfume out to give herself a quick spritz.

"Easier said than done," Cash said.

Abigail laughed in tired agreement as she tucked the Chanel rip-off bottle back into her pocket. Her despair was stale, chewed over every time she exhaled the last smoke from her throat and told herself, "This was the last one," even though she knew it was a lie.

Go to any addiction self-help group in the city and you'd probably find a wisp there in the back. Addiction was the cheese sandwich of despair, but it never ran out, and there were usually donuts.

"My mom smoked," Cash said, because his monster had been more of a dick than usual these last few days. "She was a waitress too. It helped her get through a shift without killing anyone. When she got a better job, she quit."

That was a lie. She hadn't gotten a better job. She'd worked at the same café until she got cancer. Then she died. Cash didn't visit her in the hospital. It turned his stomach to glut on his mom's death, but it wasn't something he could control.

It made Abigail feel better, though, that brief jolt of hope that she could do it, get a better job and quit, get far away from here. She was probably never clear on why she wanted away from here so much. It was a job, and it paid well, but on some cellular level, she knew what they were and that she didn't belong.

Her aura flared briefly golden as she *believed*, just for a second, that she might get away alive.

The monster retched in Cash's ear and sunk away from that flare of happiness and into his bones.

"You and Mr. Abascal, looked...." She glanced sidelong at him, as if she hoped he'd finish for her. "I thought he was straight. Him and his wife, they were always all over each other when they were here."

Cash swallowed the glass and acid in his throat. He hadn't expected that or for it to *still* hurt quite so much.

"Bisexuality is a thing," he said.

Abigail gave him an interested look out of the corner of her eye. "Are you...."

"No," Cash said easily. "I like guys. I've never—"

He paused, cleared his throat, tried again. "I'm pretty taken right now."

Abigail shrugged and nodded. "I mean, if Mr. Abascal looked at me like that? Wow."

She sighed. Cash could just taste the edges of a tattered daydream, buttercream icing and champagne as her aura fluttered like a veil. That wouldn't end well for her, but it wasn't Cash's job to scare off Arkady's prey.

"Yeah, well, it's not exactly something he wants publicized," he said. His power tasted like marsh water on his tongue as his voice lilted on the night air. "Me and him, I mean, not right now. His ex would have him over a barrel. You know what she was like. Arkady only just about agreed to be seen with me in public. If he finds out about that guy with the glasses taking photos? He'll lose his mind."

It didn't take a genius to work out that Abigail didn't like Madeline. Humans never did. Even when Arkady's ex wasn't actively courting dissent, she had contentious energy. That was the line. The hook was the chance to get closer to Arkady—even through his lover—and, well, if he *was* bisexual and obviously not *that* into Cash... who knew what might happen?

It wasn't a conscious calculation. Abigail was a nice woman. She'd never *decide* to chase someone else's man. It was enough temptation to get the hook in her throat. Cash wouldn't have been able to lead her to her death on that flimsy string, but it was enough to take the first step.

"Okay," she said. "I mean, he owns the hotel, right?"

"His mother does," Cash said.

Abigail chuckled as she handed him a warm folded napkin from her pocket. "Yeah, but he's in charge, you know. She just has tea parties sometimes."

That hurt Cash's brain. He unfolded the paper. It was full of salt. The white grains spilled out over his hands, got under his nails, and the sharp ocean smell of it filled his nose. He jerked back and let the napkin fall, lifted away on the breeze as he shook the salt off his hands.

"What the fuck?" he said.

Abigail stared at him. Her aura sagged and faded around her. Disappointment wasn't despair, but they had a similar taste. Her eyes flicked past him, into the dark. "What now?"

They salted monsters for a reason. Some of them could abide the sea, and wisps could tolerate the salty brine of marshes, but purified into thin, flat crystals it still stung them.

Fuck. *Fuck.*

Cash lunged for the door back inside, but Abigail blocked him. It was hard to tell if she meant to do it or was just in the way. Before he could decide, something cracked him across the back of the head. He had a second of hot, monstrous contempt at the fact they thought *that* would be enough, and then his legs went out from under him, and black washed over his vision.

Chapter Eight

CASH WOKE up facedown on sand. He could smell blood. His head ached. It took him a second to put the two together, but to be fair, he'd just been cracked on the head.

He groaned and tried to roll over. His hands were cuffed behind his back—real metal cuffs, not the plastic restraints that cops usually used. He managed to squirm onto his side and spit out the blood that had run into his mouth. His eyes were glued shut with it, his lashes welded together.

"Here," someone said.

Water splashed over his face, warm and fucking salty. It made his blood itch and his eyes burn, but he tried to pretend it didn't as he clumsily scrubbed his eyes on his shoulder until he could peel one open. Cash blinked against the bright light and got his elbow braced to struggle up into a sitting position.

The nondescript man with the glasses sat on a deck chair in front of him. Abigail was behind him, her arms tightly crossed across her breasts. A heavy-duty flashlight was perched on a stack of boxes, strong enough to cast a puddle of light around the three of them. It wasn't much of a cave—the roof was as much dirt as rock—but Cash supposed it would do.

Abigail's aura pulsed in time with her heartbeat, and the hot taste of adrenaline popped on Cash's tongue like sugar. The man was… nothing.

"What the fuck?" he rasped out.

"I told you," Abigail whined anxiously. "He's human. Of course he's fucking human. We fucked up. *You* fucked him."

"Iron took him down," the man said. "Monsters don't like iron."

"You hit me on the head with it," Cash said. His voice was scratchy and his throat dry. The monster tried to crawl up onto the

72

back of his tongue, but he pinned it down. If they knew enough about monsters to try salt and iron, they might recognize his tricks. "Nobody likes that, you asshole."

There was a pause, and the man grimaced his acceptance of that. He flicked Cash's wallet open and looked at the cards inside.

"Casper Davies," he read out from the driver's license. "You don't look thirty-two."

"Thanks."

"Didn't say you looked younger."

Card after card was looked at and flicked onto the sand. Credit card. Credit card. Loyalty card for that sundae place that Ellie loved. Cash knelt on the ground and tried to breathe through his nose as he discreetly worked at the cuffs around his wrists. The cuffs were a bit loose, but not enough to wriggle his hands free without dislocating his thumb.

"You're in the industry?" the man said as he got to Cash's union card. He rubbed his thumb thoughtfully around the edge of it. "Who do you work for?"

"Dustbowl Demonologist," Cash said. The man made a face, and Cash shrugged. "I didn't name it."

"I've watched that," Abigail said. Her anxiety was forgotten in an unexpected flash of fandom. "Preacher Winslow. He seems like a genuine guy?"

She looked expectantly at Cash, who hesitated and then shrugged awkwardly. "I guess," he said. "He believes he's helping people."

"You don't?" the man said. He dropped the wallet to the ground and leaned forward, his hands loosely clasped between his knees.

Cash didn't look at them. If the Hunter's mark was on either hand, he'd have already seen it, and most people wouldn't know where to check.

"We never run out of subjects," he said. "Look, what's going on here? If you think someone will pay to get me back—"

"We're not kidnappers," the man said.

Cash snorted and yanked at the cuffs behind his back. "You know what, you might be," he said.

Abigail nudged the man in the shoulder. "He was with Arkady Abascal," she said with a smirk. "I mean, *with* with, you know? He said they were a thing. Maybe we *could* get something out of this. Concrete."

Cash swallowed the laugh that scratched at the back of his throat. It wasn't the reaction they'd expect, but… they'd definitely get something if they tried to demand money from Arkady. Or kept saying his name.

"We hooked up," he said. "He's bought me a couple of drinks, but he's not going to pay a ransom for me. My kid would, but she's twelve, so her worldly wealth is what's in her pocket."

The man stood up and walked around behind Cash. Cash tensed, ready for another blow, but instead he felt dry fingers on his wrist. This close he caught the ghost of something from the man.

Disappointment. Annoyance.

"We aren't criminals," he said, as much to Abigail as Cash as he unlocked the cuffs.

She rolled her eyes at him and mouthed, "It was a joke," as she turned away.

"This was just a… misunderstanding."

"You thought I was a monster," Cash said. A lifetime of conditioning made his neck prickle as he said that out loud, as if he expected the left hand of the Prodigium to drop from the ceiling to flatten him. "Then you hit me on the head and dragged me… what… down to the shore? Into the woods? That's one helluva misunderstanding. You know this is Roanoke, right? Not some backwoods Appalachian shack in the mountains."

For the first time, he felt a solid hit of emotion from the man. Excitement. "You'd be surprised," he said. There was something familiar about the way he said that, the cadences that his voice fell into as he pulled Cash to his feet. "This area has always been a hub of infernal activity. A *bor*, a fault line in the world where evil can peek through. You know that. It's why a third of exorcism programming in the US is made within a hundred miles of this spot."

"Like I said, we never run out of subjects," Cash said. "You work for 12:28, right?"

"I do. I'm an assistant director. Harry Treadwell," the man said as he stepped around and crouched down to collect Cash's cards from the floor. "Abigail is a local hire."

His voice was dry as dust. Abigail didn't seem to notice as she grinned, her lips dark in the dim light.

"I worked here when I was a teenager," she said. "I grew up on the South End—"

"Me too," Cash said absently. He wasn't entirely sure why, but he supposed it was to be cruel when Abigail flushed and glared at him.

"Well, I guess every generation, one of us gets out," she said cattily. "Although I guess *you've* never worked for 12:28."

Cash had not. That was 70 percent lack of opportunity and 30 percent choice. It had never seemed worth the risk.

Somewhere between splatter-rite and reality exorcisms lay the respectable ground of paranormal investigation. 12:28 had followed an exorcism for a year, through every unpleasant puking, cursing, scabbing moment of it. Rumor had it the spirit involved had found the experience so intense it had actually been truly exorcised, not just cut free of the honeypot of the house, which only happened in two out of ten cases. Three years ago they'd uncovered the Hairy Secret of Candle Hollow, and tracked a dozen local suicides back to a reclusive family who lived up by the mines.

In Cash's expert opinion, the Cannock Clan had just enough monster in them to make them outcasts, but the suicides had been more down to the fact that Candle Hollow was a dead-end place to live. No one asked him, and the Cannocks had been driven out of town after the production crew left.

It was a Jesuit-run show, which would fit Harry and his hard-rind aura. Holy men and philosophers were always hard to read… real ones, at least. Fake ones were like a large print pamphlet. But in a professional believer, all the time spent thinking about the meaning of the universe/secrets of God muddied up the want-take-have of the lizard brain.

"So what? Roanoke gets a lot of wannabe Witches of Endor and possessions," he said. "That's common knowledge. It isn't worth an exposé on prime time."

Harry held out Cash's wallet, the cards piled neatly on top. "It wouldn't be," he said. "But we recently received actionable information that there's a more… concrete… threat present here. When you started to pay attention to me, I thought perhaps you were part of it. I may have overreacted."

Cash grimaced and touched the back of his head. His hair was spiked with blood, and there was a knot the size of an egg on his skull—a freshly boiled egg from how hot it felt across his fingers.

"With a bat," he said. "I should sue."

"That's your right."

They all knew it wouldn't do him any good. Harry would just claim he was an ordained cleric in fear of his immortal soul, and all Cash would get for his trouble would be an official expression of regret. Even if Harry had killed him, all he'd get would be a slap on the wrist and a month in a religious retreat.

"You thought I was a monster, though?" Cash said. He tried to sound the right level of skeptical—somewhere between blasé and theatrically shocked. "At a spa? Do you think they're here for a hot-stone massage?"

"Maybe it reminds them of hell," Abigail said snidely. Her aura sagged around her shoulders like a baggy sweater, threaded with gray in disappointment as the adrenaline spilled out of her. "Come on, Harry. An hour ago you thought he was some sort of incubus. Now you want to spill your guts?"

Cash swallowed a nervous laugh at that misidentification. A wisp was to an incubus what the flu was to the bubonic plague. The first might kill you, if you didn't take the right precautions, and the second was an unholy contamination that hadn't been seen since the Middle Ages.

"He kind of needs to convince me to hold my tongue," Cash pointed out. He slotted his cards back into his wallet and tucked it into his back pocket. "Hard to do an undercover investigation when the owner's boyfriend is howling about his cracked skull."

"Boyfriend, is it?" Harry said mildly. "I thought you said he was just a hookup."

Cash shrugged. He ignored the faint, weird satisfaction he felt when he used the term. Whether he looked it or not, he was thirty-two years old, and definitely too old to get silly over the idea he had a "boyfriend." Especially since he didn't.

"I bet if I stagger in covered in blood, he'll temporarily upgrade so I don't sue him," Cash said tartly. He paused as a wash of nausea hit him and he struggled to stay on his feet. His humanity was still thick enough not to blister under salt, but he was still allergic to it. Under his nail beds and behind his eyelids itched in irritated reaction, and his monster felt dry and thirsty around his bones. "Look, this sounds like bullshit to me. I buy there's still monsters in the world, but they're out in the woods or deadheading the rails for easy prey. They aren't at a spa. So I'm going to go, and you can deal with hotel security."

He stalked out of the puddle of light and felt his way through the dimly lit cave toward the faint sound of the ocean. Instincts strained for him to *run*, to go to ground somewhere wet and dark until the holiness passed on by, but he reined it in.

"We can't let him leave!" Abigail hissed. There was a rattle of metal on plastic that made Cash's head throb with the reminder of whatever they'd whacked him with. "The hotel will kick us out. The last thing they want is to become the Monster Spa."

There was a tight edge to Harry's voice that suggested he'd lost his patience with his coworker. "We aren't the fucking Inquisition, Abigail. We can't kidnap people. Or murder them. Put that down. Down." Something hard hit the ground with spiteful force, and Harry raised his voice. "Mr. Davies. Wait."

Cash turned around but didn't stop. He walked backward a few steps, the sand lumpy underfoot as he glanced from the bat to Harry. "Outside," he said.

He had to hunch over the last few steps out of the cave. The roots of the seagrass that grew down through the packed dirt tickled the back of his neck and the tops of his ears as he scrambled out.

The moon hung fat and heavy in the sky. It was full—a good night for werewolves and wisps. Cash wasn't tied to the moon, but travelers were less wary on a well-lit night. They took more risks. He brushed the sand off and looked around to orient himself. It wasn't far from the hotel. Cash could hear the faint high notes of music on the breeze if he strained his ears.

"My friends and I used to come here to party after our shifts," Abigail said as she joined him. She shook her head to shed anything that had gotten in her hair. "We'd steal well whiskey and beer, come out here, sit on deckchairs, and pretend we were fancy bitches like Donna Abascal and her kid."

"It's a little more... MacGyver... than our usual hub of operations," Harry said. "But we're investigating monsters, Mr. Davies. If I made a mistake, we didn't want our research to disappear with our bones."

Shame he'd brought Cash here, then.

"Hookup or boyfriend, I'm in Arkady's bed," Cash said. "Why shouldn't I tell him about you?"

Harry and Abigail traded a look for a second. Then Harry straightened his shoulders and met Cash's eyes with a steady, earnest look from behind his spy glasses.

"Because we believe that Ilyana Abascal is about to marry a monster," Harry said. "If it realizes that we know what it is—if her family gives it away through any change in their behavior—then only God will know what it does to her."

Cash was lucky that poleaxed shock was an appropriate reaction to that sort of information. He gawped at Harry and then swallowed hard, a wet click in his throat from nerves.

"That's.... That's something from a fairy tale," he said. "Monsters don't marry princesses anymore, if they ever really did."

Harry took a step closer to him. "Oh, they did," he said. "Fairy tales are just simplified history, Mr. Davies, you know that. *Beauty and the Beast* was based on a documented historical event in 1500s France, except the historical Beauty didn't have a happy ending. Her sisters weren't able to save her. She married the Beast, and they never saw her again."

"I know the story," Cash said. "And plenty of historians argue that a real girl might have disappeared, but the story was exaggerated to make it more newsworthy. Fake news isn't new."

Monsters had a different version again. It might not be any more true, but it was said that Beauty was the one who helped them find human skins to hide in. Some stories said it was Beauty's skin that Donna still wore—in her memory—but the Abascals came from Italy, not France. So who knew?

"When our source contacted us earlier this year, we were skeptical too," Harry said. "12:28 has chased a hundred stories about monsters while I've worked there, and maybe three of them panned out to anything—infant disappearances in five different hospitals along the East Coast in the last decade."

"Five," Cash said. He hoped the *only* was only audible inside his head. The Black Witch ate once a year and apparently didn't cover her tracks like you might expect. "Jesus."

Harry nodded grimly. "He also sent us to a woman who was under some sort of monstrous oppression, visited nightly by some creature in the form of a loved one that"—Harry flushed, the color deep enough to be just about visible under the moonlight—"sought some esoteric form of congress with her."

Yeah, Cash had heard that about the Worm. He supposed if he lived long enough, the more unesoteric forms of congress would get a bit same-old, same-old too. Hard to imagine at the moment, with the warmth of Arkady's skin still fresh in his memory.

"Of course, we had to get the local authorities involved," Harry said grudgingly. "For her safety. Unfortunately, that resulted in the monster's escape when it chose to die rather than be captured. Until the corpse is retrieved, we can't prove whether Ms. Fennick's ex returned from his untimely grave through magic or fraud."

They never considered both. It was always one or the other. That was what the Prodigium was created to take advantage of—humanity's confidence that they were the only ones who could get used to the modern world.

The Worm was Seated Prodigium, one of the ruling members of that terrible council. Cash was confident the old monster had covered his ass if anyone questioned what his dead host was doing up and walking. That made it more worrying that someone had not just a rough idea of the Worm's schedule but an intimate knowledge of the host he'd worn. An intimate knowledge of the business of every monster in Roanoke was bad enough, but to be able to track a council member from out of town? That was the sort of information network that required money, power, and influence.

That described the Abascals. They collected secrets like some kids collected stamps, tucked away to lube the deal later. Cash would lay odds that, between the three of them, the Abascals knew a dirty secret about every monster in Roanoke—and that included him.

If Cash believed Arkady that they weren't involved....

"Who's your source? Are you sure this isn't some prank to expose you?" Cash asked. "I've lived here my whole life, and the only secret horror story I have seen sniffed out was the contagion that spread through the Lane development."

That had been bad enough. The contractors on the housing development had known that their housing project edged onto, not just against, the cursed land of the old asylum. They'd rolled the dice that the two-foot-wide strip of land under one house would, at worst, make the paintwork crack. Instead the curse had budded and spread out to the edges of its new boundary line, taking in every sprawling McMansion and shell-white colonial bought up by social-climbing locals.

Ten serial killers had been tracked back to a stay in those placid, character-free houses, never mind the murder-suicides and home invasions that kept the turnover of ownership ticking along. Last year a podcaster went in and was never seen again.

Yet people kept buying.

"He says he's afraid of retribution," Harry said. Of course. Cash's aching head didn't earn him any favors from the universe. "My theory is that he's a penitent consort, but—"

"I think he's a Hunter," Abigail said. She traded a sharp irritated glance with Harry. "Just because the Church disbanded them doesn't mean they went away. There are well-researched books that track their continued influence—"

"Well-researched pulp fiction," Harry corrected her impatiently. He held up his hand to cut off any further dispute. "We will find out soon enough, either way. He's going to be in the hotel for the wedding, and he's promised us that he'll unveil the monsters."

That would, at least, get rid of the immediate threat. A hall full of unveiled monsters would leave nothing but shoelaces and contacts.

"We're going to livestream it," Abigail said.

Cash rubbed his head. Of course they were.

"Two days, Mr. Davies," Harry said, his voice intent. "That's all you have to give us. Two days and your faith that the Good Lord won't let any infernal creature rest in peace on his creation. Do we have it?"

Cash clenched his teeth on a bark of laughter. At the moment he'd buy that God had come back from that long sabbatical and the angels were desperate to look busy—specifically by screwing with his life.

"I'll give you that," he said. "But if you're wrong, your credibility is going to be down the drain. What the viewing public leaves of you, the Abascals will drag through court until all that's left is money and regret."

"You're already saying *if*," Harry said. "This is real, and it's a game changer. Once we reveal that there are still monsters out there—real ones, not half-starved inbreds and mangy Sasquatches? Forget Hunters. The Vatican will empower the Witch Finders with temporal authority again."

That was something new to worry about. Cash filed it behind the question of who in Roanoke was powerful enough to pull this off… and keep that power a secret from Donna.

"I guess we'll see," he said.

Chapter Nine

"IF I needed someone to get the staff drunk and fuck them, I could have hired a maenad," Arkady said in a tight, controlled voice. His "too pissed off to let the monster out" voice. Cash supposed he was flattered that he could still make someone jealous. He guessed he *was* still pretty. "Don't make me regret trusting you, Casper. Not *again*."

Cash rubbed grit and sand from his eyes and propped himself up on the narrow mattress. After his near tumble with Arkady the other day, he hadn't expected his bedroom to be where he woke up today. But the best laid plans of mice and monsters....

The inside of his head felt light and loose, and his skin was too tight. Last night had burned through a layer of humanity, rubbed it down closer toward the grain of the monster. Luckily he had enough of it to spare.

"You married someone else," he said.

Arkady stared down at him. The grip he had on his monster had dimmed the see-through amber of his eyes down to a dark, almost brown honey. That was the color he had when they first met. It surprised Cash how strange it looked on Arkady now. The arrogant tilt of his eyebrow hadn't changed.

"So?" he said.

He *knew* what the *so* was. Arkady was a monster, but he wasn't that much of a monster. Only the elders, locked in their luxurious prisons, could be that truly inhuman. The rest of them got humanity by immersion, even the ones who hadn't been born with it, whether they liked it or not....

So it hurt. So Cash realized he'd *always* be the charity boy from the South Shore. So neither of them had a choice, and that sucked the most.

"So get over it."

Arkady gave him a bleak, bitter look. Neither of them ever seemed to say what the other wanted to hear.

You could, the monster pointed out. It was loud against the tender seams of Cash's skull. *I could.*

Could, but wouldn't. It was impossible not to see the irritation that ruffled Arkady's aura or taste his emotions on the air. That was just another sense, like Cash's ears or nose. The hook was different. It might not even work—Arkady was a much bigger fish—but Cash wasn't going to try just in case it did.

"I'll get over you banging my sister when you get over the chip on your shoulder you've had since camp," Arkady snapped. He leaned down and grabbed Cash's chin between his fingers to tilt his face toward the window. "What the hell happened to your face?"

Good question. Cash pushed Arkady away and staggered out of the bed. He padded over to the mirror and peered at his reflection. The black eye and the bruise on his forehead had already started to fade, but while his skin hadn't blistered last night, it had reacted. Under the smooth layer of human skin, pale and flecked with freckles, flat grayish blotches of scarred monster showed through.

His hands were the same, peppered with dry gunmetal-gray flecks.

"You know how it is," Cash said. "You pick someone up and they turn out to be kinkier than expected."

"No." Arkady walked up behind him and pushed Cash's head forward so he could examine the knot on the back. He made an irritated sound, still not ready to let go of his temper as he wrapped his hand around the nape of Cash's neck. His grip pinched, hard enough to make Cash squirm. They both stared into the mirror as if their posed reflection might reveal something. "People are going to think I beat you. Maybe I should."

Cash snorted and tried, halfheartedly, to pull away. "They would think it was about time."

"I've never cared what they think," Arkady said as he tugged Cash back. The tension in his voice was cut with lust, like rotgut served with a whiskey chaser. "But if someone is going to bruise you, it better be me. What happened?"

Cash leaned back against Arkady's chest. Buttons scratched against his bare back, and the itch of pleasure prickled in his gut and down the backs of his thighs.

He groaned and pulled away, with more determination this time. Arkady growled, a scrape of stones in the back of his throat, but he let go.

"Yeah, well, not going to be talking much if I'm under you," Cash pointed out. He grabbed yesterday's jeans and pulled them on. The time it took him to hitch them up over his hips gave him the chance to pull his thoughts together. "I found out who our leak—your leak—is leaking to."

"Was that before or after they hit you on the head?"

Cash left his jeans unbuttoned as he reached up to touch his head. He probed gingerly at his skull. It still hurt, but the knot had gone down from a goose egg to a chicken's egg overnight. The skin had pulled back together as well, although he could still feel the seam of it with his fingers.

"Simultaneously," he said.

"Who?" Arkady said. His monster pushed up against his skin, a sheen of sickly gold that bled through his honey tan. "I'll kill them, and all we have to deal with is a traitor. Not the Left Hand and the Prodigium."

"That won't work." Cash sat down on the edge of the bed, T-shirt dangling from his hands between his knees. "It's not one wannabe Hunter, it's 12:28. Even if you kill the crew that's here, it won't stop the investigation. If anything, it will just confirm to any doubters at the network that there is *something* here."

Arkady stalked over and leaned down to take Cash's hands. He turned them over and grazed his thumbs over the half-faded marks left by the cuffs.

"I want to kill them," he said.

That made Cash's heart stutter hard enough that he wondered if Arkady could feel the skip in Cash's pulse through his skin.

"And ten minutes ago you wanted to kill me," he said. "You got over that, you'll get over this."

Arkady lifted Cash's hands and brushed a hot-lipped kiss over the marks. It made the tender skin sting and itch as Arkady's power picked at the wound.

"I didn't realize I'd gotten over wanting to kill you," Arkady said dryly as he gave Cash's hands back. He stalked restlessly around the room to burn off emotion as the gold sheen sank back under his skin. The pressure in the room changed, and the absence made it easier to breathe. "Fine, discredit rather than murder. Them, at least."

Cash pulled his T-shirt on with a wince as the collar scraped over the back of his head. He ignored the jab.

"We'll get the chance," he said. "Apparently they plan to crash the wedding."

Arkady stopped for a second and then swore through his teeth. "That makes no sense."

"Why not?" Cash asked. "No one will have their human skins on. The director is expecting to just catch Yana's husband—"

Arkady snorted something under his breath and stuck his hands in his pockets.

"—but they aren't going to stop filming because they see more monsters than they expect. Even if none of the film gets out, a breach of the law that... huge... would bring the Prodigium down like a hammer."

The Abascals would bear the brunt—even if they hadn't commissioned the exposure, just to show that no one was above the law—but everyone would suffer. Every monster involved could be relocated... to the bottom of the salt sea if any of the footage did make it out to the world.

"Exactly," Arkady said. "Why did I want you here for the wedding, Cash?"

"To piss your family off?"

A flicker of bleak humor tucked the corner of Arkady's mouth. It didn't last. "No secrets from you, huh?" he said. "Not just that, though. Any monster who *could* have done this is going to be here. If they're going to help the humans gatecrash, then they'll definitely be here. That means they'd be part of the breach, along with the rest of us."

Cash hesitated as he tried to explain that away. "Maybe that's to throw the Prodigium off their scent?" he said. "They'd assume the same thing—that no one would expose themselves."

"Would you put your faith in the Prodigium's proportionate reaction to this?"

No. Cash wouldn't. No monster with sense would. He didn't want to admit that to Arkady just yet, though, so he changed the subject.

"It doesn't matter anyhow—"

"It's the only reason you're here."

That caught Cash off guard, right between the ribs. He felt his lungs hitch in at the almost physical ache of it, and he spat the sour breath out. It was a lie. Cash could tell that, but it still hurt. Apparently, his pride was an idiot.

His monster sighed—a long sibilant hiss in the back of his head—but didn't even dignify that with a jab.

"The Worm was collateral damage," Cash said. He'd worked that out last night, and he thought saying it aloud would make his head hurt less. It didn't. "Whoever did this didn't do it to unseat him. They just wanted to convince the 12:28 crew to trust them. Whatever they want to accomplish with that, it was always going to happen at Yana's wedding. If it looks like we're going to derail that, I don't think whoever it is will just give up."

"So they reveal themselves."

Cash nodded and stood up. He didn't often have to bother, but he pushed the monster down into his bones until they felt tight with it. The gray freckles on his hands faded down to faint blotches, just a shade darker than his skin.

"When does Yana get here?" he asked.

It took a second, but Arkady sighed and answered, "Soon." He put a knuckle under Cash's chin and tilted his head back until their eyes met. "She hasn't asked about you."

"So?"

Arkady scowled with a flash of peevish irritation at having his own flat statement turned against him, and then he dipped his head down for a kiss. It was soft and unhurried, gentle—not what Cash was usually into, but it felt like… champagne. The fizz of reaction tickled his nerves and made him shiver. Cash leaned into the kiss and caught Arkady's hips to pull him closer.

This time it was Arkady who pulled away. He stepped back and smirked, his lips wet and well-kissed.

"So get over it."

He turned and strode out of the room. Cash stared after him in exasperation and ran his hand through his hair.

"I was never under it," he muttered as he looked around for his boots. "So…."

SHANKO GAVE Cash a skeptical look.

"The guest list?" he said as he hoisted a frozen carcass off a hook and braced it on one broad shoulder. Meltwater ran down his arm and soaked his collar pink. "What do you want that for?"

He shoved Cash unceremoniously out of the way as he headed out of the larder. Cash caught himself on one of the strung sides of meat and staggered as it spun listlessly on its hook. He pushed himself off the cold lump of flesh, brushed the frost from his T-shirt, and jogged after Shanko. His footsteps sounded too loud as they echoed from the frost-crusted walls.

"I just want to know who's coming," Cash said as he dodged through the hanging meat to get ahead of Shanko. His breath steamed as it left his lips, thin and gray on the cold air.

"Your betters," Shanko snorted. The words didn't fog on the air.

"That could be anyone."

"Ask your boyfriend."

The urge to debate that point caught in Cash's throat. He ignored it as he stretched his legs to duck out of the larder first. There were other ways out of there—one of Donna's more useful quirks was a dislike for any room with only one exit—but they weren't pleasant.

"Arkady knows who's been invited," Cash said. "You know who's coming."

The corner of Shanko's mouth turned up in a brief smirk. "I do."

He dumped the carcass onto the trolley with the rest of the cuts for the wedding dinner. The wheels clicked and bounced on the rough floor as Shanko threw his weight against the handle. The kitchen would be busy tonight as they spiced and dressed the meat in cutlets and rolls. It was their one chance in the calendar to show off their skills. Traditionally most of the high-holiday feasts took a rustic approach, with as little preparation as possible before the food reached the table.

Ideally the meal would still be breathing, just lightly greased with a chili rub for pep.

Weddings, though, celebrated deception. Food that looked like one thing but was another, gifts with a hidden sting, and a few oblivious humans to play the fool. Preferably the bride or groom—Harry had been right about that particular hobby—but servers would do at a pinch.

"There's some people I'd rather avoid," Cash said as he half jogged along at Shanko's heels.

"Still running on negative friends, then?" Shanko asked. "Hopefully the child takes after her mother."

"Yana doesn't have any friends either," Cash said.

"That's by choice. You couldn't make a friend if you had a Mr. Potato Head and a Hand of Glory."

Cash broke stride as he visualized that. It made him shudder. "I can live with that," he said. "Besides, they aren't enemies. They're exes."

It was the truth. Sort of. Only one of his exes was likely to be *invited* to something like this, even if they were low down the list, but there were a few who might work the event. Cash hadn't dated a lot—humans thought it was hard to date as a single parent, they should try it with guys to whom *baby* was a superfood—but even in Roanoke the monster world was small. It was hard not to cross paths with your hookups.

Shanko stopped and leaned on the handle of the trolley. He pulled a handkerchief out of his pocket to fastidiously wipe his hands and neck and raised a heavy eyebrow at Cash. "You're on good terms with them?"

"No."

"Then they're enemies." He tucked the stained square of cloth back into his pocket and shoved the trolley back into motion. "I'll get the list after I deal with the cook, have it sent up to your room. If there's anyone likely to cause a scene if you catch the bouquet, let me know and I'll make sure they know better."

Now that Cash thought about it, that might not hurt. Two birds, one stone.

"Thanks," he said. "I appreciate that."

"Why don't you fuck Arkady, then," Shanko grunted. "It might put him in a better mood."

"I'll see what I can do," Cash said dryly. They reached the heavy metal doors to the kitchen. Cash paused as Shanko pushed them open with one shoulder and braced them on his heel. The crackle of the fire was loud enough that Cash raised his voice. Something unidentifiable and multilimbed dragged heavy chains across the floor from the counters to the ovens. "Hey, you hear of anything weird going on? In the city?"

"The Abascals welcomed you back into the fold," Shanko said. He always sounded bitter. His voice was scratchy with old disappointments. Maybe it was a bit sharper when he said that. Cash had sucked as a servant, burned his bridges on the way out, and yet here he was, back on the good linen. Yet all Shanko's years of good service had kept him right where he was—because he didn't have a pretty mouth and good bones. Cash could hardly object to any resentment there. Shanko snorted and dragged the trolley backward into the kitchen with him. "And the Worm has curled up under our feet until he regrows a human skin. Don't know who I'd have expected Donna to skin and wear more—you or him. Yet here you both are, under the same rock. Maybe I should send him the guest list too."

The trolley wheels bumped over the door frame, and the door scraped along the side as it slowly swung shut.

Cash stared at the scarred metal as he took in that bit of information. It made his brain ache, and the little part of him that was still a stupid, cocky asshole twitched to "go and see." As if the Worm were a tourist landmark to take a selfie at #atleasthediedquick.

He resisted that urge. The Worm being here explained what Donna and Arkady had been doing over dinner. Although not why Arkady hadn't told Cash about it. He might not have thought it was relevant, or he wanted to keep it a secret.

Cash could just ask, but…. He was good at lies, and Arkady wasn't. Not once you knew him, anyhow. Before Cash asked any questions, he wanted to be really sure he wanted to know the answers.

Something shrieked in the kitchen, high-pitched and shocked through the heavy doors. Cash jumped and remembered to move on before he got pressed back into service. He doubted Shanko would care whether Cash called himself staff or not if an extra set of hands were needed. Last time Cash'd gone in there, the chef wanted to cut his finger off to see if wisp tasted like fish or fowl.

He strode briskly away from the door and headed out into the guest parts of the underground.

"UGH, EUROPE," the thin woman with the see-through pallor sighed as she flicked thin, matted strings of hair back from her face with long fingers. Her aura was puffed up around her like a balloon, stretched so thin with her desire to impress that it had gone translucent in spots. "It's just changed so much from the old days. Nothing *smells* anymore. Don't you miss that? That real, ripe *stink* of human meat?"

She licked wet lips at the thought, a glimpse of fishhook teeth just visible. Her need prickled on Cash's tongue with a familiar acidic undertaste. All she wanted was everything—raw meat, fresh-carved respect, anyone her eye fell on under her—and it was sharp enough to make Cash's stomach clench in sympathy.

He could eat.

Cash plucked a square of golden pastry and… what was probably?… some sort of fish smear off a passing tray. He popped it into his mouth whole. The pastry crumbled into thick, buttery flakes on his tongue, and the salt hit the back of his throat with the brackish gene-memory of a marsh.

The reminder made his hands itch, even though it was only treated salt that made his monster shrivel like a dosed slug. He scratched between his knuckles even though he knew it wouldn't do any good. The irritation was buried under layers of skin, down near the bone.

He scored another glass of thin wine from a passing server—even after all these years of legal drinking, it still felt like he'd gotten away with something—and moved on through the crowd. The siren wanted too much, too single-mindedly, to focus on one thing long enough to set up contact with a production team. Two days into the plot, she'd have gotten hungry and eaten her catspaws instead of talking to them.

Water monsters were suckers for immediate gratification. Look at Cash. He hadn't even given Arkady the *chance* to seduce him. In fact to an outsider, *Cash* might look like the seducer.

Again.

He sipped the wine and wandered through the crowd. The occasional pop of interest/curiosity/spite when someone recognized him tasted like boba in watered-down green tea—a pop of something thick, sweet, and then gone. A flicker of interest in Arkady Abascal's bit of rough, but it was only for a second. Then they focused back on their own concerns.

The uneasy weight of a fresh meal in the red-skinned yara-ma-yha-who's stomach, the outline of a shoulder and a hand still visible against the thin skin of the Australian's distended gut, and the vague, moonlit memories of… *before.* The regret was like cotton candy—the same sort of disappointment you felt over a meal you hadn't savored at the time.

Cash left the man to his fig syrup and moved on.

A rail-thin sin-eater, his face all bones and shadows, waved an empty glass in Cash's face. Half-melted ice cubes rattled in the bottom like dice. "Another whiskey, boy," he said, voice loud and self-conscious. Then he laughed and glanced at the woman with him for approval. "It's the bastard's father. Sorry, I thought you were a server. I mean, you *were* of course."

He was all self-satisfaction as he imagined the moment he'd share that bon mot with Madeline. *The wisp was crushed*, the sin-eater imagined saying as he took Madeline's hand, *I think he went away to cry.*

As if she'd care. She was a spiteful monster, but not a particularly petty one, by all accounts.

"Don't worry about it," Cash said with an easy, empty smile. "I thought you were a monster. I mean, you know, a real one."

A sort of liver-colored scald crawled up the sin-eater's throat and into his cheeks. *That*, in case anyone wondered, was what crushed looked like. It wasn't about how scathing the insult was, it was delivering it at just the right moment to puncture whatever idea they'd coddled.

"Fuck you," the sin-eater spat. "Whore."

"John."

Cash walked away. Behind him he heard the sin-eater's companion ask curiously, "How did he know your name?" He nearly choked on his own snort of laughter and covered his cough with a sip of wine. Monsters could get away with being rude, but laughing at your own jokes was the sort of thing that only Baba Yaga could get away with.

Laughing at my jokes, the monster poked at him snidely.

He ignored it as he stepped over a tail and avoided a thick spill of ruched velvet train. It was the same thing, and besides, Cash didn't care about the crack at him. That would have been hypocritical. If you dished it out, you had to be willing to take it. But people needed to learn to hold their tongue about El.

They should be grateful it was Cash who taught them that lesson. It just cost them a needle to the ego. Donna didn't believe in any lesson that didn't end with someone's liver on the floor.

It had been a whole thing when Cash sent El to a Montessori preschool. He didn't think even the few segregated monster nurseries encouraged baby cage matches. It was hardly conducive to staying under the Church's radar. Toddlers would murder someone over a sticky penny if they knew it was an option.

A slattenpatte sighed in exasperation as she lifted one breast up to dab seltzer on the hot-sauce stain on the underside of the velvet bra.

"Every time I wear white," she groused. "I get blood on it."

"So don't wear white," her trow escort suggested as he held the glass of seltzer for her to dip into. He looked bored, a thin dark gray man with an explosion of such extravagant lace at his collar that it looked like he had started to froth. "Or learn where your mouth is."

She lowered her boob long enough to give him an annoyed look from under her heavy brows. "Is that a crack about the children?"

The trow rolled his eyes and groused, "No." It had been. They both wanted to go back in time, although the length of history they wanted to unwind was different—yesterday and a decade ago, respectively.

Their discontent was small and immediate—the restrictions of parenthood, his mother, the fact they might have murdered the head of the homeowner's association… or just really wanted to. It was hard to tell if the flickering image of blood on white tiles and torn white culottes on the perfect green grass lawn were real or wishful thinking.

Cash could sympathize, although it was the PTA that always got his goat.

The banshee had fucked someone she shouldn't. A troll in a glorious cloth-of-gold suit, his tail tasseled and gemmed, had pennies in his pocket and an eye out for a rich lass. Those were just the monsters common enough to have a breed. Others were like the Abascals—a pared-down bloodline that didn't need to be named. Although, if you were young and in love like Cash had been, you might try dragon or demon and find neither quite fit—or just one horrible, solitary deed that served as their new identity. A short mercreature in pirate finery, long boots on short legs and a nest of jellyfish stingers strung from his nose down, wanted something that Cash couldn't understand, with a salt-bitter poignancy. The witch in cracked black leather whose grimy fingers made mold sprout where she touched was ripe with simple, cheerful lust for a wedding hookup.

Everyone wanted something. Most of them had secrets they would sweat through a lie to keep hidden.

None of them *felt* like Harry's contact. Surely someone who put this whole self-destructive—Prodigium-destructive—plan into play would be consumed by the Abascals' fall? Not with the question of whether they could pour another thin mushroom cocktail down their throat without puking up their last meal.

Of course, these were only the powerful. Old breeds and up-and-comings who'd gotten a foot on the ladder of power. They wanted to show off their finery to Donna, impress her or intrigue her enough to earn her interest.

The real power-players—the Prodigium movers and shakers—would arrive with the dawn. Much as she hated it, those were the ones Donna needed to show off to in order to stay their peer.

It was easy to slip. That's why Cash liked it where he was. No one wanted anything from him, and the only person he had to impress was the director with a steady shot.

Cash traded his glass of wine—still half-full, the stuff tasted worse than he remembered—with a server for a napkin. The square of fabric was thick and smooth, nicer than any of the suits he'd brought with him. He wiped his hands with it as he glanced around the room. That was the thing about the Abascals. It was hard to stay in their orbit and *not* just accept their world.

His gaze flicked over the rest of the evening crowd as they milled around and waited for the guests of honor to show themselves. He stopped on a man in the corner of the room who looked almost as out of place as Cash did. Not that Luke Kohary was. The Left Hand of the Prodigium *was* the power player in the monster world.

He didn't look it, though. Tall and sandy-haired, with an actual tan, Kohary was dressed down in black jeans and an open-collared shirt. If it weren't for the wary exclusion zone around him, he might have even passed for human.

Rumor had it that he had been.

Cash wished Donna served whiskey at these events. He didn't drink much these days—it was hard enough to function during daylight hours without a hangover added to the mix—but a shot of liquid stupidity always made things easier. In its absence, he'd just have to depend on the dumb he'd been born with.

He blotted his hands on the napkin again and headed over to talk to Kohary.

Chapter Ten

NOTHING.

To a wisp there was nothing where Luke Kohary stood but meat. No itch of regret or want, no thin hotdog-broth saltiness of yearning. He didn't even have an aura, not even a thin rind of one like Harry. It was… disorienting, like he was a projection of some kind instead of a real person.

But Cash could feel the warmth of his skin as Luke grasped his hand. There were rough calluses on his fingers and old scars on the bony back. He was here, even if Cash's monster didn't want to believe it.

"It's an honor," Cash said. It wasn't, of course. It was a nape-prickling, pit-sweating mistake that made his stomach regret that fishy bite he'd taken earlier. They both knew that, but niceties and fear were what tied the Prodigium together. "It's not often you see the Left Hand… socially."

Kohary smiled coldly. He had very green eyes, so opaque you could hardly see the monster underneath.

"Trust me," Kohary said in a soft, rough voice. "Socially is the only time a monster sees me. My professional visits are… brisk."

And the monster ended up dead. Cash took his hand back before it got too clammy for either of them to ignore.

"I guess that's reassuring," he said. Kohary looked at him curiously. It was probably the first time that *anything* about him was described as "reassuring." Cash showed his teeth as his nerves insisted that his survival required him to be an ass. "That you're here for the finger food, not our fingers."

Kohary waited a second—long enough for Cash's mouth to go sand dry—and then laughed. It was a pleasant sound, low and warm, and his eyes crinkled at the corners like he meant it. Behind him a spirit dropped out of the curtain treatment. It twitched on the floor, stunned, and the scavenged bits of it evaporated into grease and dust.

"At least not yet, anyhow," he said. "I'm surprised Arkady didn't tell you to expect me."

Cash considered the ball-pinching idea that he might have stepped on the fucking Left Hand of the Prodigium's toes... or fingers, he supposed... when he kissed Arkady. He hoped someone would lie to Ellie about how he'd died, or at least why.

"No," he said, his voice thin in his throat.

"The Prodigium isn't just a soulless council of monsters and demons. We're a family, and we attend family events," Kohary said dryly. He took a drink of wine and looked away from Cash as he scanned the room. After a moment he glanced back at Cash and snorted. "It was a joke. You can laugh."

"I knew that," Cash said. Or at least he'd thought it was an option, although his throat had not been confident enough to take a risk. He cleared his throat and tried again. "I'm trying to imagine you turning up at the hospital with a baby gro. It's not easy."

"I do gift cards."

"Good choice."

"Arkady is my finger on the pulse of Roanoke," Kohary said. That was news. Cash tried not to look like he'd been caught off guard, or not any more than he already did. Kohary looked him up and down. "And you're his wisp. You're prettier than his wife."

Cash raised an eyebrow. "I have met Madeline," he said. "I know that's not true."

Madeline had the sort of personality you expected to find under a rock—which wasn't a drawback when you were a monster—but she was beautiful. It was a weapon, of course, but just because it had a cutting edge didn't make it unreal.

The candlelight glowed fitfully in the wine with sparks of luminescence as Kohary took a sip. He wiped the moisture off his lip with his thumb, the black spike tattoo on the webbing very dark and sharp-edged. "I prefer humans."

Cash flushed. He wasn't sure if that was an insult or a come-on, or which was more disturbing.

"Half-human," he said.

If that, by now. He'd always be half-human born, and every monster who didn't like him would throw it in his face, but it didn't really matter once you survived your childhood. *If* you did. The camps had judged him monster enough, and the wisp in his bones ate his mask thinner every year.

Live long enough, and he'd be as wary of the sun as Arkady. That was the dream, he supposed, but sometimes he thought he'd miss it once it was gone—like a pulled tooth, the empty socket always some sort of surprise.

"Half's enough. More than that, and they don't... like it."

Once, when Ellie was still a toddler, she'd put a cockroach in her mouth. It shouldn't have been a surprise, since she put everything in her mouth, but Cash had still nearly gagged. For the first time, he thought he must know what it felt like, as the question *"Like what?"* tried to scramble up his throat.

He didn't want to know, but his monster desperately did. It was an asshole.

"Of course, I suppose you were already in the area," Cash said. It wasn't *safe* ground, but it was safer. At least it was only casual murder under his feet, not the question of whether what Kohary did in bed was more or less esoteric than the Worm. "I'd heard you were here about that redcap who got caught, although redcaps seem below your pay grade."

"Who told you that?"

"Camp drop-off gossip," Cash said promptly.

Kohary snorted, but it was a lie that was hard to poke holes in. A good 75 percent of every Prodigium scandal in the last century had started as drop-off gossip. Evolution—or the devil—might have designed most monsters to be solitary predators, but parents needed to unwind over liquor.

"Fine," Kohary said. "Don't worry about me, wisp, or my business. You've enough of your own to keep you busy. It can't be easy to watch your ex get married."

"You should know."

The words slipped out of Cash's mouth—which had apparently decided to unlink itself from his brain. He felt himself blanch, his face cold except for hot spots on his temples and tongue, as Kohary turned to look at him.

Black. Kohary's monster had black eyes, dull as coal.

Fuck.

Cash's tongue stuck to the roof of his mouth. He swallowed stickily and fumbled for a take back. Before he could come up dry on that, a hand touched the small of his back and he breathed in mead and linen.

"Kohary," Arkady said. His voice was tight, strung through with suspicion and discomfort but still awkwardly courteous. "Enjoying the wine? The grapes came from the caverns in Italy where my mother grew up. A taste of home."

Kohary blinked, and his eyes were green again and unexpectedly regretful.

"It's… a taste," he said. "Earthy."

"Fungus," Arkady said. "Donna always says it tastes like why she came to America, but it's traditional."

"And she's a traditional woman?" Kohary asked as he set the glass aside.

"She's a businesswoman," Arkady corrected. "She doesn't have to enjoy the tradition to see its worth."

"Out for herself," Kohary said. "Good to know."

The undercurrents in the conversation could have drowned a horse. Cash shifted uncomfortably away from the tension, and Arkady tugged him back, fingers hooked in the waistband of his jeans.

"My sister is on her way," he said. "We don't want it to look like you're avoiding her."

Black threads flickered in Kohary's eyes as he drained the rest of his wine. To his credit, he didn't grimace at the taste. Most people did until their palates accepted their fate.

"Good idea," he said. "How things look isn't something that can be ignored."

Arkady's knuckles pressed into the small of Cash's back as his hand tightened. "It can be for a weekend," he said shortly.

"Perhaps. Go greet your sister," Kohary said. He was talking to Arkady, but his eyes were on Cash as he said it. "Don't let me keep you. We can catch up later."

Hopefully not.

Cash waited until there were bodies between them and Kohary to let the full-body shudder escape him. He felt more relieved than he had when he got out of the cuffs last night.

"He's not that bad," Arkady said as he moved his hand up Cash's back. It would look less like he was dragging Cash somewhere.

Cash snorted. "That's clearly a lie," he said. Out of the corner of his eye, he saw Arkady dip his head and tilt the corner of his mouth in a wry acknowledgment. "Is the fact you work for the Left Hand of the Prodigium one of those things I would have known if I'd asked?"

"If you asked the right people," Arkady said. "Ellie doesn't know. Donna does."

"I wouldn't ask Donna if my head were on fire," Cash said.

"She likes you now."

"Somehow that's worse."

Arkady made a dry noise of agreement and slid his hand up Cash's back. He walked his fingers along the knobs of his spine up to the weird, sensitive spot between his shoulder blades. The sort of spot that only someone who knew—still knew—your body could find. Awareness prickled under Cash's skin like inverted goose pimples, and he felt his ears flush.

"It does take the thrill out of you being the bad boy," Arkady said. "Her approval, you know?"

It was only monsters who'd look at the two of them and pick Cash out as the bad influence. Good influence, he supposed, from the human side of things.

"It's a shame," Arkady murmured as he nodded a coolly distant acknowledgment to a... thing? Cash hadn't been introduced. The monster bent its great, thorn-antlered head back to Arkady, mindful of the other guests around it. "But if you can't ruin my reputation, at least you can look pretty on my arm. For a weekend."

Cash ignored the pointed restriction as he nodded polite acknowledgment to the monster—it's wild bloodred eye had already rolled on over the crowd, but it was never wise to assume that was the only way something could see. "And who should I have asked about the Worm in residence?"

There was a beat as Arkady absorbed that question. Then he smiled pleasantly and leaned down slightly toward Cash as they paused.

"Did your human filmmaker tell you that?" he asked tightly. "And mind your tongue, for once. No one is meant to know the Worm's location while he regenerates."

Cash ignored the insult. It wasn't as if Arkady were mistaken. A habit of saying the wrong thing at the wrong time was great at mealtimes when you were something that ate negative emotions, but it didn't get you many invites *back*. Cash couldn't even blame it on the monster. A lot of it was him deciding to be a dick.

"Harry wouldn't believe it," he said. "Monsters are basically extinct, remember, and if they aren't, only the plodders are left. Sasquatches and hedge witches, hex men and redcaps. If someone went into a producer's office and pitched that the... your honored guest... was still around, they'd be laughed out of town. Why is he here, anyhow? Why isn't he loaded onto a train home?"

"Because he's too weak," Arkady said bluntly. "He probably wouldn't survive the trip. He demanded sanctuary from my mother, and if anything does happen to him, then we pay."

The bottom dropped unhappily out of Cash's stomach at that bit of information. That was something he shouldn't know, that it wasn't a good idea *to* know. He tried to move away from Arkady but got tugged back. Arkady cupped his fingers, warm and dry, around the back of Cash's neck. He didn't squeeze tightly enough for it count as scruffing Cash. Not quite.

"You asked," Arkady pointed out.

"And you could have lied."

"Would you have believed me?"

No, probably not. Arkady was a really bad liar when you knew him. That didn't make the faint sick feeling in Cash's stomach go away, though. The Worm had killed people for less reason than knowing his weaknesses.

"And people wonder why I don't ask questions," Cash muttered instead of acknowledging Arkady's point. It would have been a good time to actually take that advice, but he glanced over his shoulder toward Kohary. "That's why *he's* here?"

"Well, he wasn't invited," Arkady said tiredly. His fingers tightened slightly around the nape of Cash's neck. "Should I be jealous?"

"No," Cash said with a slight shudder. It wasn't that Kohary was more powerful than him—so was Arkady—but everyone knew what the Left Hand did for the Prodigium… and how he did it. Cash glanced sidelong at Arkady and gave in to the temptation. "Should I?"

Arkady stopped in the middle of the hall and leaned down to kiss Cash. It was rough and possessive, sharp teeth and a hungry tongue. His magic slipped into Cash's mouth along with Arkady's breath, sweet and heady. It seeped down his throat and into his blood until he could feel the hot golden prickle of Abascal magic stretched out like a net between his flesh and his skin.

It was a trap of sorts, but Cash knew what he was doing when he said "Deal" to an Abascal. There was a lot they could do to you without that, but once you started to barter, that was the hook in your soul. For a human it ended much the same way it did for a trout, but it was a bit more… survivable… for something whose soul was meant to die with it. It was a lot harder to extract for consumption.

More enjoyable too, at least that was Cash's experience of the honey trap.

And the soul is still not the bit of you that he has on a line either, the monster mocked him, but lazily. Arkady's magic wasn't something that could sustain Cash, but like faerie food, it felt like it could. The dull nibble of a few days unfed was washed away by a thick, sated feeling.

Arkady's fingers were buried in Cash's hair again as he finally raised his head. His eyes were bright gold, like coins, and he looked as glutted as Cash felt.

"Maybe just stop asking stupid questions," Arkady said in a low, rough voice. He tightened his grip and tilted Cash's head back a little to get a good look at him. Behind him a thin woman licked her lips with a wet split tongue and fanned herself with a webbed hand at the display. "But this works. It's my sister's wedding, after all. I don't want her confused about which ex you're here for."

Cash swallowed the assurance that she wouldn't be. It felt like a stone in his throat, but Arkady's ego didn't need to be any larger. Yana had always known where she stood. It was where she preferred to be.

"If she misses it, I'm sure everyone here will tell her," he said.

"Good."

Arkady ruffled Cash's hair, grabbed his hand, and headed for the stairs. Halfway up, something occurred to Cash.

"Wait," he said as he hesitated between one step and the next. "Yana knows why I'm here, doesn't she? She knows what's… going on."

Arkady glanced at the two goat-headed men at the banister, goblets of not-the-best vintage in their hands. They flinched and moved their discussion down a few steps, out of easy earshot, at least.

"Of course not," he said. "You know what she's like. Yana can't keep a secret to save *your* life."

Yeah, Cash mused, that's what everyone thought.

THE CAREFULLY composed family scene in Donna's drawing room made Cash's fingers itch for a camera. Donna sat in a black leather wingback chair, dressed all in pale gray silk and velvet with a delicate scrap of silvery lace pinned into her wig. The matriarch in mourning—most monster weddings did end in *someone* dead, after all. On the other side of the chess game in progress, Arkady sprawled lazily in fitted leather two shades away from black, his eyes and hair bright even with his monster pushed down under his skin.

It made him look younger, his mother's favorite son again instead of Kohary's whatever it was Arkady actually did.

Call it the "Monsters Reception" and leave it to the viewer to pick out the *wrong* details in the background. The twisted things carved into the arms of the chairs, the fact the chess pieces were all monsters, and the candlesticks that were hands of glory—the wicks the corpse-long fingernails soaked in paraffin.

Then there was Cash, rumpled and uneasy in black as he leaned on the back of Arkady's chair. He figured the picture would definitely make more sense without him in it.

Donna finally selected Medusa from her side of the board and moved her forward.

"You can sit, Casper," she said as she positioned the queen neatly on her square. "You aren't Arkady's aide these days."

Goose bumps prickled along Cash's arms as he shook his head and tightened his grip on the back of the chair.

"I'm fine here," he said. "I'm used to it."

Donna smiled at him, fishhook teeth behind glossy red lips. Her eyes were still and dark as a bog, with the same sucking bottom. Cash found that rather lovely, of course, but it was still dangerous.

"So are we," she said. "The room finally feels right with you back at Arkady's shoulder. You always were practically one of the family, after all."

Right. Cash ducked his chin to hide the skepticism in his eyes. It used to drive Donna mad that he didn't stand up straight. She threatened to pull his spine out and replace it with spoons once. That didn't mean she *didn't* consider him family, of course. Donna had threatened her own blood with worse. She'd buried more than one ambitious son, and some of them had even been dead. The implication made him wary—that she'd missed him "making the place untidy," as she'd always snapped before she threw something.

That and the fact she was still being nice to him. Cash could feel the tension in his shoulders, tight and itchy, as he waited for the other shoe to drop.

"You once told me you'd sell him to the Yagas if I didn't pass calculus."

Arkady made his move. It was careless, a goat-horned bishop nudged into the path of a skull-faced knight, and Donna made an annoyed sound. She liked to win. It didn't even bother her if people *let* her win, but she expected them to put on a good show.

"It was a *joke*, Arkady," she said and rolled her eyes behind her froth of a veil. The bishop left the board on her next move. "What would the Yagas want with a teenage boy? The meat would be stringy."

Cash snorted. He shrugged an apology when Arkady turned to give him a dubious look. It wasn't funny. Or it wouldn't have been if Donna had trussed him up to be shipped to Moscow. That was—somehow—what made it funnier. It had been a long time since Cash had gotten to laugh at a bad thing. He missed it.

"See?" Donna said as she picked up her wine. "A joke."

Arkady frowned at the board as he finally saw the trap Donna had nudged him into. Any move would doom his king. His fingers shifted between a sacrificial pawn and his gape-mouthed queen, but the doors to the room slowly creaked open before he had to decide. Shanko stepped into the room through the gap, trussed into shirt and tails that did nothing to dress up the raw-meat planes of his face.

"Your daughter's home," he said.

Even though he *knew* who Shanko meant, Cash felt a twinge of anticipation, as if there was a chance Ellie was going to walk through the door. Ellie was on an overnight camping trip in the mountains, and even if she got fed up and decided to hitchhike home, it would be a while before she got there.

His heart still sank a little when Yana blew into the room.

"Mama," Yana said happily as she bounced over the thick, stained carpet. She stooped down and kissed the air just above Donna's dry, smooth cheek. Her hand braced on the back of the chair, and she whispered something through her smile into Donna's ear. It was too low to hear, but it was mean enough that Donna's eyes flickered mercury-flat for a second. Before she could retaliate, Yana had already pulled away and turned to look at Arkady. "And you. My *little* brother. How well you look, after everything."

They glared at each other.

Yana looked like Arkady, enough that no one had ever questioned their family connection. The line of the nose was the same, and they had the same fox-amber eyes. But where Arkady was all gold and honey, Yana was old bones and blood. Her skin was a thick creamy white, the color of powdered bone, and her hair and lips were the exact same scarlet red. She looked vivid, as vivacious as Donna had reputedly been as a young woman, before she learned that fear worked even better than charm.

Except there was nothing to Yana but the skin she'd been born with. No power under her thick human skin, no monster restless in her bones. She wasn't human—there wasn't enough of her for that—but she'd never age into anything other than what she was right now.

She was a walking, manicured coffin for the monster she might have been. Monstrous enough for the Prodigium, but not for herself.

Cash cleared his throat.

"Yana," he said.

Her eyes flicked up from Arkady, and she finally registered that Cash was there. She smiled with quick, surprising sweetness and clapped her hands together. "Casper! You made it," she said. "I was afraid you wouldn't."

"You didn't invite me."

She shrugged that off as unimportant as she bounced around the chair to throw her arms around him. Her hair was wiry as a horse, and she smelled of gas and fresh blood.

"Is Baby here?"

"Ellie."

She snapped her fingers behind his ear and tutted. "That's it. Why did I have *Jo* in my head?"

A low, slow voice interrupted from the door. "That was the truck stop, sweetheart. Jo's Gas and Dash. We ate there."

Yana laughed. Her breath was warm and somehow sticky. "Oh. That's right."

Cash looked over her head at Jerome. A slender, tall man in a good suit stepped around Shanko and offered a tip, a fifty-dollar bill pinned between his knuckles. Shanko looked at it and barked a harsh laugh at him as he turned and walked out. Left with his flashy gesture limp in his hand, Jerome casually tried to tuck the money back in his pocket.

He was….

Cash licked the salt of despair off his lips and carefully peeled Yana's arm from around his neck. He looked at Donna, who looked ruffled, but not by her visitor, and then at Arkady. Maybe that knock on the head had thrown him off more than he thought.

"He's human," Arkady confirmed for him.

"Part human," Jerome interjected. "My grandfather is a kushtaka. Once I have an heir, I will be too. And you're—"

He stuck his hand out. At least the fifty wasn't in his fingers this time. Cash accepted the handshake, Jerome's fingers cold as they wrapped around his.

"My ex," Yana said. She ran sharp red nails down Cash's arm. "My daughter's father."

Arkady leaned back in the chair and crossed his legs in front of him at the ankle. His eyes were bright and liquid, dangerous enough to make Jerome nervously shift his weight. It wasn't about him any more than it was *really* about Cash, but if Jerome survived the wedding night, he'd learn.

"And currently my lover," Arkady said.

"Again," Yana said. She smiled, bright and empty, under Arkady's glare. "Oh, don't pout. You'd put him down, and he was so pretty, and it seemed a shame to let him gather dust."

"Or Cash," Cash said dryly to Jerome. "Most people stick with that."

Jerome looked uncomfortable. He'd get used to that too.

"Okay," he said. "And *what* are you?"

There was a brief, unpleasant pause at the insult. Cash broke it with a dry chuckle as he took his hand back. Either Jerome didn't have any clue just how rude that was, or he did and he was stupid enough to show his true nature day one. Either way, it was Yana's problem.

"Late," Cash said. "Camp is going to send proof of life today, so I don't want to miss that."

Jerome laughed like it was a joke, and Cash shifted his money from "stupid" to "clueless." He turned to Yana.

"Why don't you come with me," he said. "You can catch up on how Ellie's doing."

Yana rolled her eyes. "It's camp," she said. "If they're still sending photos, she's doing fine. You worry too much. It's not like it's her first year."

Cash clenched his teeth. He was used to Yana, but sometimes her blithe self-centeredness still caught him off guard.

"Go," Donna instructed. She reached over the table and flicked Arkady's king over to cede the game for him. "Let your brother and I get to know your latest beau. Maybe he'll impress us. Stranger things have happened."

Jerome had, at least, enough common sense to look worried. After a knee-jerk glare at her mother's order, Yana gave in with a shrug.

"Fine," she said. "Show me pictures of Ellie while I unpack. I smell like gas fire anyhow."

Arkady half turned in his chair to watch them leave. His expression was unreadable, which just meant he was irritated. Cash considered an apologetic look but decided against it. He was here to help plug a leak. Being the forgiven ex was just the cover story.

That was a lie. Cash didn't even need the monster's snigger to know that. It was a useful lie, though. Just like the one Cash told himself where the ache under his breastbone was just the fishhook of Arkady's magic.

He let Yana take his arm and headed out of the hall.

Chapter Eleven

"SHE LOOKS like you," Yana said. "I mean, of course she doesn't. But she does."

Cash knew what she meant. Taken individually—her nose, her hair, the length of her legs—Ellie looked like an Abascal. She moped at him sometimes that she wasn't as *pretty* as her *dad*, and it wasn't *fair*. Taken altogether, though, no one had ever questioned that she was his.

"Yeah, well, it could be worse," Cash said. "It's the sort of thing you tell your daughter, you know. Getting married."

Yana handed him his phone back. On the screen Ellie grinned at the camera, her arms thrown over the shoulders of two other little monsters. Werewolves, from the eyebrows. All three of them were muddy, and behind them two boys were trying to get to their feet in the mud.

"Why? It's nothing to do with her," she asked.

"Jerome is going to be her stepfather," Cash said. "A whole new family to be part of."

Yana shook her head and sat down on the bed to take her boots off. They were in her suite, the mirror image of Arkady's, from the shape to the decor. A set of expensive suitcases were stacked neatly in the corner, and a tray of something sat on the dresser, the plate covered with a chased silver dome.

"That's stupid. I barely see Ellie. Why would Jerome want anything to do with her?" She kicked her boots across the room and pulled her feet up onto the bed. All of a sudden, she didn't seem old enough to get married, all bony knees and rounded shoulders. Her eyes narrowed over high, freckled cheekbones. "Besides, that's rich talk coming from the pot. My brother can't make his own spawn, so he's just moved in on you and my kid. Nice little readymade family, huh? What are you going to do? The three of you going to move to the heartlands and become cowboys?"

Cash was briefly distracted by that idea. "No. It's not like that, and why would we? I don't think I've ever seen a cow up close."

"Oh please, you were at Arkady's wedding," Yana said with a perfectly tilted lift of one eyebrow. She held the mock-confused look for a second and then snorted at the expression on Cash's face. "It was a joke, Kasparas."

Sometimes Yana was a lot like her mother, but she wouldn't thank Cash if he pointed that out. He glanced down at the photo of Ellie on his phone. Despite her grin and the camp's thin comment, clearly unsure if it was a good trait or not—that she "was uncommonly personable and made friends easily"—Ellie still looked very small and very human to him.

Even though she shouldn't, really.

Cash blanked the screen before he said anything, as if some sort of contagion were possible through a screen. Who knew, after all? It might be.

"Kohary's here," he said.

There was a pause as Yana absorbed that. She closed her eyes, and when she opened them again, her irises were flat human hazel. Her smile was tart and full of mockery as she hopped off the bed.

"Well, Mother's hospitality *is* legendary," she said. Her image in the long free-standing mirror caught her eye, and she paused to tidy her curls, as much as they'd cooperate. "If you survive it. Now that my brother is his good left pinky, I guess he couldn't overlook the chance to partake."

"You okay with that?" Cash asked. He put his hands in his pockets and shifted his weight.

With no one but herself to perform for, Yana's expression in the mirror was empty. Her eyes flicked toward Cash, and she shrugged.

"Why would I care?" she asked. Her tone was light, but there was a barb hidden under the fluff she used as a lure.

"Because, once upon a time, it was his job to decide if you got to live or die?"

She hitched one shoulder in a shrug and leaned in closer to the mirror to tidy her lipstick with the edge of her nail. "It was nothing personal. Water under the bridge."

"Because—" Cash broke off as he saw a shadow flicker, long and grayish, against the wall. A second later one of the housekeepers appeared at the door, silent in her sneakers, with a stack of fresh towels for the bathroom. He waited until she'd dropped them off, and by then the urge to be honest had passed. "It's your wedding, and is Jerome really going to be comfortable meeting the Left Hand over canapés?"

Yana smiled. It was for herself and her mirror image and therefore faded and brief. She didn't feel much, not like most people did—not hunger, not rage, not anything. It had seemed, when Cash was young, hungry, and spurned, to be enviable.

"Jerome won't have a clue," she said. "He'll shake Luke's hand and ask him what he does and if he enjoys it. Tell him the Kohary is here, and it'll mean nothing to him. He might have heard of the Left Hand, but he doesn't know enough to fear him."

The thought of Kohary's marsh-water eyes made Cash shudder.

"He's scary enough on his own," he said. "I wouldn't need to know anything about it to know he was bad news."

Yana turned and quirked an eyebrow at him. "That's only because you *are* the bad boy." She paused and then smiled at him. The expression was sickly sweet, and there was acid in her voice when she said, "When I heard Arkady had gotten divorced, I assumed Kohary would be his date to my wedding. I guess he wasn't ready for the big-league bad boys, though. Not yet."

She waited. So did Cash, for the brittle tide of self-loathing and insecurity to hit the back of his throat like bile.

They were both disappointed. Cash laughed when Yana's smile folded into an annoyed pucker.

"I get good performance reviews at work," Cash said. "The moms at Ellie's school all think I'm a sweetheart and trust me to have sleepovers. It's flattering I can even pass for bad-boy training wheels."

She sniffed and dismissed that with a flick of her hand. "Don't be smug, Cash. One raw spot scabbed over doesn't make you invulnerable."

"I thought you should know about Kohary, that's all."

Yana stepped toward him and touched his face, her fingers cool as they pressed on the salt-tender flesh under his eyes.

"That's all? You sure?"

He stepped back. "It's your mother's house," he said. "It's never *all*, but it's all I came here to tell you."

Her hand dropped to her side. "Be careful. You got away once. My family never lets prey go to ground twice. Arkady won't let you go again."

"What's he going to do? Lock me up? Tie me to the bed?"

That slipped out. It was more fantasy than fear. Yana had the grace to just give him a disparaging look and ignore it.

"I would," she said. The corners of her mouth turned down slightly. "And mother would if she thought it would keep her golden boy happy."

Cash shook his head. "You know better than that," he said. "She hated that I crawled into Arkady's bed. Some half-human charity case wasn't exactly who she envisaged on Arkady's arm at family events."

"Yet here you are," Yana said.

"Donna didn't invite me."

"Neither did I, and yet…." She trailed off and, point made, waved her hand dismissively at him. "If you're done, then? I need to unpack my trousseau, prepare the bonbonnieres, and decide what I want to say with my bouquet."

It didn't *feel* done, but Cash supposed that his conscience was clear. Technically, which was the best kind of clear. He glanced down at the picture of Ellie and decided he could definitely face her when she got back from camp.

"You'll need to talk to Ellie when you get back," he said. "She'll be upset otherwise."

Yana glanced over her shoulder at him. "She's a monster now," she said quietly. "She'll be upset by worse. Would you really want her here? With Kohary? With the great and the grim?"

No. Probably not. Not yet, at least. One day she wouldn't have a choice, the same as with camp. Right now it was bad enough she was sometimes around her grandmother. But he wasn't happy about it.

"Congratulations on your wedding day, Yana," he said to her back. "I would have gotten you a gift, but it was short notice."

He started toward the door. His foot had just touched the threshold when Yana's voice caught between his shoulder blades like a hook.

"In fact, maybe you're right," she said. "If you and Arkady are a thing again, maybe Ellie should spend more time with me and Jerome."

He turned around. "Yana—"

"See?" she said without looking around. "You're still too soft to survive this family, Casper. Just like she is."

"THEY'RE HERE," Cash said as he slid onto the seat next to Harry. It was in the café instead of the bar, but the rest of his setup was the same. Harry twitched at the company and glanced around. "I saw Yana Abascal arrive earlier. She came in through the family's private entrance."

Harry lifted his cup to his mouth and pretended to take a drink. His mouth moved behind the cover of the rim.

"We aren't supposed to know each other," he said stiffly.

Cash shrugged and leaned over, his hand braced on the edge of Harry's seat. "So, I'm hitting on you," he said. Harry gave him a dour look from behind the heavy fake glasses, and Cash smirked at him. "What? You've never hit on a cute stranger in a coffee shop?"

"I'm straight," Harry said. He put his coffee down and looked away from Cash to scan the room. He tapped the edge of his glasses twice as someone who passed by got his attention. His monster-hunting skills were fifty-fifty at the moment. "And I'm ordained."

Huh.

The steam of the lie bled from cracks in Harry's close-fitted aura. It was thin and acrid as nicotine, the taste of shame and regret.

Most lies weren't so obvious—or Cash would have known whether Yana was serious or not—but self-delusion had hang time.

It wasn't Cash's problem, although he filed it away for the monster to gnaw on. It might be useful later.

"There are cute girls in coffee shops," he pointed out. "And you weren't born with a collar."

"I had a caul," Harry said. "So might as well have been."

Cash resisted the urge to pull away. His skin crawled, and he struggled not to check Harry's hands again for the Hunter ink. Just in case it had welled to the surface overnight.

It was superstition. The caul-born were resistant to monster tricks, but that was all. Useful enough for a Hunter or a Jesuit investigator but not dangerous. That was what everyone said, but the hair on the back of Cash's neck believed in the old gory folk tales Shanko used to tell when he had a few in him. In those, the cauled Hunters could rip your monster out of your bones, screeching and gritty with marrow. That and worse.

The back of Cash's neck itched as he casually leaned back.

"I know you've watched TV. Pretend you're Tom Hardy and it's a meet cute."

A brief smile tilted the corner of Harry's mouth before he bit it back. "I suppose I can do that," he said. He took his glasses off, folded the legs neatly, and tucked them into his pocket. "How do you know it was—"

"I grew up around here," Cash reminded him. "I'm dating her brother."

"She's the mother of your daughter."

Cash's mouth felt sticky. It wasn't a secret. These days, if a monster wanted to live in the human world, they needed human identification. It could be faked, but why bother when you could get a real one if you just turned up with a baby. Admittedly, that was how some monsters got fake ones too. Yana's name was on Ellie's birth certificate, Donna was Cash's emergency contact—which always felt odd when he had to fill it in, but if something happened to him she'd take care of Ellie.

Any sort of background check would turn that up. Cash hadn't actually expected Harry to do one, but he should have. Still, he didn't like the idea that Harry had read Ellie's name. Maybe he'd even seen a photo of her.

"Cute kid," Harry said, a pro forma compliment from someone who felt they had to say something. "It sounds a bit more complicated than a hookup."

"Yeah, well, I don't spill my life story to strangers who've knocked me out and dragged me to a cave," Cash said. "Yana and I, we aren't on good terms."

"To put it mildly. She hasn't seen her daughter in, what, five years now?"

"She's still Ellie's mom. She's Arkady's sister. I don't want anything bad to happen to her. I mean, I still think someone's led you up the graveyard path, but if you were right about her boyfriend… I won't let something happen to her just so you can catch your monster red-handed."

"Pawed," Harry corrected him absently. "Red-pawed. They don't have hands, not like we do. It's one of the ways to tell that mankind was put here to have dominion."

That was so bizarrely wrong that Cash nearly argued with him. He thought better of it before he blurted out something he shouldn't know, like the fact *this* monster had enough manual dexterity to give someone the finger.

Okay, *some* of them didn't have hands. They still got by fine.

"Whatever," Cash said. "I'm not going to tell my daughter her mom's been eaten—or kidnapped, or whatever—but it's okay because Harry proved his pet theory about monsters was true."

Harry gave him a genuinely injured look. "I would never," he said earnestly. "No monster is worth spending a single human soul, not even a soul as… dissolute… as Ilyana Abascal."

Rude, but not untrue. Yana lived like someone who didn't give a damn. Mostly because that's what she was.

"Not that it matters," Cash said. "Because you're crazy."

He wasn't, of course. Wrong about the details, but not crazy. Harry smiled briefly as he took a drink of his coffee.

"You know I'm not," he said. "I've been doing this for years, Cash. Hunted down curses, exposed corrupted priests, and even went to Europe to track down one of the last vampires. And every time I could sense the... undercurrent that it wasn't over, we'd just hit a dead end. We might have won, but we'd missed something. If my contact is telling the truth—and I think he is—we'll know what. Who."

That was the sort of talk that would get you killed. The Prodigium preferred discouraged investigators, but in a pinch, dead ones would do. It was messier than they'd like—old-school rather than new-guard—but it worked.

"And if he isn't?" Cash asked. "I saw the fiancé carry Yana's bags into the house. He looked normal enough."

Harry finished his coffee. "I hope you're right," he said as he gently set the cup down on the table. "This would be the biggest story of my career, and I still hope you're right. I just don't believe you are. What do you want, Cash?"

Cash sat back and looked away. He ran his eyes over the handful of monsters and humans mostly peacefully coexisting as the need for coffee overrode anything else. The stocky, fish-faced blond throwing a fit as she demanded the lanky bloodybones behind the counter let her speak to the manager... she might not make it all the way home after her stay.

But nobody cared about Karens. They were free calories.

"I want in," he said. "You need a cameraman, and I need to make sure that you don't put anyone at risk."

Harry looked amused. "I can shoot my own footage."

"I didn't realize you'd made the guest list," Cash said. "Or been asked to do the honors when it came to photography."

A flicker of suspicion crossed Harry's face. It tasted like garlic dust against Cash's lips, barely there. It was creepier than Kohary's emptiness somehow. At least the Left Hand of the Prodigium was *supposed* to be disturbing and uncomfortable. Harry narrowed his eyes.

"That's... convenient," he said.

Cash snorted. "Sure. It's great. I get to run around all day trying to get my ex to smile at me and her drunk grandmother to stay where she's put. For the 'exposure.'"

He'd dealt with enough people who thought he should turn up for free—because they were friends, for a cut of the profits when their documentary made a splash, or someone had forgotten to budget to reshoot scenes—that the annoyance in his voice sounded real. Harry had too, obviously, as his expression softened into amused sympathy.

"Well, you're getting a free meal out of it," he joked dryly. The humor lasted long enough for Cash to roll his eyes in agreement, and then Harry turned serious again. "If I'm wrong—"

"Yana gets some very oddly shot scenes for her wedding video," Cash said. "Maybe she won't ask me to take her pregnancy-announcement photos."

"And if I'm right, it could be dangerous."

Cash shrugged. "I was supposed to be in Louisiana this weekend, tracking a loup garou around the oil refineries on the Mississippi," he said. "Last year I filmed the *Damned by Blood* splatter-rite doc up in Alaska. Just because I'm not chasing after a gig on 12:28 doesn't mean I don't know what I'm doing. If you keep me in the loop, if you assure me you won't take any risks with Yana's life, I'll get the footage you want."

"And get paid?" Harry asked, raising his eyebrow.

"It's my job," Cash said. "And I don't need to keep you sweet to impress my boyfriend. Or my kid. Just the going rate. Or I warn Arkady *now*."

Harry grimaced. He tapped his fingers on the Formica table as he considered his options. There weren't many, not with that final condition.

"Okay," he said. "Deal. You're on the payroll. I need to go into the city tomorrow. My source said there's some sort of secret meeting going on in a warehouse. Abigail is going with me. So you get to keep an eye on the fiancé, make sure nothing spooks him. If it looks like something is going to happen—anyone is going to be hurt or corrupted—call the police. I meant it, no story—not even this one—is worth someone's life."

He pushed his chair back from the table, metal legs loud on the tiles, and left without a word. Cash watched him go and tried to work out if he was being played.

Harry's source had broken the Prodigium's Cardinal Rule with malice aforethought. He'd thrown some of the monster-world's movers and shakers—the Worm, the Black Witch—under the wheels of the papal-documentary train. Yet he hadn't told him *Yana* was the monster too, not even hinted at it.

Tomorrow was the start of the wedding festivities. The Hunt would start at midnight. Anyone who knew the Worm's private movements would know that. They'd also know that Yana, as the ranking monster in the couple, would lead the chase.

So why send Harry on a wild goose chase into Roanoke? He might find a few goblins, monsters with so much human in them they didn't have a breed or a name, or a werewolf itchy in his skin during the crescent moon. The real monsters—the ones with meat in their teeth and bones that rattled—would be here. Or tucked away, sulking over mimosas so they could *imply* they were here after the fact.

The answer seemed obvious, of course. Despite Arkady's protests, one of the Abascals was behind this. No one else would care—or dare—to try and protect the family.

Or at least, that was the interpretation the Prodigium would jump to. Before they did, Cash needed to find a better one. He might not be an Abascal—by name or blood—but the only people in the world he cared about were.

Shit.

He took Harry's cup with him when he left.

Chapter Twelve

CASH PAUSED in the doorway of his room, the stolen cup held loosely in one hand and his foot braced against the heavy door to hold it open. The clothes were laid out on his bed in a creepy approximation of movement, tucked and folded so it looked as if their original owner had turned to dust midstep.

Appropriate.

Cash had worn it before. The last time, the first time, had been to Arkady's wedding. He hadn't expected anything, except for Arkady to take one look at him at the entrance to the Chapel and throw Madeline and the alliance over. Cash hadn't planned much past that point, which turned out to be a good thing. Arkady had looked at him once, then ignored him for the rest of the feast.

It had felt like he'd crumbled away, only it had been word by word, not merciful and all at once.

The clothes were in the garbage when he left.

"I was pretty once," bag of bones wheezed from overhead. The unexpected interruption made Cash twitch. He stepped to the side and looked up. An ear on a string of sinew dangled through the plaster. It twitched and tried to be a mouth, the lobe curled like a tongue, as bag of bones talked. "Or ugly? Some or the other. Hard to tell from what he left me. He took all my bits to make his suit. He could have left me some…."

The ear twitched and crumpled as the ghost complained. Cash ignored it as he yanked the wardrobe open and stashed the cup inside his bag, under a couple of old T-shirts. It could wait.

"Monsters aren't big on leftovers," he told the ghost.

It made a thin bagpipe drone of sound and reeled the ear back up into the crawlspace. For something that knew it was dead most of the time, the reminder of how it happened always upset it. Most ghosts didn't remember. They were angry, but they didn't remember why. Once they did, they kind of lost their… *colère de vivre*. Not much point to anything when you were just the nail clipping of a dead thing.

Cash grabbed the clothes from the bed, leather and silk twisted around his fingers, and stalked over to give the adjourning door a perfunctory rap of his knuckles. He didn't wait for an answer before he shoved it open… or tried to. Cash jarred his arm as his weight rattled the black wood but didn't shift it.

It was locked.

The door hadn't been locked in years. Cash *couldn't* do it, and Arkady, after the first few snarky comments about light-fingered charity cases, hadn't wanted to.

Until now.

The heavy, sour tug of rejection and frustration sank through him. His monster smacked its lips over the tang of it and its stomach rumbled. He'd need to feed soon.

First, though, he wasn't going to have this.

"Jackass."

He kicked the door. The impact probably jarred his foot more than the solid slab of wood. From the other side, the silence was pointed. Arkady was in there, a mouthful of old grudges between his teeth and his cock in his hand.

Fine. Cash bundled the clothes under his arm and stalked back to the door. He yanked it open and nearly walked into the sad-sack drooping bag of bones. The ghost hung limply from the jamb, a clammy chill sticking to it like sweat, and extended a handful of tiny dead eyes to blink at him.

"If you aren't going to use the bed—" It wheezed. "—it's cold up there, and if he finds me. Oh, if he finds me."

"Fine," Cash said as he side-stepped the fluttery lung. A human could have just stepped through it, even if it saw some shadow of the real thing, but not always best if you were a monster. Sometimes the ghosts could get… stuck places you didn't want them. Under arms, between your ribs, and one satyr Cash knew had sworn up and down he had a haunted testicle. Just the one. "Make yourself at home."

The ghost curled sullenly in on itself. "It is my home," it sulked, before it splatted to the ground and dragged itself over the floor. The collection of rodent ghost eyes it had put together slipped from its fingers and dissolved.

Cash slammed the door, took two steps down the hall, and shoved open the main doors to Arkady's rooms. The indulged son of monster aristocracy, with an army of well-paid cleaners on staff to pick up after him, he never remembered to lock his door. Arkady was sprawled out on the bed, barefoot and half undressed, with his eyes closed and a snifter of brandy balanced on his chest.

"Congratulations," Cash snarked. "I had to walk and open two doors instead of one to get in here. My lesson is learned."

"Maybe I just like you sweaty," Arkady said without opening his eyes.

"It's a couple of yards," Cash said. "I'm not sweating."

"Not yet."

Cash swallowed the hot honey-scratch of interest that dried his mouth. He crossed the room and tossed the bundle of clothes at Arkady, who swore and jerked upright as the brandy spilled over him.

"I'm not wearing that," Cash said. "Why the hell do you even still have it? I chucked it in the trash."

Arkady scowled as he peeled wet silk off his chest and tossed it aside. He dragged his hand down his chest to wipe away the amber glaze of brandy.

"You threw a lot of things away that year. I thought you might still value *some* of them." His lip curled in a sneer as he flicked drops of liquor from his fingers. "If nothing else, Yana certainly seemed to appreciate the way you looked in—"

"Oh, shut up," Cash said.

It actually shut Arkady up for a moment. Cash had always gotten away with more than anyone else, his smart mouth tolerated because Arkady liked his pretty face, but even he usually stuck to sarcasm and snide asides. *No one* spoke to Abascals like he just had.

Arkady stared at him, all sticky skin and "what the fuck" expression. He'd just pulled himself together enough to scowl when Cash started to strip. He pulled the shirt over his head, collar tight as it scraped over his ears, and dropped it to the ground. It felt oddly… vulnerable. The skin between his shoulder blades itched and tightened with self-consciousness.

A decade wasn't long for a monster in their prime, but it was a long time since Arkady had seen him naked. Cash had been lean and angry back then, all taut muscle and carelessness. Now he was a single dad who ate leftovers from the spirits' table at work more often than not.

Under his bones the monster squirmed in irritation that he'd got to that line first.

"What are you doing?" Arkady asked. The frown lingered on his face as he watched Cash kick off his boots.

Denim slid low around Cash's hips as he unbuttoned his jeans. He paused there and cocked his head to the side.

"If you don't know, then it's been too long for one of us, anyhow," he said dryly. "How long ago *was* the divorce?"

Arkady snorted and licked brandy from the palm of his hand. He swung his legs over the edge of the mattress and reached out to hook his fingers in Cash's waistband, his knuckles damp and cold against Cash's stomach as he pulled him a step closer to the bed. "I thought we were going to have a fight."

"Yeah, well, we both know how it ends," Cash said. He quirked the corner of his mouth up. "I win. So I figured we could skip it. Unless you'd *rather*…?"

"No," Arkady said. Another tug put Cash between Arkady's lean, leather-clad thighs, and Cash's stomach tightened eagerly. "You're the guest. It's only polite to make sure you get what you want."

Cash leaned down and ghosted a kiss over Arkady's mouth, the sticky apricot-and-smoke sweetness of his breath a temptation to linger. The hooks of the deal shifted in Cash's gut. The tug of it pulled at his balls and thickened his cock.

"So I'm calling the shots?" he said. "The big, bad Abascal has to do what I say?"

The chance that—*this time*—he was going to push it too far caught in Cash's throat like gravel. It also prickled the nape of his neck and dried his mouth with anticipation. It was, for him, kind of a win-win situation.

Arkady narrowed his eyes, a bright rim of gold around his pupils, but he didn't disagree. That made Cash cocky. He licked his lips and tried to decide what to do next. The possibilities were overwhelming.

"I could fuck you," he voiced the thought aloud.

Once he'd said it, the idea had its appeal. The thought of Arkady sprawled out under him, all that muscle and monster tight around his cock, made his breath catch in his throat. It wouldn't be the first time, but... not that often. Rank had its privileges, and monsters did care about rank.

Arkady leaned back, arms braced against the mattress, and smirked.

"You could try," he said neutrally.

His chest was still sticky with brandy, and a trail ran down his chest and splattered droplets over the tight leather that covered his crotch. The thick outline of his cock was visible against the scraped-thin fabric, and the shadows of something scaled and sickly gold moved under his skin. The smell on the air was still smoke and honey, but the hint of meat was under it. It was smashed hives and pillaged farms, the smoky taste of the tongue that had spat a curse at an Abascal. It was a predator's stink, like the lion house at the zoo.

Cash couldn't move. He'd always thought that one day he'd get used to how beautiful Arkady was when his monster showed itself, but he never had. It used to annoy him. He was pretty, but no one had ever lost the ability to speak while looking at him. Now he just enjoyed the cold frisson of lust and terror that curdled his guts and made his skin itch with the need to be touched.

It had been a long time since he'd been this aware that the man in his bed could hurt him. He'd missed the thrill of that.

Cash crawled onto the bed, straddled Arkady's hips, and dug his
knees into the mattress on either side. Hunger had sunk down into his
bones, sharp and hot in his marrow.

"You *said* I could do what I want," he pointed out, mouth against
Arkady's sharp jawline. "So...."

He pushed Arkady down on the bed... or tried to. The mattress
shifted under them, but Arkady didn't move.

"So," Arkady said, the edges of his voice roughened from
brandy and his mood. "You misheard me."

He rolled them both over and pinned Cash down to the mattress,
both of his hands held above his head. Cash cursed him and squirmed
in a halfhearted attempt to get away, but not too hard. Arkady's
knee nudged between Cash's thighs and his cock pressed against his
stomach. He dipped his head to chew wet, bruised kisses along the
unmarked side of Cash's throat from his collarbone to his jaw.

"I did?" Cash asked, his voice tight as sharp teeth worried his
skin and a tongue soothed the sting.

There were probably a lot of really smart, unpleasant things he
could say, and he'd regret the missed opportunity later. He could feel
the hard, hot pressure of Arkady's cock against his thigh and *taste* him
on the back of his throat. It wasn't like he was going to think about
anything else.

"I said you should *get* what you want," Arkady said. "Not *do*
what you want."

"Do *who* I want," Cash said—apparently he could muster some
smartass. "And what, you know better than me what I want?"

Arkady smiled against Cash's throat. "It's my art."

Despite the dry sherbet fizz under his skin, Cash had to laugh as
his favorite excuse for bad behavior was volleyed back to him. It was
as true—and as not-true—of Arkady as it was of Cash. He didn't pick
people's mental pockets the way Cash did, but if someone let him in,
if they took his deal, he could strip-mine their soul.

"That's cheating," Cash said.

Arkady's fingers tightened around Cash's wrists, and then he
let go as he pushed himself up onto his knees. The deal Cash had

swallowed the other day pulsed in his chest as Arkady tugged on it. Then it faded down to the back of Cash's mind.

"I don't need to," Arkady said. "Not with you. I can map what makes you whimper on your body with someone else's hands."

Cash propped himself up on one elbow and raked his hair back from his face. The back of his neck was sweaty and sensitive to the touch, and an itch of pleasure skittered down his spine as he imagined Arkady's fingers there instead. Tomorrow he could remember everything he had to be sensible about—his human life, his kid, his... his pride.

His brain stuttered over that. He could feel his monster's amusement as it licked his denial. He'd worry about that tomorrow too.

"Prove it," he said with a smirk.

Arkady sprawled back against the pile of pillows stacked against the headboard. He stretched his arms out over them, muscles pulled tight over his shoulders and across his chest, and tilted his head. The dark, heavy mantle of his aura draped over the bed like a cape, hungry but patient.

"Undress me," he said with a lazy wave of his hand in the direction of his groin.

It wasn't an order, but it wasn't a request either. The expectation was obedience. It galled Cash—a part of him had never quite ousted his mom's early lessons about apple pie, the constitution, and equality—but it also twisted his libido like a wet rag.

It was a sucker punch of wet, sticky hunger, and his shallow principles didn't stand a chance in hell against it.

"What did your last servant die of?" he groused in a halfhearted attempt to preserve his usual attitude.

Arkady smiled that odd unguarded smile that escaped him sometimes when he wasn't being his mother's son or the epitome of a good Prodigium vassal. It wasn't *nice*—it was cocky with a tilt of smug bastard—but it was Arkady's own.

"Satisfaction," he drawled out and spread his legs apart.

"Asshole," Cash said. Any edge there might have been to the insult was muted by the fact he had already started to crawl up the bed.

The leather was skintight, thin enough that the slant of Arkady's hipbones and the crease of his groin were outlined in glove-soft black. It stretched over the thick, interested bulge of his erection, not *quite* tight enough to see every ridge and vein. That was okay. Cash had a good memory.

He straddled Arkady's lap, the hard jut of leather-wrapped cock pressed against his ass, and leaned in to lick the sticky spill of brandy off his chest. The sparse coating of light brown hair tickled his lips as he laved the sweet, heady liquid off Arkady's skin. He felt Arkady's chest hitch as he sucked in a ragged breath, the thud of his heart fierce.

Openmouthed kisses left a damp trail on Arkady's skin as Cash worked his way down. He flicked his tongue over Arkady's nipple, the taut, coppery bud of it tight at the attention, and then caught it between his teeth. That got him the groan he'd worked for—a ragged sound that scraped out of Arkady's chest as he let his head fall back.

"I know you too," Cash taunted as he lifted his head. He teased the slick bud between his thumb and fingers, tender flesh hard and hot, until he got another gasp for his efforts. Gold flushed over Arkady's chest and into his throat as he arched up into Cash's touch. "In case you'd forgotten."

Arkady caught his breath and undraped one arm so he could tangle his fingers through Cash's hair. He tugged until Cash had to crane his neck awkwardly to look at him. Then he dipped down to kiss the taste of himself off Cash's mouth. The kiss was spiced with a bite, Cash's lower lip caught briefly between sharp teeth.

"The only one who's forgotten anything," Arkady murmured, "is you, with how to unfasten my trousers."

He shoved Cash away lazily and stretched out under him, the play of muscle and scale under his skin not quite in sync as he waited. The show of laziness would have been more convincing without the unsteady rise and fall of his chest and the cage of his aura as it stirred around them.

Cash swallowed and wiped his mouth on the back of his hand.

"My bad," he said. "I was looking for your shirt."

"You took too long to get back." Arkady shrugged as he tucked one arm behind his head. "I had to start without you."

The lure bobbed in front of Cash's nose, but for once, he didn't take it. If Arkady wanted to fight about Yana, he could wait.

"And look at the mess you made," he said instead as he trailed his fingers down Arkady's flat, tight stomach. The long bands of muscle tightened under the not-quite caress, skin pulled tight over them. Cash dipped a finger into Arkady's navel and licked the last drop of brandy off it. "I guess that's why you need... help."

He swallowed the *me* that had almost escaped his tongue. It scratched reluctantly on the way down. That would have been....

Revealing. The thought rolled through his head as he felt that odd moment where his monster and the rest of him were in sync. It was a jibe and realization rolled into one. It wasn't true in any real sense—Cash was useful right now, he wasn't necessary—but he'd always wished he were, hadn't he.

"I suppose I do," Arkady agreed with him, his voice guarded. "Why else would you be here?"

A braver monster would have asked what that meant. A stupider one might have assumed almost anything.

Unfortunately, Cash was neither. He wasn't built for bravery— wisps lured their prey to their deaths for a reason—and he was smart enough to know he might not like the answer.

Coward, his monster reminded him smugly as it slid away from him.

Cash pushed all that doubt to the back of his mind—let the monster have it for snacks—and focused on what he did know. That Arkady's cock wasn't going to free itself.

"Well, right now," he said as he picked at the silk laces that crisscrossed over the fly. Monsters knew zippers existed, but they weren't classy. The less you accommodated the human world, even if it was in stupid, small ways like how to do your pants, the more respected you were. In theory. The knot came loose under Cash's fingers, and he tugged impatiently at the slick fabric strips. "I'm here to fuck you. I thought we'd cleared that up."

Arkady's laugh was a low, dark sound that belonged at a midnight crossroads as he ran his own hand down lazily over his stomach. "You're just taking so long," he teased. "I thought you'd changed your mind."

The silk strips tangled around Cash's knuckles, tight around his fingers, so he gave up and just snapped them. Arkady made a rough sound of approval in his throat. He hitched his hips up off the bed to let Cash drag them down over lean thighs.

Leather peeled away from Arkady's cock. It was slick with sweat and precome, thin skin drawn tight over the thick shaft and the foreskin drawn back from the pink, glistening head. It hadn't changed. Cash wasn't sure why part of him had thought it might.

He wrapped his hand around the base and squeezed gently. The pulse of it throbbed against his fingers, fast and eager as Arkady folded his lower lip between his teeth and waited.

"What do you want?" Cash asked.

It was an old question, one that cut through rank and ignored the hand Cash *wanted* around his throat, the one that made sure this was *their* decision, outside of whatever their nature or nurture poked at.

What do you want? Do you want this? Do you want me/us?

Last time Cash asked, his throat tight with hope and resentment, Arkady was about to head to the Hunt. He hadn't turned around when he said coldly, "For you to stop asking me that."

Cash felt stupid for letting the words leave the inside of his head. It was a question for stupid, hungry boys, for stolen moments in dark corners.

"You," Arkady said. It felt raw, the honesty of their old ritual too blunt to question. He pushed himself up out of his sprawl and cupped his hand around the back of Cash's neck to pull him in for a kiss. It was awkward and a bit clumsy, not like Arkady at all. Then he pulled back slightly, just enough to catch his breath, and the low rasp of command was in his voice again. "Now."

Chapter Thirteen

SOME MONSTERS stripped off their humanity to fuck, doing it as the devil intended—in fur, scales, and loops of raw muscle. But that didn't work for everyone. Cash was too human, his skin too thick to shuck off like a raincoat, and even if he'd been able to, without their human face, a wisp was just swamp gas with evil intentions. That made them hard to fuck unless you were another wisp, and even if you were, or so Cash had heard, it wasn't that satisfying.

Others didn't have enough skin to risk damage. The Worm bought and bargained for his skin—with people who, all evidence to the contrary, thought they'd come out ahead—and they were tailor-fit to him. He squeezed himself out and he'd never squeeze himself back in. Donna's masks were works of arts, crafted to order, and took three maids and a bath of blood to remove. She wasn't going to waste all of that on a quick tumble.

As for Arkady, he'd only ever had what the Prodigium—somehow—had given the pure-bloods like him. The human shell that would do to let him move around human scrutiny and the uncomfortable squint of the sun. It was a one purchase per monster deal, and he needed to care for it. Better than he had, anyhow.

Besides, if he let his monster crawl out, it would probably end with Cash dead, or at least peeled open to see if he was wisp enough in his gooey center to survive it. He might be, by now. Probably not.

Cash was monster enough that the idea made him catch his breath with sticky, unhealthy interest. It was like candy. A little was okay, but you *wanted* a lot, even if it was bad for you.

The Abascals, taken separately or together, were a lot. It was in their job description.

"Penny for them," Arkady asked as he pushed Cash's hair out of the way and scraped a sharp kiss over the nape of his neck.

Cash laughed raggedly and leaned back against Arkady's chest. They'd both lost their trousers, the half-serious game of service abandoned as they ran out of patience and stripped off with clumsy, button-scraping haste and knelt on the bed. He could feel the press of Arkady's hard, slick cock against the small of his back.

"One deal with the devil per wedding is my limit," he said. A bitter laugh he'd have struggled to explain caught in Cash's throat and then dissolved as Arkady reached around to wrap long fingers around his cock. Pleasure flicked along his nerve endings, a hot pulse of need that staggered through his body and escaped his mouth on a whimper. He wanted this. Almost enough to make himself a liar. He twisted his head around and caught a hasty kiss on the corner of Arkady's mouth. "After that I'm anybody's."

Arkady caught his jaw in one hand, fingers curled around his chin so he couldn't slide away.

"No," he said, before he slashed a sharp-toothed, possessive kiss over Cash's lips.

One of them drew blood from the other—a bloom of copper and salt on their tongues—but Cash wasn't sure who'd bled and who hadn't. Arkady's aura folded tightly around them in bruised shadows that slid over Cash's leg and faded through his cock. It made Cash shiver, goose bumps on his inner thighs, as if it were tangible. He couldn't feel it, but his skin knew it would feel like thick, tight-woven silk—smooth and heavy and cold.

Arkady played with Cash's dick with one hand, callused fingers tight with impatience, and ran the other hand from Cash's chin down his chest. His fingers, already slick with lube, grazed over bare skin and pinched the hard bud of a nipple. If Cash had been standing up, his legs would have gone out from under him. As it was, he had to brace himself against Arkady to keep his balance as pleasure snapped through him like a plucked wire. A throaty, hungry whimper escaped him, thinner as it hit the air than it had felt in his throat.

"What happened to the ring?" he asked. His teeth nipped at the curve of Cash's ear as he scraped his nail over the tender flesh. "I liked the ring."

Cash reached back and curled his hand around the nape of Arkady's neck. He slid his thumb up into the tender span of soft skin just under his ear. "Maybe that's what happened," he said. "If it wasn't for you, why keep it."

It hadn't been. The truth was that single fatherhood with a grabby toddler was not a lifestyle choice conducive to nipple rings. After one particularly snake-like strike from Ellie, he thought he'd lost his nipple. So it had gone into a box for later, then the box had gone in a drawer, and at some point, he'd lost track of it. Inertia rather than romance.

That wasn't the sort of story that set the mood.

Arkady made a rough, amused sound in his ear and dragged his hand down Cash's cock, from the head to the base. His palm was slick with precome as it slid along the shaft. Pressure, hot and strung so tight it felt like *something* had to snap, knotted in Cash's balls as he whimpered. His skin felt too tight, pulled over bones, muscle, and bubbling, sticky hunger.

"See, that's why I thought of you when I needed help," he said. "You aren't just a good liar. You know when to lie."

He kissed Cash's throat—without teeth this time—and pushed him down into the pillows. Cash shivered, his back cold as the air kissed it, and then Arkady was sprawled out on top of him again. He ran warm, slick hands up the inside of Cash's thighs and gripped the taut cheeks of his backside to pull them apart.

Cash expected the blunt pressure of a finger. Instead he got the wet, slick push of a tongue against his ass. His surprised whine was muffled against the pillows as he pressed his face down into them. A hot tongue probed at his ass, spit-wet and thorough, while long hands stroked his thighs and pinned his hips down to the bed. Silk twisted between Cash's fingers as he squirmed—or tried to—against the spill of warm, honeyed pleasure that filled him.

His monster drank it down, drained it into his bones until his whole body hummed with want from his skull to his heels. He could feel his own breath, hot and sticky against his lips as he panted. His cock ached, so stiff it was tender, as every involuntary twitch of his hips rubbed it over the silk sheets. Hunger pulsed with dull, insistent finality in the pit of his stomach, a hollow pressure that tugged at his balls and the clenched muscles in his thighs.

"Say it," Arkady said as he finally pulled back. "Or I'll leave you to finish yourself off."

An uneasy combination of surrender and reluctance made Cash's mouth go dry. He knew what Arkady wanted him to say, but he'd only ever said it twice and only when he could claim it didn't *count*, that he'd meant it sarcastically or it had been in reference to a specific, limited moment. Exactly like this one right now, when he'd swallowed a hook that was only for the duration of the weekend.

He was a good liar, after all. Good enough that, until this moment, with the words right there on his tongue, he'd actually convinced himself to forget about them. And the fact he'd kinda meant it back then.

But not now, the snide voice in the back of his head said. He could hear it roll its eyes as it drawled, *You don't mean it now, for real.*

Cash usually blamed that voice on his monster, but it just sounded an awful lot like him right then.

"I'm yours," he said… admitted. "Happy now?"

Arkady made a low, pleased sound in his throat and bit Cash on the ass hard enough to make him curse and jerk away. His cock slid over the sheets, the cold stroke of silk almost rough against the hard shaft.

"I already knew that," Arkady said. He kissed the bite better with a quick graze of soft lips and then crawled up over Cash's body. The weight of him on top of Cash felt right, the fit of him perfect even where it wasn't. "I just wanted to make sure you did."

Under normal circumstances Cash would have snorted at that, but in the naked, sweaty moment it sounded… right. Just like Arkady felt. No matter how hard he ran—and not like he'd gone far or fast, just across the bridge to the city—he couldn't get away from that.

The blunt pressure of Arkady's cock against Cash's slick ass made that train of thought skip the track. He sucked in a breath and pushed back into the pressure as it stretched him open. For a second there was a sharp itch of pain as the warm velvet thickness of Arkady's cock slowly spread him wide around it. Cash tipped his head down into the cushions, dark curls loose around his face as he waited for the balance to slide back to pleasure.

Arkady wrapped his hands over Cash's, fingers interlaced, and trailed kisses over Cash's braced shoulders and up his neck. His voice was strung tight with control as he promised patience and ruin in one breath, as monster and man got their needs tangled up around each other. Each slow roll of his hips worked his cock deeper inside Cash, stretched him out and filled him in.

The dark wash of pleasure felt like the taste of brandy—all rich, brewed sweetness with a sharp bite at its core. It settled in his balls like treacle, heavy and restless, and caught in sharp, sugary threads around his cock. The tug of it was… almost. Cash thrust his hips against the bed to chase the peak of that feeling, but it was pointless. The bed was too soft, the sheets too slick. He could feel the sensation from it, but it teased and tempted instead of satisfied.

Arkady groaned against Cash's throat, breath hot and sharp with smoke, and tightened his grip.

"Sometimes I wonder why I missed you," he grumbled. "I'm trying to be… gentle."

"Why?" Cash asked. He tilted his head back and looked up at Arkady through sweat-tangled curls. "I won't be when it's my turn."

Arkady shifted his weight and freed up one hand to drag Cash's hair out of his face. He kept it tangled around his fingers and tugged until Cash's back arched and his breath caught.

"I don't need you to be," he said.

Cash swallowed. He could feel the gulp in his throat, like a candy he'd just swallowed whole.

"Please," he said. "I could hurt you if I wanted."

Something shuttered dimly over Arkady's eyes, and he let go of Cash's hair. It flopped back down, tangled and damp with sweat and lube, so he couldn't see Arkady's face when he murmured, "I know."

Flattering, but they both knew it was a lie. Cash would have pointed that out, but—maybe fed up with the complaints from the gallery—Arkady sheathed himself inside Cash in one long stroke. Long, lean thighs pressed against Cash's ass, the muscles clenched tight under warm, smooth skin. It made Cash tense, his ass squeezed tightly around the cock that filled it, and squeeze a grunt out through his teeth. He wasn't sure if the warm throb in his guts was the pulse of Arkady's cock or his own exaggerated heartbeat.

They lay there for a moment, stretched out on the bed in one long, sweaty line of flesh. Arkady moved first. He shifted his weight to the side and freed up one hand to hook around Cash's chest. His fist, clenched so tight his knuckles showed through his skin like raw bone, tucked into the hollow of Cash's collarbone. The bar of his forearm across Cash's throat tightened with each rough thrust that shoved him down into the bed, the ache of his frustrated cock twisted through every misfired pleasure/pain neuron in his head that got off on the... sharp edge of it.

He wasn't a masochist. Pain on its own was just unpleasant. It was the adrenaline rush. Fucking Arkady felt precarious, the same dizzy temptation that people on the edge of cliffs must feel. Only Cash had jumped nearly every time, when most people showed better sense.

Arkady shifted again, his knee cocked under him to change the angle of his thrust. This time when he thrust home, thighs pressed tight against the slick curve of Cash's ass, the head of his cock bruised against his prostate and plucked a hot, stupid jolt of pleasure along his nerve endings. It fried Cash's brain and made his cock throb.

The second time it knocked the breath out of him and left him boneless, a *fuck* dry and silent on his tongue. The rhythm between them felt clumsy as Cash tried to regain the pace of Arkady's thrusts, their bodies out of sync as the sheets tangled around them.

Somehow it didn't matter. It didn't need to be perfect. Imperfect— the grip of Arkady's fingers on Cash's hip as he yanked him up onto his knees and thrust into him, the way Cash's knees slipped on the silk sheets—didn't matter when you needed it this much.

Cash clenched one fist in the wet sheets as Arkady thrust roughly into him. His cock bumped against his stomach with each stroke, precome wet against his skin. Cash reached down and wrapped his fingers around himself. Pleasure tugged at him, almost painful as it scraped along strung-tight nerves, and he dragged his hand along the shaft from base to tip. His balls pulsed in rough counterpoint to Arkady's rhythm as Cash worked his way toward the slick, wet spill of orgasm.

He closed his eyes and bit the inside of his cheek. The tart salt metals of his own blood always helped him make it over the edge. Sweat itched in the small of his back, wet and clammy between his and Arkady's bodies, as his muscles tightened, ready to come.

"Not," Arkady said in his ear, "yet."

He pulled Cash's hand away from his cock, and the orgasm wriggled free and slipped away. Cash spat a "Fuck" out, finally enough air in his throat to make it a word.

"It's not *all* about you," he spat irritably as he tried to pull his wrist free. "You know that, right?"

"I've heard it said," Arkady teased him. His voice was rough and ragged, breathless. "I haven't seen any evidence to support it."

He hooked his arm around Cash's stomach and took him with him as he sat back onto his knees. His cock slid deeper into Cash's ass, spread him painfully, ecstatically wide as his weight settled into Arkady's lap.

"Son of a bitch," he gasped as the muscles in his thighs and stomach jerked under the skin in reaction.

He leaned back against Arkady's chest for support, sweat slippery and cold between their bodies.

"Yes," Arkady agreed. He rocked his hips, and Cash sucked in a ragged breath at the jolt of pleasure that stuttered through him. "I am. So?"

Cash braced his hands on Arkady's thighs, muscles clenched in tight bands under his fingers, and pushed himself up. His tightened around Arkady's cock as it slid out, a dull hollow in his stomach, and it was Arkady's turn to groan.

"Doesn't mean you need to act like one," Cash muttered.

It made Arkady laugh, but the sound choked off as Cash pushed back down onto his cock. Arkady's mouth moved silently against the back of Cash's neck with each slow, deep thrust, his cock buried to the hilt each time. Cash expected hands on his hips to set the pace, but—for once—he got to ride Arkady's cock without interference.

Who said people didn't change?

Arkady reached over Cash's hip and grabbed his cock. He smeared lube over the shaft, cold against hot flesh. Long practice guided his strokes as he jerked Cash off just a *little* faster than Cash fucked him.

It felt like a race… one that Cash was going to lose.

He closed his eyes and tried to concentrate on anything but the cock that filled his ass and the scrape of slippery, callused fingers over his own cock. It was impossible. Maybe he could have done it at twenty. He hadn't always come off worse in these competitions then, but he'd been *twenty* and having a lot more sex regularly.

Arkady squeezed his balls—*fuck* too hard—and the sticky knot of pleasure in his balls cracked open. Cash's head dropped back against Arkady's shoulder as he came, a whiskey hit that washed through him. It was all smooth notes with a rough bite in the backwash.

"I don't have to do anything," Arkady said. He wiped come off Cash's cock and lifted his hand. Out of the corner of his eye, Cash saw him lick his fingers clean. "I choose to do it."

He tumbled them back onto the bed again, tangled in sweaty sheets as he finished the race last—and won—with rough, impatient strokes that shoved Cash down into the sheets. His come spilled hot and sticky into Cash's ass, and he sprawled out limp on top of him.

From somewhere in the hotel, the dinner bell rang. Even fucked out and boneless, the sound made Cash twitch. Arkady's growl was an inhuman flutter of sound as he pinned Cash down with a leg slung over his hip.

"You keep telling *me* you don't work for me anymore," Arkady said. "So why still dance to my mother's drum?"

Cash shoved an elbow into his ribs. "I don't," he said. Arkady grumbled disbelief into his neck, and Cash was annoyed enough to put enough effort into his next shove that he could wriggle free. He sat up, naked and sticky and bruised, and pulled his tangled hair back from his face.

"Since when?" he asked. "I've been the thorn in her side since she took me on."

Arkady stretched on his stomach and dragged one of the pillows down to rest his head. "You mouth off," he said, his voice oddly cold and precise. "You stay *just* on the right edge of defiance, but have you ever *actually* put my mother out? Have you ever cost her *anything*?"

The answer to the question prickled on Cash's tongue. He had. He'd cost all the Abascals something they would have held very dear. So Arkady could kiss his ass. The problem was that if he told Arkady that, then it wouldn't be a secret. It was a lot safer when it was a secret.

"I cost her you," he said instead, as the monster snatched his tongue. "For a while."

Cash winced as that picked an old scab. His worse half didn't care if it hurt him, someone else, or both. He did appreciate being able to blame it for stuff like this. Cash left Arkady to the sting of that as he scooted toward the edge of the bed, but Arkady caught his elbow and dragged him back over to his side.

"What?" Cash asked warily. He could still see Arkady's monster, fat on whatever part of this satisfied him and too restless to sink down to his bones. It was always a good idea to be wary around an Abascal monster. Even if it liked you. *Especially* if it liked you.

Arkady rolled onto his side. He ran his hand up Cash's arm, over the fine bones of his chest, and down to his nipple. It was still tender, and Cash flinched as Arkady scratched a sharp nail around it.

"You said the nipple ring was mine. Just for me?" Arkady said.

Sharp. Cash glanced down briefly at the thin black claws that tipped Arkady's fingers. They looked like sharpened smoke and had points like needles.

The monster said. Cash licked his lips. They tasted like salt and sex. The question hung between them. He could back down, admit himself the liar they both knew he was. It would get him out of whatever this was about to become.

"Yeah," he said instead. "I did."

Arkady and the monster both smiled at the same time, with the same mouth, and… pinched. Black nails punched easily through the raised nub, and Cash whined a high note in the back of his throat as he struggled to stay still. Muscles trembled under his skin as he locked them and sucked in a sex-musky breath through his nose.

The flash of pain snapped through him, from his head to his heels. It caught the after-tremors of orgasm on his nerves and fooled them it was one of them. Cash trembled as the pain slipped over to pleasure in its confusion, dark and drug-heady as it roared up toward his head.

He felt blood wet against his skin, and then Arkady leaned in and breathed on it, his breath wispy and gray as it left his mouth. It felt like a poison ivy rash for a second. Then it faded to a chill numbness, like when your foot went to sleep.

Cash swallowed and looked down, his mouth dry. It wasn't beyond possibility that he had lost a nipple. The addition of a little humanity had not made monster relationships any less weird.

Luckily it was still there, bruised dark against his pale skin, but there. A heavy garnet ring was threaded through it, thicker than the ring he'd taken out and with flickers of smoky darkness at the core of it. His blood and Arkady's magic.

That was… not what he expected. Cash poked his nipple with a finger and flinched when it hurt. It was real, then, and any monster who saw it would think he was married to Arkady. More than married, actually. Marriage could be dissolved by either party, for good reason or because it would be funny.

This—Cash turned the ring gingerly—was a claim that only Arkady could dissolve, since Cash had been cock-struck and stupid enough to just agree to it on the assumption that Arkady wouldn't do something like this. Not to him.

"What the fuck?" he spluttered.

Arkady rolled away from him and got out of bed. His back was long and lean, strapped with bands of wiry muscle that ran from his shoulders down to his lean waist. What it wasn't was expressive. Even Cash couldn't read much from the tight curve of Arkady's ass. So, under the circumstances, he reminded himself, he really shouldn't be so distracted by it.

"You're here to solve my problems," Arkady said over his shoulder as he opened his wardrobe. "Not make more. I don't intend to save the family name from the Prodigium only to have my name become a laughingstock when my lover throws me over for my sister. Again."

The flash of old hard-done-by irritation was a familiar distraction from the knot of… whatever it was Cash felt. Uncertain, maybe.

"For fuck's sake—" he started.

Arkady cut him off. "It doesn't matter if it's true or not. You know that. The perception would be enough. So now it doesn't matter how many private chats you have with my sister, everyone will know you're mine. Which is why you'll wear the clothes I left out for you."

Cash could feel the frustration in his jaw. He hated being out-angled. "Did you plan this?" he asked.

There was a pause as Arkady considered the question. "I don't know," he admitted. "I didn't mean to, but it all kind of fell into place, didn't it? Does it matter?"

"Yes. No." Cash scrambled off the bed and grabbed the clothes from the floor. He ached dully in all the right places, a satisfying feeling of being *thoroughly* fucked, and he was sticky where he didn't sting. "And after this weekend?"

His breath caught in his throat like he didn't know the answer. Except they both did. It was a deal, and the Abascals kept their deals to the letter. It wasn't a matter of choice.

"After this weekend, everything will go back to normal," Arkady said. "As agreed. Nothing has changed."

"No," Cash said. "I guess it hasn't."

It never did, but the hope that it might one day had always been the hook his heart hung from. The admission—that he had never had his cock or his pride, or at least not *just* them, at risk—dropped like a stone in his brain. His temporarily sated monster let it settle without comment. It didn't seem worth its while to comment on the obvious.

"You worry what they'll say if they think I'm still sweet on Yana?" he said sourly as he stalked out the door. "What, and see what they say when they see you dragging mutton dressed as lamb around the floor."

Chapter Fourteen

As IT turned out, Cash still looked pretty good in leather. In the humid, unwholesome lair of monsters, anyhow, where mouse-nibbled ruffs of tea-colored lace came straight from the best underground fashion houses and brocade was evergreen. If he turned up at Ellie's school gates in skintight leather, his shirt cut down to there and his pants laced up to just about decent, he'd look a bit more desperate.

Not any sweatier, though.

Cash wiped sweat off the back of his neck, his freshly washed hair damp again under the rough ponytail he'd pulled it back into. Had it always been this sticky down here, or had years of air-conditioning just spoiled him?

"The child is at camp, of course?" the bogeyman said to Arkady. He was tall and thin, stretched out like a child's drawing in a stylish gray suit nipped in to exaggerate his exceptional boniness. Cash could have told how many buttons there were on his frock coat, but not the color of his eyes or the set of his mouth. There was definitely a face there, but it refused to *stick*. A human would have seen something to upset them—a hated teacher, diseased features, his own death—but the bogey's powers didn't work on monsters. His aura was shriveled and starved, all rags and tatters that picked and plucked at everything on the way past. "My son goes next year. His first time. How has s… the child… found it?"

Behind him the party was in full swing. Everyone had stuck to their human forms for now, draped in capes and designer shrouds. Some of the jewels that sparkled on fingers or around throats still had the grave dirt on them. Things that could live for centuries didn't value aged things as much. A bit of fresh graverobbing showed a certain rakish style.

"Ellie," Arkady said. He stole a blood-red crisp from Cash's plate and popped it into his mouth, his fingers stained pink from the seasoning. "My niece. Cash's daughter. My mother's granddaughter. *That* child?"

The bogeyman ducked his head. Somehow the shabby stovepipe hat he wore didn't shift on his head as he did so. "I meant no offense, Arkady. It is just hard to navigate such… civility. In my day, the child would have been fostered out to peasants, and at least two people would have been dead or buried alive. But I suppose one must move with the times if one wants to kill with them."

He laughed. The teeth caught in Cash's memory—small, rounded, and creamy white. Baby teeth in a grown thing's mouth. His flicker of disquiet came from his mom, and the bogeyman's aura rustled in response. Tendrils of pallid gray shuffled toward him and picked at his… aura, although he couldn't see his own.

Cash poked the monster out of its sleep. It reluctantly uncurled, and the dull ache of its hunger came with it. He'd need to grab someone real to eat, not just drink a full bottle of lust and hope it solved anything.

The bogeyman's aura sagged in disappointment as it realized the mistake.

"Civility is one word for it," he said. "Ellie's doing well at camp. She missed her friends—"

That made the bogeyman's eyes widen. Probably? That was Cash's take, but he couldn't pin down the actual expression.

"Human friends? She's… popular?" he asked as he leaned in. "My boy couldn't make a friend out of a corpse, popsicle sticks, and a free plug socket. Is there a *trick* to it?"

"I don't know," Cash said uncomfortably. He wasn't used to being the one spoken to. Usually he was either behind a camera lens or, back when he'd come to these more often, at Arkady's heels. One step up from a servant, one step down from someone who mattered. "I think she's just a cool kid. She's fun to be around."

The bogeyman sighed and took a drink of whiskey. "That's not going to work for Grub…. Greg." He made a face. "Apologies. Your mother's hospitality takes us all back to the old days. Sometimes it is hard to remember the new rules."

It was. Donna had been known to use that to her advantage.

"If you keep them, no need to remember them," Arkady said. His tone was mild, his words weren't. "The Prodigium's edict on names is not new."

Despite the general impression of pallor, the bogey managed to blanch. "Of course," he said. "It's just a pet name for the boy. Not one the humans would understand, is all."

"Not exactly wise," Arkady remarked.

"Maybe he can come over for a playdate with Ellie sometime," Cash said, before the bogeyman said anything worse. "I'd like her to have some friends who aren't human, even if they can't cut loose like they do at camp."

The bogeyman's spine straightened. "Oh yes, that would be… good for them both," he said. "I'll get my assistant to email you the boy's schedule, but we can make it work whenever the child—Ellie— is free. So important for them, isn't it, to make the right connections at this age?"

"She'll mostly want to talk about horses and K-Pop, on past experience," Cash said.

The bogeyman probably winked at him. "Thanks for the tip," he said. "I'll set him some homework on that tonight. Excuse me."

He ducked away, and a faint dimness to the air and the smell of mold trailed behind him. Arkady snorted.

"Look at him," he said. "He thinks his Grub is going to marry into the family now, thanks to you."

Cash moved his plate out of reach of Arkady's fingers. He wanted to eat some of it, and there would be plenty of bones for Arkady to crunch once the party got into full swing.

"Most monsters in Roanoke think she's a liability."

"Then they're stupid," Arkady said calmly. "Mother can't use Ellie, so it's possible to just love her. As much as she's able, at least. If someone made Ellie happy, they would have Donna's support in life."

He plucked the plate out of Cash's grip and handed it off to a servant on the way past.

"Hey," Cash protested as he grabbed for the yakitori skewer on the way by. "I was going to eat that."

Arkady tipped his head down and pressed a toothy kiss against Cash's ear. "And once this is over, I'm going to eat you," he said, his voice low with the sort of promise that could be dangerous. Just because he probably didn't mean it literally, didn't mean he couldn't *do* it literally. "Until then, we'll both have to go hungry. Come on. The Hunt starts soon, and I want a dance."

For a second, Cash resisted the tug of Arkady's hand, old excuses and reasons tart on his tongue. Servants don't dance with their masters, after all, but it had been years since he'd had a paycheck from them, so he supposed he could do what he wanted.

And that, more than he wanted to admit, was to follow Arkady out into the dizzy reel of velvet and scale that spun on the time-worn stone.

Let it be, he told his monster as he laced his fingers through Arkady's. *I know it's pretend, so let it be.*

For once, it listened to him, the sour little voice that refused to let him lie to himself quiet as they threw themselves into the crush. He clung onto Arkady, his freshly pierced nipple tender as it was pressed against the rich red brocade of Arkady's frock coat, and he struggled against the feverish throb of the music.

It wanted him to spin and dip, breathless and mindless, until his feet were bloody and his heart ready to burst. To dance until the music stopped or he dropped, whichever came first, was fun at one of the monster-run clubs, when you were soaked with sweat and running on adrenaline until the musicians fumbled and faltered to a stop with bloody fingers and raw throats. In the halls of the Abascal, the musicians were made of bone and sinew, strung together by Donna's will, and they'd play until she said stop.

There was already blood on the floor, a long smear of it where someone had been dragged out of the way. It stuck to the soles of the other dancers and picked out their footwork in damp, sticky prints on the stone.

The monster's waltz winnowed the weak from the strong. Unfortunately, Cash was one of the weak. The strings of the violin pinched at his heels, and the heady wheeze of the organ's pipes urged him *on, on, on* until his heart stuttered in time with it.

Arkady pressed a hand against the small of Cash's back, fingers spread to claim as much skin as possible, and held firm against the fever of music. If he wanted to, he could probably match the other dancers' frenzied, desperate pace, but it wouldn't impress Donna if anyone kept up. That was the least she expected of her guests, to not die of her hospitality.

The point was to see who ignored the pull of stolen humanity as the music pulled it out of their blood and danced to their own beat.

"I forgot that sound you make when I'm inside you," Arkady murmured, soft and filthy, against his ear. "That *whimper.* Like I gutted you and you liked it."

Cash shivered at the brutal immediacy of that image. He could feel the sound in his throat, scratchy and hot, and in the taut flick of pleasure that tightened his ass. One hunger to counter another, and it was one that had *always* worked to distract Cash.

He curled one hand around the back of Arkady's neck and grazed his thumb over the tender spot where his pulse lived. It made him feel better to feel the quick throb of blood under his touch. Arkady looked calm and collected, but the music had as much of an effect on him as it did Cash.

"I don't recall," he said primly as he rested his head on Arkady's shoulder. He waited for the hitch in Arkady's chest as he got ready to argue. Then he added, "Maybe you can jog my memory later."

Arkady slid his hand down to cup Cash's leather-covered ass and squeezed roughly as he tugged him—somehow—closer. The play of lean, long muscles under velvet and leather distracted Cash as Arkady guided them through the muddied steps of the waltz.

"Oh, I'm definitely going to make you whimper," Arkady promised. He spun them out of the way of a high-stepping Jersey

Devil, its head tossed and nostrils red and wet, and finished his promise against Cash's ear. "And sooner rather than later."

The ragged breath that Cash sucked in tasted like Arkady. He could feel Arkady's warmth on his tongue. It didn't exactly help him focus.

"We're supposed to be looking for your leak," he said. "Not—"

He stumbled over what else Arkady might want to look for—on Cash, in Cash—because apparently he either had denial or nothing. Sometimes being too human sucked more than others.

"Pleasure?" Arkady said. His earlier mood had lifted and been replaced by smug good humor. He turned and brushed a kiss over the thin skin on the underside of Cash's wrist. "Your human is showing, Casper. Any monster worth his salt can keep more than one hunt in play at a time. Especially when the prey in one has already tasted the… hook."

Cash blushed. The hot wash of color made Arkady chuckle with low, dark appreciation. That or the clash of pink cheeks against the pure red shirt amused him.

"Besides," Arkady said before Cash could come up with something clever to say, "if you want a good oversight of the wedding guests, where better to get one than here?"

It was a good point. Cash lifted his head enough to glance around. The music throbbed in his head, between his eardrum and his jawbone, as he took in the hall. It was like being in the heart of a kaleidoscope as the jewel-bright colors gyrated around them.

The dancers' auras flared to the music, stretched up from flesh and bone until they were only tethered along the spine. Nobody with a secret that big would risk the loss of control that came with the waltz. But there were a few who moved against the tune, like Arkady. In the middle of the floor, Yana danced on bloodstained silk slippers with her still-human lover, her smile practiced and set at *just* the right curve to be happy, but not stupidly so. He clung to her, dazed and off-balance from the assault on his senses.

It gave Cash pause for a second as he loosened his grip on Arkady's shoulder. Was that what he looked like? Out of his depth? Desperate.

"No," Arkady said.

"What?"

"It's not the same," Arkady said as he glanced over at his sister. "You belong."

It wasn't clear if he meant Jerome or Yana didn't. Cash didn't ask. It was one argument he could dodge.

They turned again, and Cash lost sight of Yana, the flip of the grubby hem of her dress the last thing he saw. Donna sat primly on an ornately carved leather-upholstered seat that *somehow* managed to stop an inch short of trying to be a throne, next to a frail hunch of a man in a stained gray robe. She cracked a leg bone open with her nails to scrape out the peppered marrow and offered him half. The hand he extended to take it was thin, gray, and membranous—newly grown. His aura was thick and heavy on his skin, like a layer of slime.

The Worm.

Cash looked away before the Worm saw him. That was the sort of notice that wouldn't end well for him. Behind them, the few who hadn't dared the dance floor picked at the platters of banquet food, ignored the servers, and jostled for either attention or anonymity. None of them tugged at Cash's monster. None of them wanted more than any other monster.

"Nothing," he said. The frustration of it caught in his throat. He hadn't *wanted* to come back—not that he'd admitted to himself at least—but now that he was, the old need to prove his worth scratched at his teeth. "If the traitor's here, I can't find them."

Arkady hissed under his breath in frustration. "Damn," he said. "But it doesn't matter. We know what the plan is, and as long as we stop your human from exposing us, I can talk Kohary into giving us more time. We *will* find out what they have planned, and who they are."

He might. Cash would be gone with the confetti, swept back to his normal life. That was definitely what he wanted, and it didn't make the back of his throat hurt with salt.

"And what if it's Donna behind it?" he asked quietly, his voice muffled against Arkady's chest. "Or Yana."

"Or me?" Arkady asked.

"If it were you, you wouldn't have gotten me involved."

"Would I be scared that you'd find out my secrets?" Arkady teased, his voice light and cocky with bred-in aristocratic confidence. "If you did, would you turn me in?"

"You wouldn't risk me or Ellie in a plot like this," Cash said. Whatever else they had been, might have been, would be in the future—Arkady wouldn't have dragged him into this as a patsy. "If anything, you'd have sent us away."

The sharp clap of Donna's hands silenced the musicians midnote. They let their hands drop to their sides, instruments clutched loosely in torn fingers, and stood patiently. The echoes of music bounced off the high walls and arched ceiling as the dancers staggered—bloodied, winded, flushed—to a halt.

"A toast," Donna said as she lifted a thin ivory goblet in one hand. The tusk was ground down thin enough that it glowed pink from the liquor within. "To my daughter, may she survive her birth and her first husband."

A ragged round of applause quickly died away. Yana tilted her head with an expression of wry appreciation for her mother's careless cruelty, one hand on Jerome's forearm to shush his attempt to protest. Glasses were snatched from tables and trays—sometimes from hands—and raised in the air.

"Until the key to the pit is found," Donna proclaimed, her voice rich and layered with her birth tongue's accent. For effect. "Until the angel opens the gates. We will endure, thrive, and multiply. We walk in darkness so that, one day, our grandspawn shall walk in the fires of hell."

At the edge of the dance floor, Kohary, elegant and alone in unadorned black, raised his glass.

"To the Prodigium," he said, his voice cool, composed, and pitched to carry, "who will take us there."

The silence was brittle and felt like it would be sharp when it broke. Donna stared at Kohary for a drawn-out moment and then smiled. It looked genuine, which was scary.

"To the Prodigium," she acknowledged, "and all our children."

It was a lot to toast. The cheer from the crowd was a little confused, uncertain exactly what they were meant to celebrate, but the burn of alcohol as it hit the back of their throats steadied them.

"To the Prodigium!"

"To the Abascals!"

"Sláinte!"

The cheers stuttered over each other. Next to Donna, the Worm pointedly downed his glass in silence. He snapped the stem of the glass when he finished and dropped the goblet to the ground to crush underfoot.

In the center of the hall, surrounded by a ring of empty space as the dancers stepped back, Yana picked up her skirts high enough to flash scarred knees and curtsied.

"To me," she agreed, her voice chill and clear. "At long last, Mother."

The two Abascal women stared at each other for a second. Then Donna turned and gestured to the musicians. They jerked to life under her attention and prepped their instruments, bruised fingers poised over aged keys on the piano and the violin tucked under a blistered chin.

"An instructional for the happy couple," she said. "Play 'The Auld Wife.'"

She gathered her skirts, all heavy gold shot through with ivory threads, and stepped up onto the stage with them. As the bow was scraped over the strings for the introductory skirl, she lifted the remnants of her dinner and licked the bony knuckle of the thing.

"For she loved her husband dearly," she sang, with a pause as she wiped her mouth on her sleeve. "But another twice as well."

Her voice was high and sweet, with a chorister's purity to the notes as they soared. Whoever she'd plucked the talent from had been truly gifted, so no wonder she held it close. Yana pulled a quick, ugly face as she registered the song her mother had picked—an old Irish murder-ballad about an incompetent husband-killer—but then offered her hand to Jerome. He looked nervous but gulped and took it.

The assembled monsters jostled each other—teeth bared and elbows jabbed into ribs—as they pulled back to give the happy couple room to move through their paces. No one wanted to lose their position at or near the front of the mob.

"A beautiful couple," Kohary's low, rough voice remarked over Cash's shoulder. "The Worm regrets he won't be able to stay for the wedding."

Arkady didn't look away from his sister's dance. Neither did Cash, even as the back of his neck crawled with nerves.

"A shame."

"I'm sure he'll be missed."

"We were expecting great things from his wedding present," Arkady said dryly. He finally turned, and despite a brief resistance, Cash turned with him. "How long do I have before the Prodigium sends you back?"

Kohary actually looked regretful before he schooled his face back into unreadable lines. "Not long," he said. "Once the Worm is out of Abascal territory, he'll rally the Prodigium Seats to act. I'll have no choice."

"For the first time in her life, my mother *is* innocent," Arkady said.

Kohary glanced down at his feet, as if he expected the devil himself to come up in protest at that slur. Cash had as well.

"Or at least, not involved," Arkady said with a flicker of tired amusement.

"It doesn't matter," Kohary said. "The Worm has wanted this excuse for a long time. Your mother has gone unchecked for too long, and he is… concerned… about her ambitions."

"Who isn't?" Arkady asked.

"What will happen?" Cash asked. "To her family. To my daughter?"

Kohary looked at him for a moment. "I don't know," he admitted. "At best, she'll be made the Prodigium's ward."

Cash swallowed. His throat hurt, and something he suspected was guilt scraped at the back of his ribs. That wasn't a *best* he could accept, and that meant *worst* was going to be terrible. He had already known that, which was why he should have focused on who did this.

Maybe he did love Arkady, but Ellie was his daughter, and she had to come first.

"For what it's worth, I believe you," Kohary said. "Your mother is hardly part of the human world. How would she even get in contact with some human TV show? But it doesn't matter. The Prodigium keeps order. Not justice. Once the—"

The doleful toll of bells interrupted Kohary. He paused as he cocked his head to listen and then shrugged the rest of his apology as he put his hand on Arkady's shoulder.

"Your sister's marriage might be short, but I hope it's happy," he said.

Then the gates were dragged open—the scrape of iron-shod wood as it dragged through the ruts in the stone somehow caught up into the music—and the Abascal Hounds bayed their way into the party. All bones and pale hide, with bloodshot human eyes in overlong Saluki hound heads, they tore into any monster not quick enough to get out of their way.

It should have grabbed Cash's attention—it was certainly meant to—but his mind had grabbed on to something else. How *would* Donna get in touch with Harry, or whoever had passed the story up to Harry? How would any of the Prodigium's old sour monsters? It wasn't like they could look it up.

Behind the Hounds, the Hunter came, hunched over the weed-slimed neck of the kelpie as they galloped through the gates. A bone mask hid his face, yellowed and crusted with lichen, and a hangman's rope dangled from one hand. The monsters laughed, gasped, and shoved their way out of his path as he goaded the horse forward. Cash lost his grip on Arkady as the crowd surged again to watch the Hunter snare his prey. He lost sight of him too as well-dressed things shouldered him out of their way and toward the back of the press.

Cash let it happen. He dragged his fingers through his tangled hair as the Hunter, Jerome tossed over his thighs, charged out of the hall.

Shit.

Cash had asked the wrong question.

151

Chapter Fifteen

"WHAT?" ANNA-BETH said—yelled—down the phone. The dissonant screech of death metal vocals made the line fracture with static bursts. "Did who ask?"

Cash pressed back against the wall. The roughly carved stone was cold through the thin fabric of his shirt, and the knobbly edges jabbed into his shoulders and spine. He could hear the excited yelps of the wedding party as they got Yana ready for the chase to get her groom back. It wouldn't take long before they spilled out onto the shore.

"Anyone." He tasted salt on his tongue and wiped his nose on his sleeve again. A troll had caught him across the nose with the end of her tail, the tuft braided and banded in gold. He wasn't sure if his nose was bleeding or the skin had split. "Forget who asked about local horrors. Did *anyone* want to know who to contact with a big story?"

Anna-Beth blew air out between her lips on the other end of the line "People ask all the time, Cash," she said. "Everyone's got a granny with a cursed puppet or a spirit in the sink that they wanna get on TV. How many 'for reasons unbeknownst I have found myself cursed' letters does Winslow get a week?"

Sacksful. Most of them were just spite over the disposition of a will or an attempt to ruin/mend a marriage with the cudgel of hell. There was a whole team of researchers to sift for the few that had genuine desperation worked into the weave of the paper.

"This one wasn't crazy," Cash said. He pulled the threads of the idea apart in his head as he worked out how *he'd* have done this, if he'd decided he wanted to burn down the world with him. "He knew what he wanted, he didn't explain himself, he didn't *justify* anything. It was a simple trade, money for information."

He paused for a second as he thought about who'd have the information they'd sold so far. "And he was *off.* You know what people say about you? That's how you felt about him."

There was a small pause. Cash supposed he should feel bad, but he didn't have time. Anna-Beth sucked in a breath that she let become a laugh.

"I'd tell you to go fuck yourself," she said. "But when you put it that way, I know exactly who you mean. And when you put it like that, why should I tell you?"

Cash pushed himself off the wall and walked back down the hall to peer through a crack in the door. The room was chaos, full of monsters ready to head out to the hunt in heavy velvets and delicate silks. In the middle of it, Arkady stood with Yana, his hand on her shoulder as he told her something urgent. Probably not to set anything on fire. That was a problematic hobby when she was a teenager.

He didn't have long. Tradition said the length of the Hunt predicted the duration of the marriage, so Donna was going to be miserly with the traditional head start. She might tolerate Yana's marriage, but it wasn't *useful*, and she'd want Yana to remember that.

"I'll pay you."

Static and a raw-throated howl made Cash jerk his head away from the phone. When he put it back to his ear, Anna-Beth was halfway through forgiving him. More or less.

"… have that than an apology," she said. "I don't know his name, though."

"I'll pay for what you've got," Cash said. A humorless snigger caught in his throat as it occurred to him that if Anna-Beth gave him the wrong answer, he'd have no one to submit his expenses to. And maybe no need to worry about it, since he wouldn't have a kid to send to camp. That pinched off the air to the brief, bitter flash of humor. He forced himself to focus. "Did you meet them?"

In the background there was a howl from the audience and an ear-piercing smash of chords. "Hold on," Anna-Beth said. "Let me get outside. They're starting to get loud in here."

Two doors opened and closed, and a brief exchange with the bouncer. Cash chewed the inside of his cheek in impatience.

"Okay, mostly I spoke to him on the phone," she said. "He was from round your way, sounded like, and a rude bastard. Called himself Mr. Kane, but that was probably an alias. He talked like he thought I gave a fuck who he was."

Kane. Or Cain, Lilith's first-born and the monster's King Arthur. Definitely an alias, but a weird one for a traitor to pick.

"Mostly?"

She sighed. "I paid good money for these tickets, and I'm going to miss them pissing blood on the audience, thanks to you."

"If you want to go back, talk faster," Cash said coldly. It was Shanko's voice, the flat disinterest in courtesy. He didn't use it often, but it worked when he did. Over the phone, at least. He didn't have the bones for it face-to-face.

"I met him once, just to feel him out," Anna-Beth said. "I didn't want to burn my contact, you know, send him some para-stalker who believes in the secret monster government or something."

Cash resisted the urge to point out she should have maybe asked him some more questions, then.

"And?" he poked instead.

He could feel her shrug down the phone. "We met at that trailer park on the poor end of the island. I don't think he lived there, but he had the keys to one of them. Just some old guy in a nice suit, probably an ex-con. He looked like he'd been beat up enough over the years."

Cash's throat had gone tight and dry, because he *knew* he was on another wild goose chase. He had to be.

"What did he smell like?" he asked anyhow.

It was a question that would have given most people pause. Anna-Beth didn't hesitate. She answered as if it was a relief he asked. As if it made it less weird that it had stuck with her.

"Like *meat*," she said. "Old meat. Not spoiled, just old."

"Like a butcher's shop."

"Yeah," she said. "That's it. You know him?"

"Like you said," Cash answered her. "He's from my neck of the woods."

He hung up, shoved the phone into his pocket, and went back into the great hall. It was hot. The blood of a hundred monsters was up with the thrill of the chase, and it sweated out of them into the air. A banshee, gaunt cheeks and hair the color of crayons, swung on him as he pushed by. Her hand raised to backhand him to the floor, but the fat white thing with her grabbed her arm to pull her back.

"Idiot," it said, out of a prim, pink mouth. "He's the Abascal boy's now…."

The banshee glanced at Cash's throat and then down to the dull glitter of the ring that was just—even without undoing another button—visible under his shirt. She couldn't blanch any more—her skin was already the color and texture of old bone—but the blood drained from her eyes.

She opened her mouth, and Cash's death squealed from her lips—somewhere far, somewhere lonely, somewhere *wet*. "Sorry," the round white thing translated. "She didn't recognize you. We are just eager for the chase."

Her tongue flicked, long and curled as a fly's nose, from her mouth and then back in. The banshee pushed her hands together in apology and backed away.

Cash didn't know if it pissed him off more to *belong* to the Abascals again in the eyes of the world, or that on some level it felt right. Stupid human heart and asshole monster needs.

He shoved the rest of the way through the crowd to the dais where Donna perched. Her heavy overskirt had been unbuttoned and left in a puddle on the ground, revealing thin legs in tight leather and small split goat hooves instead of feet.

Donna did always leave off the feet if she could get away with it. Stubbed toes were just too much of a ridiculous indignity.

"There he is," she said, with what might have been mistaken for warmth as Cash scrambled up to join them. "I told you he was fine. Our Casper has always been a survivor, Arkady. Like a handsome little cockroach."

She reached out and patted his cheek with a dry, slightly too-warm hand. Not *hot*, just a few degrees high enough that you noticed. Cash flinched back because that was weird as hell.

"Okay, that is very disturbing," he said. "But we can talk about it later. Where's Shanko?"

Donna raised an eyebrow at him. "Manners, dear heart. I know you've seen them beaten into the slow to learn."

"Where's Shanko? It's important," he said.

Beside her the Worm chuckled. It was a thick hiss of sound, like a snake with phlegm caught in its throat. He pushed his hood back to reveal a narrow, not-quite-finished face of tender skin. His true face was just visible behind it—through it. What passed for his face, anyhow.

"Even the wisps don't respect you now, Belladonna," he said. "You should be grateful when Kohary comes back with the Prodigium's weight behind him. At least an object lesson is remembered, not consigned to irrelevance."

Donna gave him a sudden fierce look as her gracious-host mask slipped. "I know you like to be beaten, Helminth, but tonight isn't about you, so hold your tongue," she rasped, the burnt-meat-and-stone smell of her power suddenly thick in the air. "Or I'll scrape you back down to the wet. If I am to be an object lesson, might as well be a colorful one, after all."

Lust bloomed through the Worm's aura until it was the color of fish guts.

Cash grimaced and dragged his eyes away. Some things he could do without knowing, and what turned the Worm on was one of them.

"Madam," Cash said, the use of her formal title—one of them—unusual enough to make both Arkady and Donna look at him. "Where's Shanko?"

"Cash?" Arkady asked quietly.

When Cash didn't answer him, Arkady glanced at him and then at the Worm. He grimaced unhappily but didn't push. Donna pouted but followed his lead. She mimed unconcern as she strapped a dagger

156

to her thigh and held out her hand to a waiting servant. The shaft of the pike slapped against her palm.

"I don't know," she said. "His last task of the day was to prepare the Hunter and the Hounds for the chase. Perhaps he's still in the kennels."

HE WASN'T, but the Hunter was.

It had been a man once. Probably a venal or a greedy one, definitely a stupid one to make the final Crossroads Deal with the likes of Donna Abascal. That was a long time ago, though, and there wasn't much left of that man. A human soul still, pinned and displayed behind bloodshot eyes, but the body had remade itself to Donna's service.

She gave him his hands back when he was chosen to be the Hunter tonight, roughed out a facsimile of a human face. Or one that would do, seen through a mask.

Cash didn't think he was human enough to be sure, but maybe the delusion he'd be human again—free, because that was always promised—had been some comfort before Shanko put a railway spike through his head. Or maybe death had been a relief all on its own.

"Shanko did this?" Arkady said. He crouched down to check the Hunter was dead. The pat he gave its scarred shoulder was almost respectful, but then, he'd have his own kennel one day. "Why?"

"He took the Hunter's place?" Cash said. He folded his arms behind his head and stalked back and forth frantically. On some level he'd recognized Shanko on the kelpie's back, but it hadn't clicked until Anna-Beth described the butcher's block stink that got in your head and lingered. "Shanko's the one who leaked information to the humans."

Arkady straightened up easily. He looked calm as he unbuttoned his jacket and stripped it off to toss it over the harness hooks that studded the walls, but his aura had lifted like hackles.

"I worked that out," he said sharply. "*Why?*"

Cash opened his mouth on the off chance the answer would fall out. It didn't. He shook his head and admitted, "I don't know." Shanko was sour and foul-mouthed, gross with bitterness, but that was his nature. His loyalty to the Abascals, to his Belladonna, was centuries old, as much a part of what held him up as his bones. "Does it matter?"

It should, Cash could feel that, but Arkady just grimaced his agreement.

"In the end, I suppose not," he said. "Whether I understand or not won't change anything. He'll pay or we will. I prefer him."

So did Cash. The Abascals would still be censured for one of their household being involved, but not excessively. Monsters understood how hard it was to control your instincts, never mind someone else's. Unless Donna confessed out of the blue to being involved, the family would survive.

Ellie would be safe.

"How's the child?" he caught the echo of Shanko's question from memory, the closest to kindness the old man had ever shown. Cash had thought that was real, that it meant something. Shanko was the closest thing to a dad he'd ever had.

Shitty as the cruel old bastard was at it, it still hurt to realize he was going to die.

Arkady grabbed his shoulder and squeezed it gently. "You won't have to do it," he said. "I promise."

It was a monster's kindness. Cash appreciated it, but there wasn't time to do more than brush a quick, grateful kiss over Arkady's knuckles.

"We need to find him," he said.

Arkady flashed a cold, sharp smile as he took his shirt off. His skin was mottled with gold scales and bruised-smoke grays, his nails sharp and black as he shredded the heavy silk. "There is an entire hall of monsters ready to do just that. Donna has hosted a lot of weddings here, Cash, and the Hunter has always been kenneled again come dawn."

"I know," Cash said. He poked around in his pockets for a hair tie. Most of his clothes had one stashed away in a pocket—just in case

Ellie needed an emergency braid—but of course, these predated her. The last few days, he'd felt like that kid again—sometimes—but it still felt strange to trip over the evidence. He stooped down, grabbed Arkady's shirt instead, and pulled one of the torn ribbons out to tie his hair back. "But we have to find him before Yana does. Whatever his plan is, she's the key. Why else do it like this?"

Arkady grimaced. They didn't just have to find Shanko, they had to find him first… ahead of a pack of the most dangerous monsters in the US and with the Worm just waiting for his excuse.

"God damned us long ago," Arkady said sourly as he grabbed one of the heavy leather dusters used when they had to handle the hounds. It hung stiffly off his shoulders as he dragged it on over bare skin. "You'd think he'd have stopped screwing with us by now."

Cash could only shrug.

IT WAS a beautiful night for the chase, with damp in the air and a thick gray bank of clouds to hide the moon. Not so good to be *chased*, but Cash thought that maybe being caught was part of Shanko's plan. He might have played a good game so far, but he couldn't think he'd get away unscathed, not even if he succeeded in bringing the Prodigium down on them.

The dull drone of the emergency siren carried on the still air from the petrochemical plant down the shore. It wouldn't do to keep everyone inside, but most people would have either battened down for the night or headed over to the mainland. A few belches of sulfur-yellow smoke from the vents and no one would question it. Over the years chemical leaks had caused a lot of people to see strange things out here.

Like monsters in their gaudiest finery, drunk as lords on the promise of blood, in full chase of a stolen groom along the shoreline. Pookas and boggarts jostled to the front of the pack against a Jersey Devil and a Black-Eyed Child on a mountain bike they'd been allowed to even the odds. They were not actually children, they just passed as them if you weren't observant, but they were short.

It was bad form to beat the bride to the kill, but traditionally there were gifts and favors in it for anyone in the… ah… "splash zone."

Right at the front, the bloodstained spearhead of the Hunt, Yana ran in bloody slippers through the surf.

"He's taken what's mine," Yana had snapped when Cash tried to reason with her. "My husband from my arms and under my own roof. I don't care what his plans are, I'm going to drown him like an unwanted twin."

She refused to listen to reason. Yana didn't care if the Abascal name was dragged through the dirt and the Abascal scions went up in smoke. She would eventually—for Ellie's sake, and Cash needed to believe that—but not with the bit between her teeth.

Even Arkady wasn't able to convince her to fall back and let them corral Shanko. She wanted to watch the old man squirm for his affront against her, prove that she wasn't the Abascal to dismiss as a threat… oh, and get Jerome back. He might not be in her top five motivations tonight, but he did make the long list.

Cash wished he'd changed before he left the hotel. Despite what the old Hunter movies tried to claim, skintight leather wasn't the best thing to run through the wilderness in. It rubbed. He sweated. Monster-bred strength and stamina was impressive among humans, but around other monsters, he was reminded he *could* have worked out more.

Despite the sweat that soaked him and the stitch in his side, he still managed to stay near the front of the pack. The back of the front of the pack, at least. He could see Arkady's back from here.

Nothing much had changed around here, so he still knew the lay of the ground. He also had a wisp's instinct for where to stand.

When your race fed by luring travelers into bogs at night, being clumsy and falling into puddles meant the Hunters got you.

Cash sprinted along the scrubby grass near the dunes. It was uneven footing, all matted hunks of dead grass and old bottles, but it was better than lumbering through sand. The air was sharp with salt. He could feel it in his lungs as he sucked in each breath and forced it out to take another.

A grim, molten blood dripping from his one dinner-plate-size eye, cast about on the sand. Grains stuck to his slobber-wet jowls as he snorted for the scent. The other monsters jeered as they passed him or cursed him as they misjudged and slammed into the dog's iron-muscled side. He lifted his head and turned toward the sea as Cash reached him.

... on a kelpie.

The Hunt came out of the sea like the tide and punched through the slack middle of the chase. Hounds, cut loose for the first time in years, tore at stomachs and legs with steel-crowned fangs. They fell under fists and claws, torn apart by a now-one-eyed troll or eaten whole by a rawhead in a torn party dress—but they kept coming. Shanko had emptied the kennels for tonight and lured out of their holes even the old, crust-hided favorites from Donna's childhood. At their head the kelpie smashed through the startled monsters. Sharp teeth and heavy stone-shoed hooves cleared its path. Anyone who dodged the snakey strike of its head got hammered into the dirt by the black-clad Hunter, by Shanko, who'd always appreciated straightforward violence over grace. They dropped to the ground, and the dogs overran them, before they turned their attention to the guests still standing.

One of them, a delicate gold locket buried in the folds of her throat, slammed into Arkady. He got his arm up in time for her teeth to sink into the padded sleeve of his coat. A terrible, broken growl gargled out of her as she thrashed her heavy, muscled body violently enough to make him stumble. It was enough that the next hound that hit him put him on his back in the sand.

It didn't matter. Even if he had been caught off guard, a couple of hounds weren't going to do any sort of real damage to Arkady. Couldn't do any real damage. That didn't stop the sick wave of fear that washed over Cash at the sight of Arkady down in the sand.

He darted between the fighting monsters, dodged the snarl of hounds and the occasional wildly unaimed swing of a panicked tentacle, and grabbed one of the hounds on top of Arkady by the scruff. Loose, clammy skin folded between his fingers and pulled tight around the hound's throat as he hauled on it.

"Off," he yelled as he braced his feet in the shifting sand. The old command words that Shanko had taught him, back when he was sent down to scrub out the pens for being smart, bubbled to the top of his mind. "Madra. Off."

The hound made a confused sound at the familiar command. It didn't obey, but it loosened its grip enough for Arkady to get his knee up and kick it off him. He scrambled to his feet and yanked the other hound off his arm. Skin came with it, enough that Cash saw a glimpse of the actual hard-scaled flesh under the rind of meat.

"If you weren't my grandmother," Arkady snarled through sharp teeth as he held the hound up, "I'd have you skinned to mend my coat."

He tossed the hound back into the fight and gave Cash a quick, furious look. "Don't do that again," he snapped. "I want you to kiss my wounds better, not be stuck with you laid up in bed for a week."

Cash smirked.

"There was a time you'd have been all for that," he joked. Fear almost made him run off at the mouth. "Getting old, Arkady? Or just not that into me anymore?"

"I won't be if you have no nose," Arkady snapped. He shoved Cash roughly back, nearly onto his ass, and slapped a hound out of the air with a clawed hand. "I like you pretty, Casper."

Was it more stupid to be afraid your pure-blood-monster lover might be hurt or to get flustered in the middle of a fight because he said you were pretty? As long as you kept your nose, at least, Cash reminded himself as he punched one of the hounds in the throat. It gagged and choked, eyes bulged out in surprise as it went down.

Another, muzzle furred with gore and hair, lunged at Arkady from the back of a pissed-off werewolf. A split tongue slavered between its sharp teeth as he snarled out something that could have been a word. Or the hound just thought it was.

The carved ivory tip of Donna's spear stabbed through that open mouth and into the hound's throat. It spat blood as she hoisted it upright, dangled it for a second like a gory flag, and then flicked it away into the dunes. Half her face was gone, the hard work of her maids shredded, and the horribly beautiful face underneath was twisted with anger.

She looked… like an Abascal—a demon—beautiful and stomach-turning all at once. Cash's monster wanted to follow at her heels, and his humanity wanted to run and never stop. His smart mouth split the difference.

"I think that's the first time I've seen someone yeet a hound," he said.

He didn't expect Donna to know what he meant, but she gave him a dry look. "Ellie *will* be proud," she said.

A stray bit of skin dangled from her eyebrow. She picked it off and flicked it away, then wiped her bloody face on her sleeve as she scanned the beach. The guests had gotten over their surprise at the tables being turned and whooped with glee at the taste of something new.

Donna's eyes weren't golden like Arkady's. The one exposed was black and fringed with thick, rustling lashes, but the flicker of fear that flashed through it was oddly human.

"Where's Yana?" she said. Where's my daughter?"

Chapter Sixteen

GONE.

Her bloodied slippers were left behind, the satin ripped to pieces and full of sand, but no sign of her. Cash swore as he looked around. The hot red hunger of the wedding guests burned the back of his tongue like cinnamon as they split up to chase the stolen couple and the hounds that scattered into the night. Whoops and shrill thin howls cut through the silence as they headed into the town.

"Someone congratulated me on my most successful soiree to date," Donna said dryly as she stabbed the spear into the dirt to clean it. "Apparently expectations are high for the ceremony tomorrow. I don't know what would be worse, the truth coming out or having to think of a way to top this."

Arkady, the sleeve of his leather duster pierced and torn, gave his mother a rare, openly sour look.

"How about your daughter's corpse found floating in the sea?" he asked. "Where does that rank in what's worse?"

Donna braced a hoof against a half-buried rock and yanked her spear out of the ground. She ran her thumb along the head of it to check for chips.

"That would obviously come under 'the truth coming out,'" she said. "And if I wanted her dead, I'd have done it myself."

"Would you?" Arkady asked.

"Of course. I brought her into the world with my own hands, and I'll do the same if I need her out of it," Donna said. "Humans disparage kin-slayers, Arkady, but monsters know it's the least you can do for your own blood. Cash understands; he's a father."

They both looked at him.

"Oh, yeah, no," he said. "I'm either too human or too common to get that."

Donna inclined her head slightly. "Or both," she said, as though it were a concession she'd generously made just for him. "But you'll see. One day."

He hoped not.

"Where would he go?" Arkady asked.

It took Cash a moment to realize the question was for him. He shook his head and shrugged.

"Ask Donna," he said. "He's served her for centuries."

Donna spat in the sand. It bubbled and stank, a thick gray fizz, as it melted the grains into a pebble of dark sea glass. If a human found it, supposedly, they could look through it and see past glamours and into the future. The future, almost always, involved them being killed by the Prodigium, so... that part might be made up.

"I tell him what to do," she said. "We don't... converse. Arkady's right. Of everyone, you were closest to him. Where would he go, Caspari?"

Cash started to deny it, but he realized he was wrong before he got the first word out. He *did* know where Shanko had gone.

Probably. A hunch was a lot to prop all their lives up on, but it was why he was there.

"The trailer park," he said. "Where I grew up. He's there."

He was ready to justify the answer, but it turned out there was no need. Donna nodded her shredded head as if he'd agreed with her.

"Go," she told Arkady. "I'll round up the hounds and make sure our guests don't get overexcited. The last thing we want is to resolve this and have Kohary call down judgment on us because a hound was taken by the dogcatcher or some idiot was caught peeping through curtains."

Arkady scowled but silently extended a hand toward Cash. The casual curve of his fingers made Cash's twitch for contact, but he hesitated as he realized that....

Oh, that was how they would travel.

HE'D PUKED here before. Cash was almost certain of that. He emptied out a party's worth of finger food onto a woody hydrangea, the bile in his throat hot with stomach acid and wine. Arkady's wings made a soft, papery sound as he folded them back under his skin.

"Are you done?" he asked. His voice was impatient, tight with angry concern, but the hand he put on the back of Cash's neck was gentle.

It wasn't *flight*—not like birds did and people, including minor monsters, always dreamed about. There was nothing graceful or natural about it, nothing fun. It was just fast and forceful, like a punch to the air. Cash had never opened his eyes during a trip, not when he was a kid and not now.

His monster wanted to snigger, but it rolled belly-up with reflected nausea in his gut. It served it right.

"I hate that," Cash said as he straightened up. "We could have taken a car."

Arkady ignored the complaint as he looked around. His slightly confused expression made Cash realize that it was the first time he'd come here. Cash had always been willing to remind people of where he'd come from back then, but only on his terms. He hadn't actually brought anyone down here, not served his mom up to them. And what other reason could an Abascal have for being here? Rich monsters, like rich people, rarely ate their dinner out of tin cans.

"This way," Cash said. He wiped his mouth on his sleeve and broke into a tired jog through the maze of half-planned "streets" and cul-de-sacs that governed the layout of the trailers. The sound of TVs or radios turned up loud filtered through a few of the thin sheet-metal walls—someone too tired, poor, or stubborn to evacuate—but none of them came out to see what was going on. They knew better after a lifetime.

His mom's old trailer was still on the lot. He paid for it for a few years after she died, but after Ellie, he'd let go of that bit of sentiment in favor of baby food. Yet nothing had changed. The stubbornly optimistic daffodils still grew in big, colorful plastic pots along with the weeds, and the scrape of red where he'd crashed his trike into the side of one when he was a kid was still there.

"Cash," Arkady said. He put his hand on Cash's shoulder and squeezed roughly. "Whatever happens—"

Cash took a deep breath. The air smelled like it always had—of sea-salt, grease, and despair—a lot like greasy burgers. "If you're going to be all noble and say you won't stand between me and Yana getting together, you can stick it up your ass."

Arkady dragged him back a step so Cash was pressed against his chest. His breath was hot against Cash's ear, that particular wet, blood-hot huff of a predator's mouth, as he said, "I wasn't going to say it, and I wouldn't do it. Yana had her chance with you, with Ellie, and she didn't take it. She doesn't get another one."

It shouldn't have helped—what did it matter who was going to fuck who in the middle of this—but it did. Something in Cash's chest unknotted, warm and loose and even slightly horny, and he let himself lean against Arkady for a second.

"So what were you going to say?"

"You've spoiled the moment," Arkady told him with a kiss to Cash's ear to soften his dry tone. "It can wait until tomorrow. Stay behind me."

He pushed Cash behind him and climbed up the rickety steps to the door. It was already open a crack. That could be an invitation, or the crappy lock had finally given up the ghost. Cash shifted his weight onto the balls of his feet and clenched his hands into fists, nails sharp against his palm.

"You knew we'd find you, Shanko," Arkady said calmly. He pushed the door open with one hand and cocked his head to look inside. It was black as a cave or the kennels under the hotel—too dark for inside the trailer, even with the thin curtains pulled and taped together. Cash started to say something but hesitated, because it was Arkady. What could Shanko even do to him? "That's why you took Yana in the middle of the Hunt. We'd have no choice. What do you want? Why do this after years of loyalty?"

In the dark, Shanko laughed—a thick, mushy sound. "And what the fuck has it got me?"

"Exactly what you asked for," Arkady pointed out calmly. He pushed the door open all the way. "Yana?"

The door slammed back on him. It nearly caught his fingers in the jamb.

"Run, you idiot!" Yana screamed.

Arkady threw his shoulder against the door instead and threw himself inside. It was like he hit a wall and bounced off. He flew backward and crashed onto the ground, taking out one of the daffodil pots with his shoulder. Blood, black in the moonlight, dripped from his nose and mouth, and his monster, all greasy gold scales and leather wings, bulged through his skin in painful torsion. Arkady screamed, and the monster did too, voices out of sync by a second as he arched his back in agony.

"You should have listened to her," Shanko said as he stepped out of the trailer. Or most of him. The gray, lumpen figure that Cash had known for most of his life—bogeyman and then boss—had fallen apart. Thick slabs of flesh hung off and dragged behind, a wasted skeleton of a man in mildewed funereal best. Mushroom-pale skin was pulled tight over his bony face, and his eyes were a faded, bleached-out yellow. "It would have given you a few more days."

Cash started toward Arkady, and Shanko swung his arm up. The heavy *sleeve* of meat that had covered his scrawny arm flew out on the end of a thin, snotty cord of plasm and hit Cash in the chest like a hammer.

It must have knocked him over. He didn't remember that. The slab hit him in the chest, and then he was on his back, lungs tight as he stared up at the cloudy sky through watering eyes.

Bag of Bones. Bones and Flesh.

The monster jibbered at him in a panic. Wisps weren't fighters, and Cash probably had more humanity left than either of them expected. Enough to still be in love.

"Pathetic," Shanko spat. "Look at you. They used you up and cast you out, cast you *over* for someone new and fresh. Yet you still come crawling when they snap their fingers."

He didn't sound angry, just upset. His voice was thick and wet, as if he had to choke back tears.

Cash rolled over and propped himself up on his elbow. He spat blood onto the dry gray grass and wiped his mouth on his shoulder.

"What business is it of yours who I fuck?" he asked. His monster crawled up his throat and took over his tongue, because even if it got them killed, it wanted to draw blood. "You aren't my dad."

This time it was a fat slice of salted thigh, gray and hard with rind, that smashed a dent into the ground just next to Cash's head.

"Shut up," Shanko yelled, a crack in his voice. "You always had a smart mouth. No one could beat it out of you, scare it out of you. I thought that you were… different, but they just fucked you loyal, didn't they? Everything they did to you, stuff you don't even *know* they did to you."

Cash wiped dirt off his face and scrambled to his feet. He glanced over at Arkady. The great leathery wing that had jutted out of his spine had been folded away again, although the skin bulged oddly around it, but a thick shoulder and a long writhe of tail still squirmed naked and tender in the air. It looked like a man trying to get a too-small shirt on.

"I might be an idiot, Shanko," Cash said. "But I'm an idiot with my eyes open. No one did anything to me that I wasn't willing to have done. Hell, I was usually the one who started it."

Shanko stalked toward him. His stolen flesh dragged along with him, heavier than the little bits of eye and rat that bag of bones cannibalized from other ghosts.

"They seduced you, ruined you, used you," he said. "I tried to protect you—"

"You did not."

The flash of anger that spat out of Cash's mouth caught both of them by surprise. Cash had never held any grudge against Shanko for not protecting him, because why should he. But the idea that the old man was patting himself on the back over some imaginary virtue raised his hackles. Shanko hesitated at the rejection, his peat-mummy leathery face creased in confusion before he recovered.

"I chose you, not them. It was me who took you away from this shithole." He gestured violently around him at the trailers. "I could have killed you if I wanted—who'd have stopped me, but I took you to the Abascals. I told Donna that you had potential."

"And what, it was for my own good?" Cash snorted at him. He took a step back, trying to—adjust the kid's memory of the space to an adult's legs. "You did what you were told to do, Shanko. Don't get me wrong, you did a good job of it, but what the hell have I got to do with any of this?"

Shanko backhanded with a side of his stolen flesh and slammed Cash through the low fence he'd shuffled toward. This time Cash managed to dodge most of the impact. He landed on his ass, a sharp pain in his ribs, but managed to drag himself back to his feet.

"I did all this for you," Shanko said. "Or for us both, but because of you. Everything we gave to them over the years, everything we cut out to offer to them on a silver fucking platter, and they don't care. You had a chance to go when the boy got married. To be whoever you wanted, to live your own life, and they couldn't bear that, could they? The Abascals. Even if they didn't want you anymore, even if you weren't useful, they have to keep you on the hook. To know that when they snapped their fingers you'd come back. But do you know what I found out, Cash? The child isn't even yours. A decade you've spent raising another Abascal cuckoo for them, some passing monster's brat. So. Do you still want to stop me? Or are you going to let me bring them down?"

"Ellie's my daughter," Cash said. He ignored Shanko's attempt to interrupt. "She's not my blood, but I knew that."

Yana's tears burned her own skin. Her face had been raw when Cash stumbled over her in one of Donna's underground gardens. Two miserable people who couldn't—ever—have what they wanted and the sort of deal that put a hook through your heart.

"I wish it were mine," Cash had said of the newt that had landed in Yana's stomach and screwed her life. "It would be easier."

Maybe she should have hesitated, but she didn't. That this would hurt Arkady as well as solve her problem, only made it better. "Deal,"

Yana had hissed, her hands tight around his as her nails drew blood. "You can't take it back now."

She might only be the human coffin for Donna's real daughter, but a dead monster was still a monster. The deal took. Cash had never slept with Yana, never even kissed her, but when Ellie was born, she was his. Her jaw looked like his, her smile could be pasted on Cash's face and no one would notice, and she had the hunger of a wisp. Once she was old enough for her monster to come into her own, that might change, but she'd still be his daughter. Cash was the one who'd sat up with her and learned algebra for her, and he wasn't going to let someone else take over when it got easy just because of *genetics.*

That was a human obsession.

"It was a lie," Cash said. "But it was my lie, Shanko."

Shanko blinked dry red-rimmed eyes in confused doubt. "You… you knew? No. If she wasn't yours, why would you take her, give up everything to raise some other monster's by-blow? You're just lying to protect them." He nodded in agreement with himself, the rise and fall of his voice almost hypnotic. "That was what I taught you to do, but it won't work this time. The Abascals took us, and they used us up, boy. Look at me!"

He stepped out of the tangle of protoplasm and cured flesh, arms spread in display. It did not make him look any better. He was a dried-out thing, all tendon and withered skin. His fingers were curled into his palms, stitches on his arms stark where they'd sliced the tendons and closed the wounds, and old, *old* bruises stained his face gray and grainy. It was a striking look for a monster. Unique.

Except he wasn't.

Cash glanced at Arkady again, his monster half yanked out of his skin and flopping around like a gaffed fish. It had been Shanko who'd told him that story, about the awful things a cauled Hunter could do to a monster.

"What did Donna promise you?" Cash asked.

"That if I kept her safe, we'd be together forever," Shanko said. "I thought she meant we'd be lovers. Instead I'm her dog."

"Yeah," Cash said. "That's something you should have nailed down right from the start."

Shanko showed his teeth. "Yes," he said. "But you don't, do you, Cash? Not when it's love."

"Especially then," Cash said.

"And who taught you that?" Shanko asked with a flicker of pride that faded back to frustration. He pulled the heavy slabs of meat back in around him, slotted over his arms and ribs like a jigsaw. It looked… sweaty. "Not that you ever did anything you were told, like keeping your head down and staying out of their business. If you'd done that, you might have survived this."

Behind him, in the unnaturally black doorway, Yana staggered out onto the steps. Her hair was torn and her dress stained with blood. She looked ill and thin, hollow as a bell. Wild eyes fixed on Shanko's back, and she grimaced, her pale lips pulled back from bloody teeth.

"Go suck my mom's crusty tit," she spat as she swung a frying pan in a short, vicious arc. The rim of it caught Shanko right across the side of his head. Despite what he'd *just* seen, Cash expected the sick crack of bone and brain. Instead, the thick knots of flesh just dented as the pan was buried in it. It was still enough to distract Shanko as Yana wrenched the pan and swung again. "Run, you idiot. Go!"

Cash went. He spun on his heel and took off at a run through the narrow avenue between the trailers. Behind him Shanko screamed with rage, and something hit the side of the trailer with a loud thunk. Cash tried not to think about what it was.

He focused on his feet instead as he followed a mental map nearly two decades old. It was just lucky for him that this place had struck on a winning combination early—rent cheap, buy cheaper, rent to the desperate—and didn't waste money on change. Cash swung around the mailbox in a concrete tub at the end of the Fernyal trailers. It used to be a flamingo, but they'd changed it to a seahorse at some point. From the taste of the house, the Fernyal mother—all harsh Presbyterian features and a well of horrifying, bubbling anger—had died, but her daughters had filled it with more despair.

172

The monster grabbed a snack of it on the way by, just threads between its teeth and a shot of teenage anger about cheerleaders.

Cash ducked across the street on a diagonal and nearly ran into a new trailer. So *some* things had changed. He hit the ground and scrambled under it, the axle too close and too greasy for comfort, to the glimpse of open space on the other side.

Behind him glass broke, and then a car alarm went off. He could hear the wheeze of a man not built to run on the road behind him. Shanko went around the trailer rather than through it.

"I would have spared you," Shanko yelled. "You're human enough to dodge the Hunt."

That was the voice of someone who'd never lived with humans. Cash jumped over a low fence and squirmed between the overgrown roses that crawled over the two trailers. He lost some skin—and really wished he'd changed his outfit before this started—but stretched his head start out a few seconds more. The Church might start with the Worms and the Abascals of the monster world if they were exposed, but they'd work their way down. Eventually, once they really had wiped out all their hidden predators, it would be people like Anna-Beth on the pyre. Just odd, not quite comfortable.

Cash would have had his throat cut on camera by Winslow long before that. The network would call it *The Monster Within* or *Our Friend, the Monster* and posthumously make him way more important than a contract employee.

No back pay, though.

That was okay. They had just given Cash an idea, although he'd started this race with no plan other than to give Yana and Arkady time to recuperate.

Cash pulled his monster up into his throat, "That's why you didn't just turn the Abascals in," he said. His breath was pale and bright as it left his mouth, and it carried the sound away from him on flickers of pale blue flame. Wisp tricks. The thrown words wouldn't fool Shanko for long, but they might give Cash just a few more seconds. "Because you promised you'd save Donna. No time limits apply."

"Save her and love her forever," Shanko said bitterly. Something smashed against a trailer, hard enough to shake it on its brick foundations, as he followed the voice. "I threw that in as a freebie, like a fool. She thought I'd be her slave forever, but love curdles like milk, given enough time. And given enough time, you find the loopholes."

"Like the fact that the Prodigium have never trusted Donna," Cash said. He hushed a Jack Russell tied up in the kennel out back of Jimmy Frank's trailer on the way by. It couldn't be the same dog—it would be damn near thirty now—but it looked the same as it warned him off with a low growl. "So really, by exposing them you were, what, doing her a favor? Protecting her against any future moves against her?"

Somewhere in the park, a door cracked open and a woman yelled out, "Fuck sake, take it inside!" before she slammed it again.

One.

Cash edged down the narrow strip between the trailers.

Two.

Three.

And… fuck. A slab of meat punched through the trellis someone had put up, bits of stick and flowers stuck to the gray creases, and Shanko stepped through ahead of him.

"Wisp tricks," Shanko said contemptuously. "You think I've never seen them before?"

Cash threw himself backward, landed hard on the ground, and rolled under a trailer. A cold, slimy *something* grabbed at his leg, but he kicked back blindly and scrambled loose.

He crawled out the other side and ran.

Chapter Seventeen

THIS HAD been his hunting grounds as a kid. It wasn't as impressive a maze as the estate the Abascals had cultivated under the island, but it had provided. And not just for him.

The trailer park was easy prey, and some things needed easy. Most of them hung out near the heart of the park, around what could be a crossroads if you squinted at it. It made them feel more at home. Besides, the sea might not usually bother monsters, but the tides pulled at spirits.

"Stop running," Shanko yelled as he shoved his way between the trailers. He waved an arm and flattened the fence and a handful of faded decorative flamingos on the lawn in front of him with a swipe of flesh. "Just come and take what's coming to you. I still like you, boy. I'll make it quick."

Cash spared the breath to spit on the ground as he ran. He reached up and wiped the blood off his neck in a messy swipe that left his fingers covered in it. That would help. He slapped the sides of the trailers as he sprinted along, the metal rough as he smeared it with blood.

Hey. He rattled the spiritual bars on his way through, loud and noisy and offensively alive. *Wake up. Come out. Help me.*

Something sighed and poked a squid-fox face out through the wall of a battered trailer. It blinked blearily at Cash and yawned, and a fat worm turned tongue wriggled between its lips. Something else stretched and chuckled under a car, thorny black toes and twenty bloody fingertips just visible between the tires.

Spirits and ghosts. The dead and the never technically alive. Not exactly the cream of the crop out here—it was the old, the decrepit, the not-really-that-good-at-shit generally—but there were a lot of them.

Fingers with too many joints slotted through lattices, and eyeballs on thin stems wriggled up through holes in the ground.

Eh?

What?

That wisp boy wants help.

The cacophony of muttered conversation filled his head with bagpipes and wailing cats as he staggered to a stop in front of the office. His lungs burned, and the stitch in one side jabbed through his spine to reach the other set of ribs. The oldest thing that lived there opened the door and looked out. It was jammed into the body of Mrs. Park, a tiny elderly Korean woman in house slippers and yoga pants. Most of it didn't fit. A great fat slug of flesh scuttled frantically along behind her.

No one was entirely sure how much Mrs. Park knew about her squatter. She had to have noticed she was too old to really be alive, but it seemed rude to ask. Her grandchildren never questioned it when they visited.

The old spirit—old and mean enough to be a real demon if it didn't live in a grandmother in a trailer park—angled its head so it could peer at him with one raw-meat eye through her slightly parted lips.

"Why," it rumbled thoughtfully, "should we?"

Cash sunk down onto his knees and stared up at it. It was a good question. Humans might think monsters and spirits were one and the same, but they didn't think so.

"For the Prodigium," he said.

The thing scratched itself with Mrs. Park's hand. Or scratched Mrs. Park with its hand. "Fuck them."

It started to close the door, and Shanko's laugh was thick and smug.

"Did you really think they'd help you?" he asked.

Cash braced his hands on his thighs and leaned forward over the ache in his ribs.

"I can get you on TV," he said.

Those were the magic words. Every spirit in that place wanted to hit it big as the next reality-rite star, thought that all they needed was their fifteen minutes to take a one-way ride from here to the big leagues.

The lure of it dragged them out of their lairs. They huffed cold, sour blasts of air as they lurched, crawled, and lunged at Shanko. His eyes went wide in surprise as they mobbed him. Beaks sawed at the snotty strings of plasm that held him together. Thin things of bone and twigs clung to the hammer-lumps of his flesh and drooled on it to make it bubble and rot. One thing got a finger in his mouth and pulled, the flesh of his cheek brittle enough to crumble as it stretched. Another crawled into his shadow and picked at his heels with bony, needle fingers to unstitch it.

If Shanko were a monster, it would have worked. Same went if he'd *just* been human.

Unfortunately, he wasn't exactly either, and that gave him an advantage.

He pulled at the spirits with ruined hands and pinned them down in the dirt with his heel on the back of their necks. Scripture didn't work for him anymore, but it wasn't as if he was up against Legion or one of the big hitters. He tore them apart in shreds and chunks until they gave up and scuttled away back into the dark.

Better to be a small fish in a puddle than undone. It wasn't as if they had an afterlife to look forward to.

Cash glanced up at the Old Thing in Mrs. Park. It shrugged at him. "She only watches K-dramas anyhow," he said. "So we don't care."

It went back inside and closed the door after it.

"Did you really think they'd help you?" Shanko spat. He staggered forward, his shadow loose and flapping from one heel. "Do you think they could? Even if it were in their own self-interest, it goes against everything they are. You should have embraced your human side, Cash. Maybe I can help you with that."

He thrust a skinny, clawed hand through to grab at Cash. His fingers scraped across Cash's breastbone, and it felt like salt poured into the raw cavity of his open chest. Pain scored down his bones, and his stomach twisted like a fist until he could taste bile and blood in the back of his throat as his monster was scraped out of him.

"You can probably live without it, you know," Shanko said as he peered through the broken trellis. "Half-human is enough for heaven, they say. You'd finally really belong somewhere."

Cash tried to hang on to his monster. He'd cursed it sometimes, wished it mute, but it was him. The thought of being without it, of being like Yana with just a space in you, made him cold. It didn't work. Shanko pulled it out of him, thin and gray and vaguely amphibian, while Cash arched his back and tried to scream.

Then the monster caught on something. It hurt—a sharp tearing pain in Cash's spine where man and monster met—but it stapled them together. Shanko tried to reel it out, his face twisted with frustration, but the line already set pulled it back.

He sucked in a breath to scream, and then Arkady was there.

The monster part of him anyhow. The flare of his aura was now a mantle of heavy leathery wings, and golden scales crawled in elegant patterns over his chest and down his thighs. Beautiful enough to stop someone's heart. To stop Cash's, anyhow.

"He's mine," Arkady said in a voice like cracked bells. He rammed his claws into Cash's stretched, weeping wisp and tore it out of Shanko's grip. "Find your own."

The monster squirmed out of Arkady's grip and scrambled back under Cash's skin where it belonged. He flopped back onto the ground and tried to breathe through the pain. His insides felt all… misplaced… and his skin itched like he'd been lying out under the sun.

Arkady stepped over him and backhanded Shanko into the delivery truck parked outside. The metal dented in, and Shanko slumped, dazed, to the ground. To his credit it didn't take him long to pull himself together and lash out at Arkady. Bu this time it wasn't so easy. He might have had the advantage when he could pull Arkady out of his human skin, but that wouldn't work when Arkady had left humanity behind.

He was a demon on a—more or less—crossroads, and no little human Hunter had a chance. Not even an undead cauled one.

Arkady tore the shield of Shanko's meat suit away piece by piece. He tore them apart like old wood and left them to rot on the ground. Shanko lashed out with what he could grab. A tire whistled through the air where Arkady's head had been, and the raw end of his plasm raised welts.

It wasn't good enough. Arkady closed his claws around Shanko's throat and lifted him off his feet. There wasn't blood left to shed, but something thick and pallid oozed from the wounds.

"If you want freedom so much, you should have just killed yourself," he said.

Shanko spat in his face. "I tried."

"I'll try harder," Arkady promised him and tightened his grip.

Cash scrambled to his feet and nearly fell over again. "Wait," he hissed through the wash of nausea. "Don't kill him."

The plea didn't set Shanko free, but Arkady stopped closing his fist. "Why not? He betrayed my mother, betrayed the spirit of his deal, and hurt you. What value does he have now?"

Shanko cursed desperately and kicked at Arkady, his heels scraping over lean, scale-covered muscle. His despair tasted like roast beef and crackling, thick and sticky on Cash's tongue.

"Because that's his plan," Cash said. Despite everything, he felt a pinch of guilt at Shanko's accusing glare, but he ignored it. He limped over to put his hand on Arkady's arm. It had been a long time since he saw the monster without his skin on. He'd forgotten the smell of it, the thick musk of scales mixed in with Arkady's magic. Cash considered all the rules of decorum and class and decided to hell with it. He stepped under Arkady's wing and leaned against his shoulder. "That's why he took Yana. He promised your mother that he'd always protect her and her family, and you can only lie to yourself for so long. The minute the Prodigium really threatened you, he'd have to fix it. Wouldn't you, Shanko?"

Shanko spat at him. "They'll use you up and turn you out," he rasped. "You should have let me kill you."

Arkady pushed Shanko's chin up with a clawed thumb. "If you had," he said. "I'd have kept you alive and screaming forever. At least this way, we might kill you one day."

He snapped Shanko's neck, and the man went limp. It wouldn't end him, not for long, but it shut him up.

THEY FOUND Jerome in a chest in Shanko's room, folded double and tied with twine. He still wanted to marry Yana, which seemed to surprise her as much as anyone. It might actually be love.

Now all they had to do was fix everything else.

"If he insisted on his pound of flesh," Donna said coldly as she examined her perfectly applied nail polish and how it matched her powder-blue mother-of-the-bride dress. She sat with Cash in the front row of seats set out in the great, curved-metal-and-glass house attached to the hotel. Lush, overgrown plants, all dark green leaves and huge, jewel-bright flowers, had been pushed over to line the walls, leaving enough tiled space for an intimate wedding ceremony, "I'd have preferred you let him carve it from closest to my heart."

After a lot of work by her maids, she looked like a middle-aged woman who'd had a lot of work done so she could deny being middle-aged—extensive work but expensive, with the telltale signs that gave it away nothing more than subtle tension and sharpness. Donna refused to just be a middle-aged woman. She wanted her face to know that no version of her would accept a wrinkle with grace.

"And where are you keeping that these days?" Cash asked dryly.

Donna laughed and put a hand on his knee. His skin, still too tight and too tender, crawled unhappily at the contact.

"I always liked you," Donna said. She dug her nails in enough to hurt even through his trousers, and it was at least more normal than her pleasantries. "I was going to have you killed once, of course, but I always liked you. Shanko talked me out of it, funnily enough."

Cash felt various shades of bad. There was still some guilt, but then he remembered the horror stories that Shanko had told him about... Shanko, it turned out... as a kid. He wondered how much the cursed Hunter had enjoyed that fear.

"Well, we've all got regrets," he said dryly. "Is that why you're being so nice to me? So the moment when you slide the knife home is more satisfying?"

Donna laughed. The genial, practiced murmur from the other wedding guests stopped for a heartbeat and then carefully, politely picked up again.

"Oh, the moment you feel that last beat is always satisfying," she said. "Never trust anyone who loses track of the simple joys in life, Caspari. No, letting you live was the right decision. Shanko might be a traitor, but he was never a fool."

She sounded fond. Proud, even. Cash wondered if Shanko understood that, in her way, her weird, gross, definitely bloody way, Donna had loved him. But monsters loved like children picked off scabs—there was pleasure in the rip.

"Are you going to tell me why you're being nice to me?" he asked.

"Can't I just be glad to see you?" she asked. "Happy that you're here, because you make my son happy?"

Cash snorted out a laugh. "It doesn't sound like you, madam."

She smiled, sly and cool. "No. It doesn't, does it?"

Speakers mounted high in the arched glass roof scratched to life as they started to play the wedding march. The sound dripped down through the high, misty windows until the whole place seemed ready to vibrate. It made Donna glance around at the doors and move her hand. Cash followed suit to watch Arkady walk Yana through the door. She was slim and pretty in gold, the bruises from last night hidden under thickly applied powder, and he looked elegant and cold in shades of gray that didn't suit him.

Everyone stood up. Cash offered Donna his arm, but she looked daggers at him and stood up under her own steam, giving her dress a disdainful swipe of her palms to straighten out the wrinkles.

It was a much more subdued wedding than the last one Cash had gone to. Not that Jerome, at the front of the crowd, seemed to care. From the dazzled look on his face, he might as well have been at the most elaborate wedding in the world. It wouldn't last. No one could live with monsters and hang on to that odd, bloody-handed innocence, but Cash could see why Yana wanted to keep it close for a while.

Cash tried to keep his eyes trained on Yana as she paced down the aisle, but his gaze flicked back to the door every few steps. If it was him, with a camera and one chance to get the best shot, he'd wait for the music to hit the last few bars.

Da da da DAAAA *da da da, da…* and now… *da* dah

A beat after Cash would have done it—with Jerome and Yana already hand in hand—the doors flung open and Harry burst in.

"Stop!" he said, his voice loud as it bounced back and forth off the windows. People gasped on cue, and a few leaped to their feet with indignant rumblings. "I'm here to stop this wedding, on the authority granted to me by the Catholic Church and the Washington See."

Someone fainted.

That was not scripted. Cash jumped to his feet and ran down to block Harry's path forward, his arms out.

"Damn it," he hissed. "Didn't you get my email? You've been played."

Something made Harry give Cash a look with a lot more suspicion than Cash expected. He clenched his teeth and didn't flinch, even as his monster cringed down nervously into his gut.

"My apologies, but I don't think I'll take your word for that," Harry said. He turned his camera around in his hand to face him and narrated his decision as he walked forward. "No one's wedding ceremony should ever be disrupted, but this was an unholy union."

Yana laughed and nudged Jerome in the ribs. "Told you," she said. He looked uncomfortable. Apparently, Jerome wasn't much of an actor.

Back at the doors, Abigail slid in, still in her uniform, and filmed the audience as they reacted to Harry's presence. *Perfect.*

"We don't know yet whether Ilyana Abascal was seduced or deceived," Harry said as he reached the end of the aisle and reached into his pocket. "But we know her bridegroom is a… monster."

He pulled out a bottle and dashed holy water, seasoned with salt and blessings, in Jerome's face. It would never have had much effect on him—still human in all but his ambitions—but the spray that caught Yana would have pocked and stained her skin.

If Cash hadn't swapped it out last night with plain tap water, that was.

Yana still squealed in a facsimile of girlie surprise and clung closer to Jerome.

"That's a lie!"

Arkady wiped water off his sleeve and glared at Abigail. "You," he said, his voice tight with anger. "Are you behind this, Amy? You've gone too far now. This was my sister's wedding."

"W… what?" Abigail spluttered as she nearly dropped her camera. "This isn't… I'm… I don't know what you're talking about. I… I don't know you."

Arkady rolled his eyes in slightly over-the-top disgust, but for a bad liar he was doing well.

"That's right," he said bitingly. "You don't, and no matter what you think? You don't know my sister either. I let you keep your job last time because Yana should have known better, but not interested is not interested."

That was the cue, and Cash's contribution to the plan. Abigail looked around nervously and then focused on Harry.

"Don't listen to them," she said loudly. "He's a monster. You can't let them get married. It's a travesty. I told you that, Yana. I told you it wouldn't happen."

Well, they'd originally hired her to serve wine. It would have been too much to expect her to be a good actor too.

Harry closed his eyes for a second. Then he threw water on Jerome again—who spluttered in surprise—before he turned to glare at Abigail. "What did you do?"

"What had to be done!" she said. "This marriage is *wrong.* It won't happen while there's breath in my body!"

Luckily the collapse of Harry's hopes and dreams for his career blurred his judgment enough he didn't question the drama of that. He lowered the camera and glanced at Arkady.

"I can explain."

Epilogue

"YOU'RE LETTING him live?" Kohary asked with a hint of surprise as Shanko delivered a cup of tea to Donna, still in her human wedding drag. She took it from him, sipped neatly, and left a bright red smudge on the china.

"He wants to die," she said. "And I'm in no mood to indulge him. If he wants death, he needs to earn his bonus, and this year's is already down the drain."

Kohary considered that and then nodded. He stood up and fastidiously straightened his cuffs. "Fair enough," he said. "The Worm thought you'd forgiven him."

"Then he's delusional with regrowth," Donna said. "I've never forgiven a debt in my life. Caspari, show the Left Hand to the door?"

Cash considered arguing but pushed himself up out of the chair instead. He opened the door for Kohary and politely ushered him out. They walked in tight, wary silence through the halls, until Kohary broke it.

"How is she?" he asked with an odd hunger in his voice. Then, to remind himself, "Your daughter."

"Ellie," Cash said. "And she's okay. She liked camp, as it turns out. She said it was like twenty-four seven ice hockey. Only everyone is the goon. If she'd ended up your ward, she'd have probably thrived."

Kohary nodded stiffly. "I am glad she didn't," he said. "It's no life for a child… or a partner. Your Left Hand isn't expected to want something the Council doesn't."

It was a very old secret, and it felt insane to talk about it like this, even veiled as it was.

"She's my kid," he said. "Humanity suits her."

"I know," Kohary said. "One day, something else might too. If you need… anything? I owe you, for Shanko. You saved me a chase."

That wasn't it, of course. Cash *had*, but that wasn't the marker he could lay down in front of the Left Hand if he ever had the balls for it.

"I won't," he said. It sounded cruel, felt cruel in his throat, so he softened it. "But if *she* does, she'll know who to ask for."

Cash walked Kohary into the aboveground hotel and through the mortal guests. The indentured servants that Donna had pressed into nice suits and the role of partygoers mingled discreetly. A night and a day up here was their bonus for the year.

In reception, Arkady waited in one of the big wing-backed leather chairs. He didn't bother to come over to say goodbye to Kohary. They just traded nods and a hard look. Then Kohary took his leave.

Cash supposed he could too as he watched Kohary go. His job here was technically done, although it was a shame to miss the wedding feast.

"You gave me the weekend," Arkady said. His fingers touched the back of Cash's neck in a featherlight caress that tickled. Then he hooked them in his collar and pulled him back a step, out of the sun. He'd lost a whole layer of skin to Shanko's attack. "And I have plans for it."

Cash turned into his arms and looked up at him. He didn't know how much Arkady had heard at the trailer park or what he wanted him to have heard.

"Still want to rub Yana's nose in me?" he asked.

Arkady kissed him, sweet and so desperate it knocked Cash off balance again. "I nearly lost you, idiot," Arkady said. "Shanko could have killed you. All I want is you, alive and where I can touch you when I want."

"For the weekend. Until things go back to normal," Cash said. It would hurt, but less than if he fooled himself.

"Idiot," Arkady said in exasperation. "You know better than to make a deal with me without parsing it thoroughly. Do you know why I kept that outfit, the one you wore to my first wedding?"

"Because I was hot, still?"

185

Arkady swallowed. "Because the first time you wore it, I couldn't even look at you or I wouldn't have been able to go through with my vows. You were so beautiful, and all I could think about was what it would have been like to marry you."

Cash drew back slightly. "Are you asking me to—"

"No," Arkady said. He twisted his fingers through Cash's hair and tugged affectionately. "Not yet, anyhow. But you? You're my normal. So, this? After this weekend, this is going to be your new normal too."

He ducked his head for another kiss, careless of their audience. Cash didn't care either. He doubted any of the parents from Ellie's school would be here to make a complaint. He curled his hand around the back of Arkady's neck and leaned in.

DONNA ACCEPTED a glass of mushroom gin from a servant—just because she'd let them aboveground didn't mean she'd given them the night off—and watched her son and his lover. Love would die eventually, of course. Even the most smitten of lovebirds would peck the other to death one day. It was still sweet, and more importantly, it got her what she wanted.

Her son, happy, and her granddaughter under her roof—where she belonged.

She savored the mealy taste of her drink.

And Cash thought that none of them were good liars.

TA MOORE is a Northern Irish writer of romantic suspense, urban fantasy, and contemporary romance novels. A childhood in a rural seaside town fostered a suspicious nature, a love of mystery, and a streak of black humour a mile wide. As her grandmother always said, "She'd laugh at a bad thing, that one," mind you, that was the pot calling the kettle black. TA studied history, Irish mythology, and English at University, mostly because she has always loved a good story. She has worked as a journalist, a finance manager, and in the arts sectors before she finally gave in to a lifelong desire to write.

Coffee, Doc Marten boots, and good friends are the essential things in life. Spiders, mayo, and heels are to be avoided.

Website: www.nevertobetold.co.uk
Facebook: www.facebook.com/TA.Moores
Twitter: @tammy_moore

Also from Dreamspinner Press

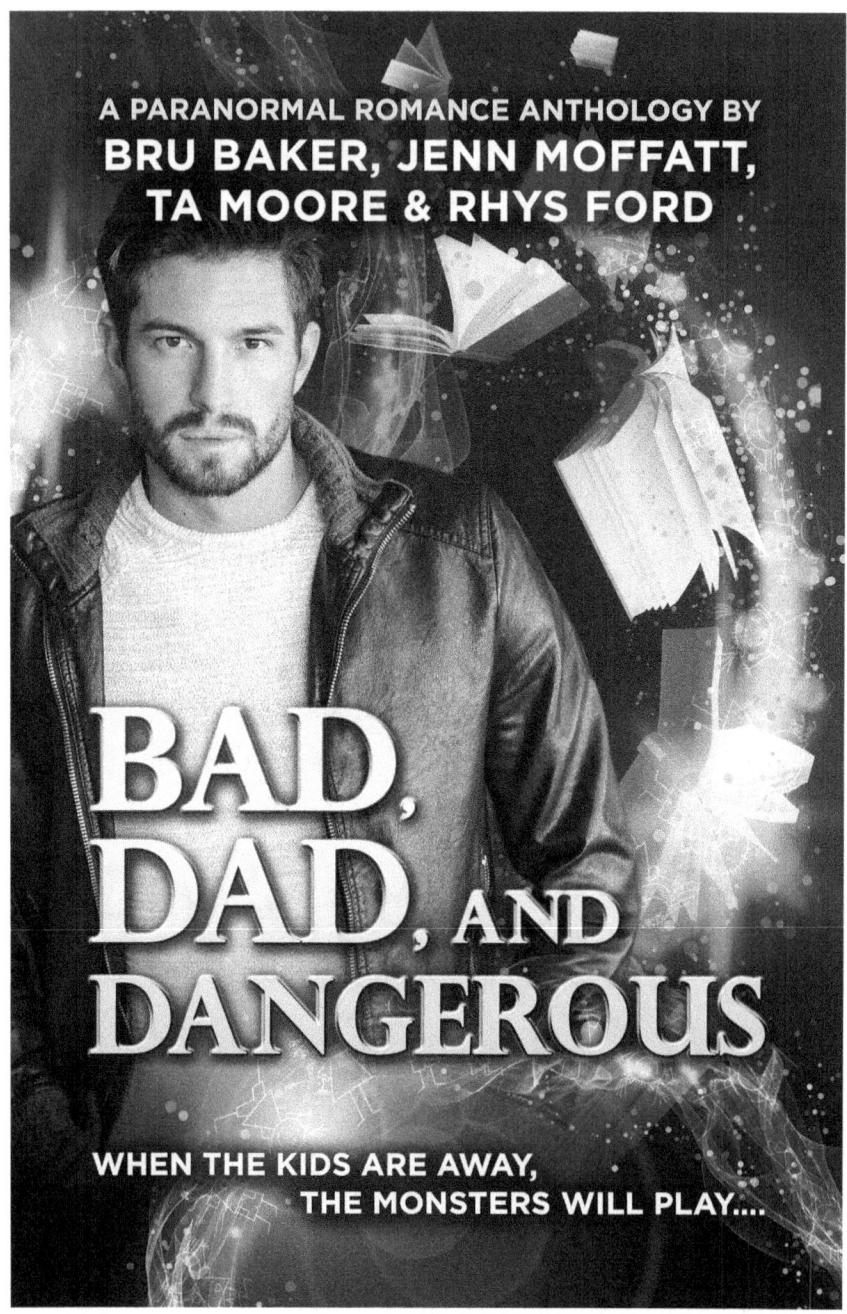

A PARANORMAL ROMANCE ANTHOLOGY BY
BRU BAKER, JENN MOFFATT, TA MOORE & RHYS FORD

BAD, DAD, AND DANGEROUS

WHEN THE KIDS ARE AWAY,
THE MONSTERS WILL PLAY....

www.dreamspinnerpress.com

When the kids are away, the monsters will play.

School's out for summer, and these dads are ready to ship their kids off to camp. Not just because their kids are monsters—whose aren't?—but because they're ready for some alone time to let their hair down and their fangs out. You see, not only are the kids monsters—their dads are too.

Even the most dangerous of creatures has a soft spot. These bad, dangerous dads love their kids to death, but they need romance.

Every year, for a few short weeks, these hot men with a little extra in their blood get to be who they truly are. And this year, life has a surprise for them. Whether they be mage, shifter, vampire, or changeling, these heartbreakingly handsome dads might be looking to tear up the town… but they'll end up falling in love. All it takes is the right man to bring them to their knees.

www.dreamspinnerpress.com

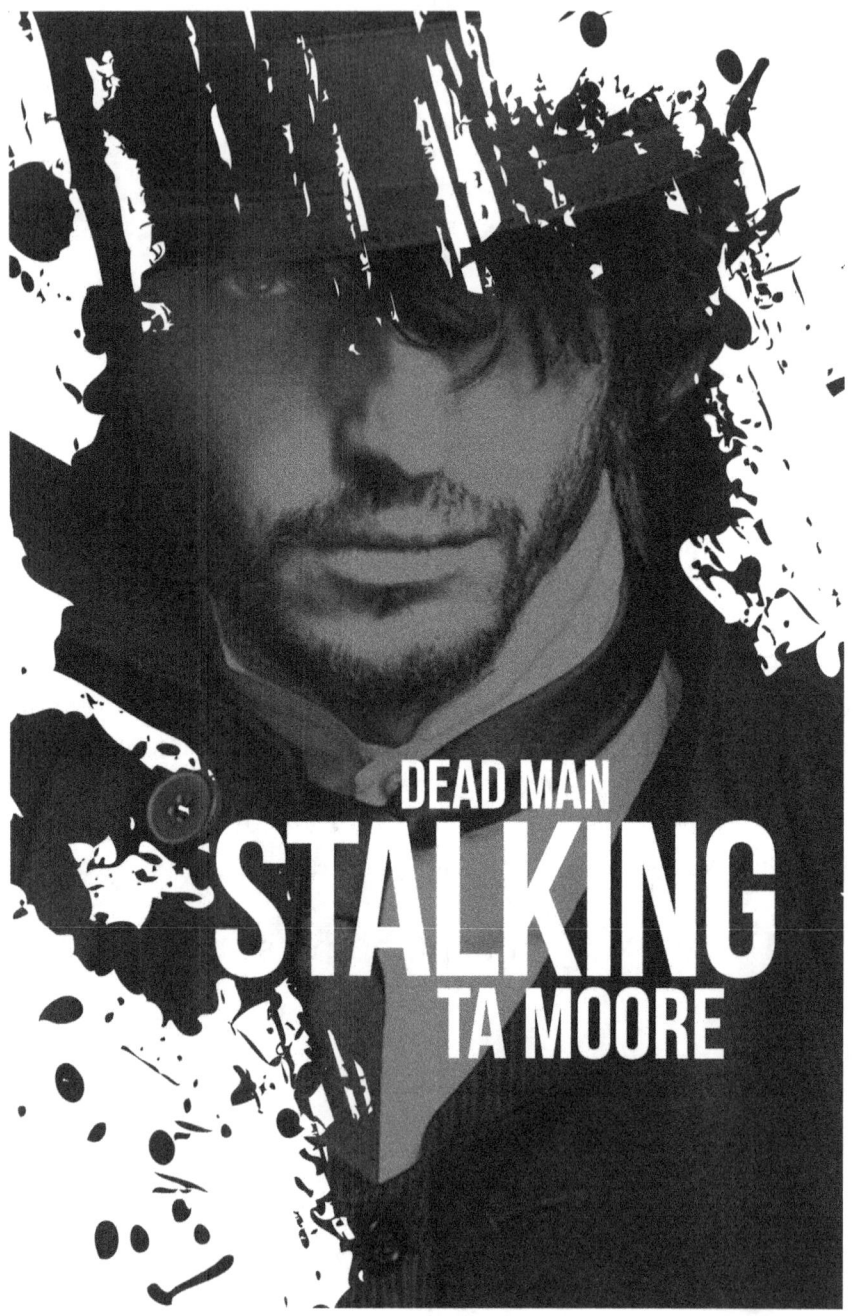

DEAD MAN
STALKING
TA MOORE

A Blood and Bone Novel

Agent Luke Bennett proved that humans could rise just as high in the ranks as their vampire colleagues—until a kidnapper held him captive for a year and turned him without his consent.

Now he's Took: a reluctant monster afraid to bite anyone, broke, and about to be discharged from his elite BITERs unit.

When an old colleague suggests he consult on a BITERs case, Took has little to lose. The case is open and shut… but nothing is ever that easy. As he digs deeper, he discovers a lot more than one cold case is at stake, and if he wants to solve this one, he'll need the help of the BITERs team. Even if that brings his old commander, Madoc, back into his life.

www.dreamspinnerpress.com

You don't end up an ex-car thief and ex-con because you're good at resisting temptation… and Cal Tate's rich new boss is very tempting.

Cal has always been the bad boy who lovers don't bring home to Mom, but now he'd like someone other than a debt collector waiting for him. He has a legit job as a driver with his brother's company, and he's got a doctor on the hook, but he still can't help crawling into bed with Joseph Bailey.

Joe has never met anyone as easy in their own skin as his new driver—or as ridiculously beautiful. He's in London to downsize the family business… and to investigate the abusive emails that imply a dark secret around his mother's death. But unpicking the lies he's been told makes Joe realize he isn't sure who he is without them.

When his life falls apart, the only person he can be himself with is Cal. But with the escalating threats from his anonymous stalker, Joe doesn't know if there's any chance for a happy future for him and Cal.

www.dreamspinnerpress.com